Praise for Vivian Arend's *Rocky Mountain Angel*

"While this is a very sweet romance, there is no shortage of smoking hot sex. From their first kiss this couple burns up the pages. Wow."

~ *Fiction Vixen*

"*Rocky Mountain Angel* is a superb addition to the Six Pack Ranch series and once again proves that Vivian Arend is an outstanding author."

~ *Guilty Pleasures Book Reviews*

"I thought this was a beautifully written story and excellent addition to the series."

~ *Sensual Reads*

Look for these titles by *Vivian Arend*

Now Available:

Granite Lake Wolves
Wolf Signs
Wolf Flight
Wolf Games
Wolf Tracks
Wolf Line
Wolf Nip

Forces of Nature
Tidal Wave
Whirlpool

Turner Twins
Turn It On
Turn It Up

Pacific Passion
Stormchild
Stormy Seduction
Silent Storm

Xtreme Adventures
Falling, Freestyle
Rising, Freestyle

Six Pack Ranch
Rocky Mountain Heat
Rocky Mountain Haven
Rocky Mountain Desire
Rocky Mountain Angel
Rocky Mountain Rebel

Takhini Wolves
Black Gold
Silver Mine
Diamond Dust

Bandicoot Cove
Paradise Found
Exotic Indulgence

Print Collections
Under the Northern Lights
Under the Midnight Sun
Under an Endless Sky
Breaking Waves
Storm Swept
Freestyle
Tropical Desires

Rocky Mountain Angel

Vivian Arend

Samhain Publishing, Ltd.
11821 Mason Montgomery Road, 4B
Cincinnati, OH 45249
www.samhainpublishing.com

Print ISBN: 978-1-61921-505-4
Digital ISBN: 978-1-61921-121-6

Editing by Anne Scott
Cover by Angela Waters

First Samhain Publishing, Ltd. electronic publication: November 2012
First Samhain Publishing, Ltd. print publication: October 2013

Dedication

To the Group That Shall Not Be Named because you know the special balance between posting spew-worthy snark, earnest encouragement and silently working your individual asses off.

Acknowledgement

Dee Carney is my go-to-gal when it comes to medical questions. I love that she takes the time from her own writing and responds with nary a blink when I IM her yet again with a starting line like: "So if you were going to kill someone…"

All mistakes, however, are mine alone.

Chapter One

Neither of them blinked.

Dust motes hovered in the sun streaming through the open barn door. Gabe Coleman leaned back on a wall and took a deep breath. The heavy scent of farm animals filled his nostrils. Familiar as it was pungent, the aroma that had been a part of his entire thirty-one years calmed his nerves.

The conversation was going about as well as he'd expected, but damn if he'd give up yet. He resisted muttering *stubborn jackass* and scrambled for a new tack. "Look, I showed you the receipts for the past year. Expenses went up, our projected revenues are still far less than they need to be."

The face before him remained motionless. Shit. Definitely not working.

Another idea struck. "I read an article in the *Calgary Herald* last week. Rancher down by Pincher Creek was ready to go bankrupt..."

Gabe trailed off. Suggesting their section of the Coleman ranch was getting closer to that same situation was not the way to make his father listen to reason.

Three feet across from him, broad nostrils twitched for a second then the ancient donkey reached down to grab a mouthful of grain before turning his back on Gabe.

Even the animals seemed tired of listening to him try to come up with a way to save their lives.

He pushed himself up and headed toward the tack room. If nothing else, the ranch itself provided a million distractions. The reality of working the land sucked—enough damn property to make a man look rich, and not enough money coming in to keep putting food on the table throughout the year.

Giving up wasn't an option, but hell if he knew what was at this point.

The saddle had barely landed on Hurricane's back before his mother's voice carried from the house side of the yard.

"You got any spare time today?"

Gabe tossed her a smile even as he wondered why she hadn't made her request to his father. "Was going to go check the creek and fence lines, but there's no rush. You need a hand with something?"

She nodded. "I want to plant the garden this week and need more room. Can you turn over another few rows?"

Shit. Now he knew why she'd waited until Ben had headed into town after breakfast. "Ma, you already have enough garden you can barely keep up. You sure you want more to deal with?"

Dana Coleman looked her age that day, but the determined jut of her chin warned him he'd be breaking sod before long. They came by stubbornness honestly in their family, from both his parents' sides.

"Every bit we grow is less we buy, Gabriel. And I figured a little extra wouldn't go amiss—there are always people who want fresh produce."

They stared at each other for a minute. Gabe hated the entire situation with a red-hot passion. He had ideas he thought could improve their circumstances, but beyond ideas were only half-started and hidden projects, none of which were going to bail them out of trouble. Using the donkey to practice talking about finances was supposed to make talking to his family easier, but hell if he wanted his ma to be the one worrying. "You can't save the ranch by growing more carrots."

"Well, I can't save it sitting and complaining that the cost of feed keeps going up either, can I?" She snapped her mouth shut and glanced out over the fields as Gabe hid his surprise. She never, ever complained about the way Ben ran things, and the small slip stunned him.

Dana shook her head then made deliberate eye contact. "I ain't saying another word, and neither will you. About me growing things to sell, you understand?"

Argue with her when she used that tone of voice? Hell no. He laughed inside. Well out of his teens, and still under his mama's control. At least he understood her reasoning. "I'll figure out a way to make things work. I promise."

She sighed. "You'll do your best, just like we all will, but there're no guarantees, Gabriel. Ranching's a dirty, hard and often thankless task. Something's got to give, and this time it might be us."

The lack of bitterness as she spoke burned like crazy. She wasn't talking about giving up on a childish dream or a last-minute whim. This was their share of the Coleman ranch they were oh-so-casually discussing, land that had been in the extended family for three generations. Thirty years ago four sons had split the inherited spread, and now it looked as if Ben and Dana were going to be the first to fall short of making a go of it.

His ma forced a smile, the lines around the corners of her eyes softening her expression. "If you break the ground before Raphael gets home from school, he can spend the next few days adding manure with a wheelbarrow and the rototiller. I wouldn't have interrupted you except Ben's put him on restriction from using the tractor and harrows."

Thinking about his younger brother's most recent escapade made him chuckle. "Rafe didn't hurt anything."

"The tractor's not a car to drive on the highway, even if he took back roads. Your father was right to give him hell."

That Ben was right to give Rafe hell *this* time was unspoken. Would remain unspoken between the two of them, and the thought was enough to wash away Gabe's amusement at his brother using the ranch tractor to get to his friend's house.

It was enough. All his held-back longings made him nod more briskly than usual before turning away. He hauled off the saddle and let his horse loose in the corral outside the main barn. Methodically he completed his mother's request, watching a little more of his day slip away. A little more of his life.

By the time he had Hurricane prepped again and thrown himself into the saddle, hightailing out the gate felt more like the start of a race than his usual even-paced ritual for confronting his endless chores.

The spring air on his face was a blend of cool and warm, clean dirt and green growing things mixed with rotting compost, and the remnants of last year's bales. The musty scents mingled with the fresh for a second before the breeze stole them both away, and he tipped his hat to block the sun from his eyes. Hurricane knew the route as well as he did and after turning toward the creek, he let him set the pace.

He'd been dragging his heels for nearly two years. Things hadn't gone to shit around the ranch overnight, and they weren't about to lose everything tomorrow, but the most frustrating thing was he'd seen this coming. Had tried to plan for a future that would be brighter for all of them, but between Ben's stubborn refusal to share any of the decision making and the poor weather conditions last season, things were coming to a head.

The challenge he'd had with his cousin Daniel to stir up and shake up his life seemed a million miles away at times. Yet, if he really thought it through, that wasn't true. The good-natured poke in the butt had inspired the one positive thing he'd managed to accomplish over the past year—he'd built a house of his own. It wasn't fancy, but it was his, free and clear, and a place to be independent.

His mother had fussed when he'd announced he was going to build a cabin, Ben had scoffed, and his then-seventeen-year-old brother had eyed him with understanding and helped every chance he got. If the original Coleman brothers could start with log shanties, Gabe figured he wasn't too bad off. He'd called in a few favours from the rest of the Coleman cousins, and at the end of the day he had a log cabin tucked up near the dividing line between the Angel Coleman land and the Whiskey Creek side of the family.

With four Coleman families all still ranching in the area, the locals had gone to town giving them interesting nicknames.

The creek was running higher than usual, and he stopped to clear away debris from the hoses they used to pull water for the watering tanks. The Alberta sunshine seemed determined to do its damnedest to cheer him up. How could he stay down when he was surrounded by wide-open spaces and the mad sound of June birdsong? The contented lowing of cattle carried from somewhere over the nearby ridge. Calves at their mamas' heels made noise that added to the familiarity of the day.

This land was his home and the idea it could be taken away killed him.

He worked for a little longer before the sounds from the other side of the hill changed to complaining. Restless fear. Something had spooked the beasts, and this location was remote enough the trouble was bound to be a predator. Just what they didn't need—a coyote or a cougar coming to grab a snack. Gabe scrambled up the creek bed and grabbed his shotgun off the saddle, topping the crest of the hill to see the lay of the land.

The cattle were disturbed all right, but from someone driving where they had no right. A long trail of dust rose as some idiot sped down the private connector road between the main highway and the secondary road that led past their land. His stomach turned as the truck shimmied on the loose gravel. Stupid fool obviously didn't realize how dangerous it was to drive at those speeds on the easily moveable road crush. Gabe returned his gun to its place and mounted, turning Hurricane toward the herd to settle them once the trespasser was gone.

The truck wasn't the only thing out of place. Gabe gazed in dismay as he realized a horse in full gallop raced just ahead of the vehicle, trapped in the narrow ditch between the road and the seemingly endless barbed-wire fence to the side.

Another irresponsible fool—only this time it wouldn't just be the rider who broke their neck in an accident, but the horse as well. Gabe kicked Hurricane in the flanks and set a course to intersect with the trespassers.

Bad enough when people cut through their land at a slow and even pace, but this was reckless and stupid. The spring freshness around him was forgotten as his temper flared harder when the truck got close enough to be recognized as one of Rafe's teenage friends. Gabe leaned forward and held on, guiding Hurricane on a safe path as rapidly as possible. Ironically, the three of them were all headed nearly straight for his log home.

He was no more than a hundred metres from the road when the rider must have spotted him. To his shock, they pulled their horse up hard and slipped off, dropping the reins. The rider basically dove under the barbed wire. Their cowboy hat fell off as they scrambled upright to run straight in his direction, long dark hair tumbling around the woman's shoulders as she moved.

And all his assumptions changed. Maybe he'd been wrong in presuming the kids were on a reckless joyride. Maybe they were looking for him to tell him something was amiss with his family. Gabe rushed forward, heart pounding in his throat.

The truck slowed to a stop beside the abandoned horse. Everything became a rush of images and faces. Someone opened the truck door, shouts rang out, the runner drew near. Gabe reined Hurricane in but didn't bother to wait until the horse stopped, instead swinging his leg over the saddle and hitting the ground at a run. He landed on his feet a split second before his mind registered the face of the woman who threw herself into his arms and latched on like a burr.

"Allison?"

There was an argument happening down on the road and one of his high school classmates trembling in his arms. Just when he thought the situation couldn't get much crazier, she buried her face in the vee of his neck, hiding against him. Her warm breath fanned his skin, tickling and heating him up.

Which wasn't altogether unpleasant, but getting distracted when potential trouble waited at the fence line wouldn't be the smartest move ever. Gabe held on tight, but made sure he could see the road clearly.

The fact she smelt like wild cherries shouldn't be the foremost thought in his brain.

He should be concentrating on why someone he hadn't seen in over a year was holding him like a lover. Why the kids at the roadside were taking off like a bat out of hell, the horse dancing away skittishly from the kicked-up gravel. Why Allison was clinging so tight that even through his long-sleeved shirt he felt the cut of her fingernails digging into his upper arms.

All those would be logical to focus on instead of her delicate perfume and the sudden longing for her to use those nails on his back. Damn if he wasn't getting turned on like some sick bastard just from having her in his arms.

He held her gently but forced her farther away, needing answers to the weird scene he'd interrupted. "Allison? What the hell?"

She met his gaze, her torso shaking. "Oh God, Gabe. Sorry—"

He caught her before she crumbled to the ground.

Something soft cushioned her head, and the smell of coffee lingered in the air. Allison rolled slowly until the memories rushed in.

"Shit." She jerked upright to find her cowboy boots were missing, but otherwise she was lying fully clothed on a bed in a log cabin. That she was alone helped her take a slow breath and relax a tiny bit.

What a totally mucked-up day. By any standard.

She assumed this was Gabe's new place, but until she knew for sure she wasn't about to do anything stupid like call out. She made it to her feet and approached the open doorway warily. One quick peek revealed a tidy if plain living room with a river-stone fireplace, and basic kitchen along another wall, a solid log table with four chairs dividing the two areas.

A thermos right smack in the middle of the table held down the edge of a piece of paper. Allison stepped forward to examine it closer, grabbing for support as blackness threatened to make her knees crumble. She leaned a shoulder on the wall and hoped the head rush would pass quickly.

The door opened and Gabe stepped in. One glance, and he was across the room, his arm slipping behind her back as he guided her to a chair. "You have trouble walking these days, Allison?"

She blew out a long breath. "Hello to you too."

"Thought we'd decided to skip the usual 'hello and nice to see you' bit after that wild greeting you gave me out in the field." Gabe dragged out the chair kitty-corner to her and leaned back, stretching his long legs under the table. "Hello, Allison. I'd say it was good to see you, but you fainted and scared me half to death. What the hell is up?"

She laughed softly at his dry tone. At least part of that was easy to answer. "I can't believe I fainted. I'm sorry. I haven't eaten in a while—that must be why."

Gabe stared at her for a moment, his green eyes examining her. It was a thorough, one-piece-at-a-time inspection, but she refused to drop her head and avoid his gaze. His intense scrutiny gave her an opportunity to look him over as well. He seemed more rugged than the last time they'd visited. The strong flex of his biceps stretched the fabric of his T-shirt, his chest broader than she remembered. His hair was longer, slight curls showing along his neck and his temples where the blondish-brown locks escaped the brim of his cowboy hat.

He rose and placed his hat on a peg beside the door before heading to the fridge. He pulled out items, working silently.

She stood to help him, and he glared. "Sit. I don't need you taking another nosedive."

He plopped a glass of orange juice on the table in front of her and turned back to the stove.

The ringing in her ears made her reach for the juice without hesitation and drink deeply. She needed a clearer head than she currently had to present her case. Her plan had been for an organized meeting under reasonable circumstances, not him having to rescue her from total panic when her horse—

She shot to her feet, glass in hand. "Oh Lord, Patches. Where is she?"

Gabe held out a hand and pointed firmly to the chair. "Sit down and drink your juice. Patches and Hurricane are shooting the breeze like old friends. I've got a small lean-to and a corral outside for them. I took off her saddle and brushed her down. That's where I was a minute ago—you were riding her damn hard."

Anger flashed along with guilt. "Stupid kids spooked her. And then I couldn't get them to stop chasing me, and I'll admit it—I lost it. Sorry for making more work for you."

He made a sound that was nearly a growl, pausing in the middle of cracking an egg into the pan on the stove. "You certainly don't need to apologize for a bunch of out-of-control brats. I'll talk to them, and their parents. They won't be driving again for a while."

The nervous anxiety that had set in on top of everything else eased a little. "Is it bad to hope they get grounded until they're like twenty-five? Idiots."

"Doubt that long, but yeah, I'll deal with it. Driver especially should know better. Shit for brains. What the hell was he thinking?"

"You say that a lot." Allison wasn't sure why the repeated phrase had registered, but it was so like what she remembered of Gabe, she had to smile.

Gabe frowned. "Shit for brains?"

"What the hell."

He nabbed toast and popped it on a plate. "Used that phrase a lot with you this morning. If it fits..."

"What the hell fits too well, I'm afraid." She took a moment to calm herself before smiling hesitantly. "I should start over. Gabe, it's good to see you again."

He slipped a plate in front of her, the smell of warm buttery toast making her mouth water. "Good to see you too. Now eat. You can explain the 'what the hell' business when you're done."

God, it tasted incredible. She shoveled the food in, barely taking time to breath. When she realized what a pig she must look like and glanced up in concern, it was to discover he was back at the stove making more.

Screw looking ladylike, she was hungry.

When he offered her a second helping, though, Allison shook her head with regret. "If I eat more I'll explode. Only, do you have any coffee left? My caffeine levels are dangerously low—that might be why I have a headache."

He grabbed a couple cups and a sugar pot, pushing them and the thermos her direction. "Pour me one as well. Black."

Then he tucked into his own food and ignored her. Allison fixed him a cup and eased back in her chair to sip the dark liquid and figure out what she was going to tell him. Her past forty-eight panicked hours had come to a head, and now, with food in her stomach and safety at hand, exhaustion overtook her.

When he pushed aside his plate a few minutes later and looked up at her with interest, she still hadn't managed to do more than mentally rumble through the same thoughts again and again. She was tired enough to be stupid. Tired enough to throw all caution to the wind and simply blurt out the words.

"I need you to be my fiancé."

Chapter Two

Gabe was thankful he'd already swallowed his mouthful of coffee or he would have spewed it all over.

"What the hell...?"

Allison leaned her elbows on the table and covered her face with her hands. "Oh Lord, don't make me laugh or I'm going to get hysterical."

"Trust me. That wasn't an attempt to make you laugh. It was an honest-to-God question." Still, Gabe smiled. "You feeling okay?"

She dragged her hands over her head and straightened her tangled hair, pulling it back into a ponytail and securing it in place. "Seriously? I'm exhausted, but I need to talk to you. This wasn't how I planned it. That's why I was riding Patches. I was going to leave you a note to contact me, and then—"

"Never heard of a phone?" Gabe pulled out his cell and tossed it on the table. "You've got my number. Voice mail, email. Haven't changed since the last time we used them."

"I'm sorry."

Allison bit her lower lip, and Gabe had the sudden urge to lean over and smooth his hand over her cheek, to force her to relax. Actually the stronger urge was to take her in his arms and hug her because she looked so damn miserable. He'd tried to give her a little room while she ate, allow her time to get more comfortable. They had enough of a history together that he was concerned, but after that insane comment?

He was going bat-shit crazy with curiosity.

"I don't mean to push, but you think you can get back to the fiancé thing? Because you lost me."

Allison nodded slowly. "I'm sorry, that wasn't fair. My..." She swayed from side to side for a second then growled with frustration. "I cannot figure out the best way to say this. I've been going for two days straight, and I thought I would have all the right words by the time I got here, but every time I start thinking everything rolls in circles and gets all muddled together."

"I'm not going to throw you out for misspeaking. You don't have to get it perfect. Just tell me. You want us to get married?"

Allison's eyes grew wide. "No."

"But that's what a fiancé usually means."

"I need you to pretend to be my fiancé, so that my mom will think I'm coming back to Rocky Mountain House to be with you."

This wasn't getting any easier. Gabe didn't mind puzzles—he played a damn good game of chess, but it looked as if he was going to have to pull information out of her one bit at a time and assemble the pieces on his own. "You want to come back to Rocky. Why do you need an excuse? Just come back."

"Can't. My mom would never accept it. It's not like I hated Rocky, but I was pretty vocal about not wanting to run the family restaurant. She'd know something was fishy if I just show up and announce I'm here to help take care of things."

"But you don't want to... Allison, you're not making any damn sense. You don't want to work at Parker's Timberline Grill. You've got a good job you enjoy in Red Deer, or at least you were having a blast the last time I talked to you. Why the hell are you trying to set up some elaborate hoax to fool your mother?"

Allison leaned back in her chair and crossed her arms in front of her. Her tired expression made her look lost, like a little girl, sad and hopeless. "She's dying, Gabe."

Shit.

He went with his earlier instinct, reached forward and pulled her into his lap. She was stiff for a moment before she tucked her face against his neck, wrapped her arms around him and squeezed tight. He pressed one hand to her back and rubbed slowly, cradling her as he let her cry.

Surreal. He'd gone from worrying about the ranch to comforting a grieving woman in less than three hours, and the day wasn't half over.

"I'm so sorry to hear that." Gabe had never had a ton of dealings with the Parkers, but he knew of them, including seeing Elle and Paul, Allison's siblings, around town. Their father's death years ago had been long and horrid, even watching from the outside. "Your family must be devastated."

She sniffled then leaned her cheek against his shoulder to speak quietly. "They don't know. Mom hasn't told them."

He sucked in air. "That's harsh, having to keep that kind of a secret from them."

"It gets worse. Mom didn't tell anyone. I found out—oh damn." Allison sat up straight, her tension returning in a rush. "You can't tell anyone this, or she'll get fired."

"Your mom?" Gabe reached behind him and nabbed the Kleenex box from the window ledge, dropping the box on the table for when she wanted it.

"My snitch."

Hell. "Someone spilt the beans to you about your mom being sick?"

Allison nodded, that bottom lip of hers back between her teeth.

"That's probably wrong in all kinds of ways."

She nodded again.

Gabe thought quickly. "How about for now you don't name no names, just, are you positive they got the details right?"

He let her go when she reached for the tissues. "This isn't some clerical error or wild idea, I saw paperwork. Even without that, it's someone I trust completely, someone who would know. She only told me because it's serious, and she's worried about us losing Mom without any warning."

Another piece of the puzzle fell into place. "Mothers don't always need much more of a reason than they think it's best for us. Maybe she doesn't want you guys to remember how hard it was to lose your dad."

Allison sniffed. "I think that's it. She's wrong, but...she's right. Losing her is going to be painful. I don't know how Elle and Paul will take it."

"So you need an excuse to come back. Your suggestion to fake an engagement seems extreme."

"I know my mom. I'm pretty sure she's doing this for our good and all, and yet—the fact she's keeping it a secret allows her to hold on to her dignity. To remain in charge of her life. How can I barge in and rip that from her? I'll confront her when necessary, but if she's only got three to six months left, and I have to lie my ass off during that time to make her happy, I'm willing."

Allison paced the space between his kitchen and sofa. Half her dilemma made sense to him now, but there were a hell of a lot more answers he needed. He spoke slowly. "So you'll willingly lie to make her happy. But...and don't take this the wrong way, but why would I lie to everyone I know? I like your mom plenty, Allison, and I'm damn sorry you have to face this, but..."

Even thinking that it wasn't really his issue made him feel like all kinds of an asshole for not wanting to go the extra mile for Allison. Yet putting on that kind of a charade in front of the entire clan? What would his ma think when they called it off down the road? What kind of grief would his cousins give him, and how difficult was it going to be in the duration to actually pull it off?

She was right. The situation was tangling his brain into knots, and he'd only been dealing with it for a few minutes.

He sighed. "I'm wondering if you thought this through beyond making your mom's last days easier. What about your brother and sister? How are they going to like finding out you've lied to them?"

Allison paused in the middle of wearing a hole in his hardwood floor. "The plan is to let them know eventually, but the most important part is making sure my mom is all right. I have gone over this again and again. I know you'd have to lie as well, and while I feel terrible about it, I don't feel bad enough to give up asking. I'll make it worth your while to help me."

Gabe pulled his jaw off the floor. "Did you just offer to pay me to pretend to be your fiancé?"

Allison snorted and leaned back on the fridge. "I'm so about to pass out, I couldn't be doing a worse job explaining this if I were drunk. No. No money, but if you're still interested in making your section of the Coleman ranch turn organic? I promise that I will do everything I can to help you. I know regs, I know who works the front lines and can fast-track inspections. I will advise and work with you, and save you time and money. Nothing illegal, but very valuable if you're serious about going green."

It was the one thing she could offer that was more valuable than money. The one thing that could render him speechless. He sat without saying a word because suddenly his brain was flooded with all the ideas and information he'd researched over the past two years. All the things he'd longed to put into place to make the Angel section of the Coleman ranch a success.

He'd have to convince his father.

But...not even Ben could turn down this kind of help. The realization that the fake relationship between him and Allison might help move them past the current stalemate hit like a load of bricks.

Ben didn't accept advice easily from anyone, especially not a woman, but if Gabe was getting what came down to valuable expert advice for free from a family member? His tight-fingered father would have a difficult time turning away that kind of an offer.

"Gabe?"

Allison stared at him in concern, and he realized he'd been silent for a lot longer than he planned.

He shook his head slowly. "You said you weren't sure how to tell your story, and I'll toss that right back at you. I'm not exactly sure how to respond."

"You still interested in making changes?"

"Like you wouldn't believe."

Allison nodded. "I can't guarantee anything, Gabe. I don't know the specific details of your land's history or anything yet, so I can't tell you timelines or even if you can successfully make the switch. But if you do this for me, I promise to work with you until you're happy with the results, or you say you've had enough trying. I'll even add a contract for you to provide as much as we can use at the restaurant. Standard prices for standard product for five years. No matter how long our fake engagement lasts, you'll have that."

Gabe rose to stare out the window over the nearest section of Coleman land. He imagined it producing enough to support his family, no worries if this was the year they'd have to beg for a handout. He swung to examine Allison again, taking in the sadness and frustration that clung to her like a thick coat. "You're not a very good bargainer. That's far too open-ended and generous an offer, and now I feel like a shit for needing to be convinced to help you."

She closed her eyes and breathed out slowly. "Then you'll do it?"

He was closer to an answer than he should be, but he wasn't going to let her rush either of them into something they'd regret. "Hang on a minute. I ain't saying no. I'm still not a hundred percent sure I should say yes, but you've made it damn tempting."

She shot across the room to grab his hands. "I know it's crazy, but Mom's been everything to us, Gabe. She kept us together after Dad died, and she's always been there for us. Losing her is going to be so hard but..." her voice hitched once before she pulled it back together, "...but making her last days extra special is what I want to give to her. Please?"

Great. She'd been reduced to begging. That hadn't been part of the original plan, or at least she was pretty sure it wasn't on her list. Exhaustion poured over her in waves, and she was barely keeping vertical. This first step had to be finished now, though, if she was going to pull off the entire ploy.

Sneaking out on horseback to Gabe's had been a bit of a wild impulse. He was right, she could have called him, but calling wouldn't have let her double-check that he really had a place of his own like she'd heard through the grapevine. That was a vital discovery to make, because while she liked him, and their background interests overlapped so well, no way she would have asked him to join her in the facade if living next door to his parents for any length of time had been part of the deal.

Overall, the four Coleman clans were well respected in Rocky. Some more than others—some of the boys had earned a reputation for troublemaking. Like any big family they had their black sheep, and to Allison, that phrase conjured up images of Ben Coleman. Ben Coleman in a devil suit carrying a pitchfork. He had always scared her a little. That Gabe was related to the rough man made her shake her head and think even better of the son for making his own decisions and marching to his own beat.

Allison glanced around the cabin, her second reason for wanting an up-close-and-personal peek coming to the fore. "You're not seeing anyone, are you?"

His hand cupped her face, his touch surprisingly gentle and warm, and it felt so good she was tempted to nuzzle in tighter. She sighed softly.

Gabe's wicked, low laugh raced over her. "You're asleep on your feet, girl. No, I'm not seeing anyone. How long since you had eight hours of shuteye?"

"Tamara stopped in Tuesday to tell me the news. I started packing my stuff that night, and gave notice when I went into work Wednesday."

"So now it's Thursday and you haven't taken any time to rest, have you?"

She had no time to waste. "Gabe? Are you going to help me?"

"More than you know. Where's your car? At your mom's house?"

She nodded, embarrassed to find she was still clutching his hand. When she attempted to let go, he chuckled again and tugged her after him.

"I'll take care of your car while you take a nice, long nap."

There was some reason she should be saying no to this, but damn if she could figure out what it was. "But, Gabe..."

"No complaining. I'm not giving you any kind of answer until I know your brain is working as well as your heart." He led her back into the bedroom and pushed her toward the oversized mattress that looked far too comfortable. "When you wake up we'll talk through more details, but in the meantime I'll nab your stuff and bring it here, just so there's no bridges burned until you're sure what you want."

She was sure. Allison sat on the edge of the bed, the mattress giving slightly under her hips. "Keys are under the floor mat."

"That's what I figured."

She must have already been falling asleep, because she swore he helped arrange her on the bed, a light quilt pulled up to her chin. He brushed a hand over her forehead, which was awfully nice.

"Night, Gabe."

That addictive laugh stroked her again, and she decided if he did agree to the charade? That sound was going to be what kept her sane through the entire chaotic situation, because the low rumble made all sorts of interesting reactions happen inside her.

Comforting, yet dangerous.

Sleep wrapped itself around her, and her eyes were so damn heavy. "I like your laugh."

"You talk a lot when you're sleep-deprived. What're you like when you're drunk?"

"I sing. Badly."

Something warm caressed her face again. "Stop talking and go to sleep."

Fighting to stay awake seemed like far more work than she could manage at the moment, so she listened.

Chapter Three

Considering everything else that had happened that day, Gabe was surprised his cautious switch went off without a snag. The Parkers must have all been working at the Timberline Grill, giving him the opportunity to sneak over on Allison's horse, exchange the low-speed steed for her stuffed-to-the-gills Toyota, and slip back to his cabin without being stopped for grand-theft auto.

While he traveled, he got hold of the idiot truck driver's mom and informed her that her baby had been driving fast and loose that morning. It might have been wrong to gloat over the punishment coming he heard in her voice, but hell if the kid didn't deserve it.

He parked Allison's vehicle directly behind his cabin where it couldn't easily be spotted unless a person was right in the yard. Once she'd gotten enough rest to straighten out her brain, she could reconsider and no one would even have to know she'd been over. And if they did go forward with the ploy, he could move whatever stuff she needed into the house...

Hell. He was as bad as her, jumping ahead, totally obsessed with the one idea that up and filled his brain.

Turning around the family circumstances was a powerful incentive, but the offer she'd made to help needed to be weighed against the downside of this ruse. How did he really feel about helping her pull off a con that would deceive a shit-ton of people? Or did it matter what people thought when her motivation was driven by the singular goal of giving to her mom?

Yeah, if it were his mom, he'd be willing to do just about anything to make her final days happier.

Gabe debated staying home until Allison woke, but that was akin to twiddling his thumbs and worrying like a granny. Instead, he tossed a few things into the Crock-Pot before spending a couple minutes straightening up his shit that had taken over the extra bed in the spare room. He wrote her a note in case she woke before he returned then headed back out to complete his chores. If she'd been burning the candle at both ends for two straight days, she should sleep until at least dinnertime.

Watching her snuggling up against his pillow, all soft as she fell asleep, had caused uncalled-for reactions in his body. It was a damn good thing he had the tiny extra room—he'd built it as an office space, but Rafe had argued long and hard until he'd given in and let the kid bring over a single bed. Rafe escaped as often as possible for some time away from home.

They both knew which parent he was avoiding.

Nope, having Allison in his house was going to be difficult, that was all there was to it. He snorted. He was probably leaping to conclusions he shouldn't. Maybe Allison planned on moving back into her mom's house for the duration.

Bullshit on that.

His brain twisted into tighter knots than he thought possible. Concentrating on the business side of her offer was far easier than imagining sharing the confines of his small cabin with Allison for months on end and keeping things platonic. Seeing her lush figure every night and every damn morning—screw being stereotypical, but he was a fucking male, and fucking was on his mind. He'd appreciated her curves and sassy attitude long before this morning when she'd thrown herself into his arms, and if they'd ever been in a situation where they might have dated, he would have had no issues keeping them both happy in bed. Or up against the wall. Or over the back of the goddamn couch for that matter.

If this wasn't one of the most awkward situations ever. Demanding she stay with him made it sound as if he expected her to whore herself out, and she would no doubt rightly react stronger to that suggestion than when he thought she'd offered to pay him to lie.

This was going from bad to worse in a hell of a hurry.

When his phone rang, he was half-anticipating it to be her on the other end of the line.

Nope.

Gabe stared at the call display with a sense of looming disaster. Keeping secrets in the Coleman clan was a difficult task at the best of times, although he'd done it for years. He hadn't had nearly enough time yet to formulate alternative explanations about Allison if he got backed into a corner, but on the line was the one person he couldn't simply blow off. He straightened and wiped his free hand on his jeans as he put through the call.

"Hey, cuz."

"I'll pick you up at seven." Travis's slow drawl rose a notch in volume to carry over the background noise of a tractor. "I need this so goddamn much, you wouldn't believe it."

Shit. Right there, Gabe's initial intent to beg off their previous arrangement was hog-tied, unless he could convince his cousin to delay for a few nights. "You sure you're up for it? After spending the day seeding maybe you should make it an early evening."

Travis swore loudly and creatively before switching to less volatile words. "What kind of pansy-assed comment is that? Sure, I'll just have a cup of tea and knit some doilies for you to shove up your ass. If you don't want to come along then bloody well say so and I'll go alone, but—"

"No, it's not that. I'm coming with you. We made a deal, remember?" Of all the lousy timing. Now he had to abandon Allison for the evening, although...maybe giving her a little more space would be for the best. They could talk over supper, then she'd have all night to figure out exactly what she wanted. Only one fire to avoid—making sure Travis didn't see any signs of her until that final decision had been made. "I'm driving though. Where you want me to nab you?"

"Pick me up at my trailer. Jackass."

Gabe laughed in spite of himself. "Asshole."

Travis hung up, and Gabe shoved his phone into his pocket, recovered the pliers he'd dropped and got back to the fence post. If he used a little more force than necessary, he figured no one was there to complain.

With a shitload of Colemans in the community, there was always someone to hang out with, to shoot the breeze or get pissed with when needed. At eighteen Gabe's brother Rafe was the youngest, but there were cousins all over the age range. They fought and supported each other in turn, with only a few situations that required peacekeeping to keep fists from flying.

Family, the kind that supported you in the tough moments and made you so bloody mad at times you couldn't see straight. They had it all in the extended Coleman clan.

He'd be pulling a fast one on this close-knit group if he and Allison went ahead with the ploy. What would the extended clan think when the truth came out?

It only took a moment before he laughed out loud. Honestly? It would be like every other situation that had ever gone down. Some folks would be upset, some would think it was the best joke ever. The improvements to the ranch would be the most talked-about part, as well as the final results with Allison's mom.

It was like a light bulb went off. His family, other than his father, would want him to make up his own damn mind and not base his decision on getting anyone's approval. And it wasn't as if he did anything to try to impress his father—at least not for years. The only reason he and Ben didn't come to blows more often was out of consideration for Dana. Gabe didn't want his ma hurt, or Rafe, and nothing in helping Allison would ultimately harm either of the two most important people in his life.

His father? Who gave a shit what the bastard thought?

Gabe looked over the fields, the familiar and comforting land he'd grown to love. He'd figured that a little time out here was what he needed to clear his head and get a straight focus on what was key. He had his answer to part of his dilemma.

If Allison still wanted his help, he was in.

What to do about the potential sexual situation between them? Well, that was an issue he would deal with as it arrived. If it arrived. Maybe they'd be so busy with other things that the attraction between them wouldn't even come up.

Gabe pulled himself onto Hurricane's back and ignored the taunting voice in his head that called bullshit.

For the second time in less than twelve hours Allison woke in Gabe's bed. It wasn't the scent of coffee teasing her senses as a wakeup call, but something savoury and rich. The sound of running water registered as well, and she sat up and stretched before looking around for the source.

Holy moly. She shouldn't have been so curious. Allison averted her gaze, but not before she'd gotten an eyeful.

The bathroom was off to her right. There was no door but instead an open archway revealed a long counter with a sink and a glass enclosure housing the shower. Which meant nothing but slightly foggy glass stood between her and a very naked Gabe. She was positive she'd spotted soap bubbles clinging to his body.

The urge to take a second peek and double-check the entire firm package rushed her, and she squirmed off the bed and fled into the living room.

Oh boy.

Sadness, a sense of loss, anxiety for her family. Those were supposed to be her concerns. Not the rush of sexual attraction that jumped her, or the tingling in her core that had nothing to do with being tired, hungry or worried. Had everything to do with what the pretence of having Gabe as a fiancé meant in a physical sense.

Maybe she was stupid, but until now? It hadn't even registered. She'd concentrated on her mother, on how to deal with her siblings. On who would be the perfect person to ask to join her in the fake engagement. She hadn't even once considered the physical attraction between them. She'd been so focused on their common interest in organics that the sensual longings he'd caused without even trying when they'd gone out for lunch so long ago? She'd totally forgotten that part.

She was remembering rather strongly now and feeling stupider than ever for not having taken sex into consideration. And pondering questions, like did she really expect him to be a monk—did she really *want* him to be a monk?—during the entire time they were acting, didn't make anything easier.

Allison turned to the kitchen counter and ignored the bit inside calling herself a coward for closing her eyes to the issue. Instead, she stirred the stew in the Crock-Pot, breathed deeply and enjoyed the aroma.

To keep her hands busy and distract her mind from everything—her mom, her job, the gratuitous images of a naked Gabe that kept leaping to mind—she opened cupboards and drawers until she'd managed to set the table.

Might as well make a few assumptions and make herself at home. Because after the extra sleep, she still didn't see any better solution than the one she'd come up with in the first place.

She was in the middle of transferring bread onto a plate to go with the stew when he stepped into the room. His hair was tousled and damp. Wearing a tight black T-shirt and faded blue jeans, Gabe was the epitome of the classic Canadian cowboy.

Wranglers never had a representative like this one, but could they ever have used him.

"You find everything okay?" He opened the fridge door and pulled out a water jug he deposited on the table.

Allison swallowed to find enough moisture to de-stick her tongue from the roof of her mouth. "I hope you didn't mind me getting things ready."

He shook his head. "It's a kitchen. I figure you know your way around one."

She froze in the middle of pouring pickles into a serving bowl. "Gabe Coleman, did you just make a macho-asshole comment about women and kitchens?"

He blinked in confusion. A moment later that addictive chuckle of his flitted across the room, only this time instead of turning her on it pissed her off that he wasn't taking her seriously.

Gabe reached over and captured the pickle jar, the one she'd considered throwing at his head. "Allison, your family owns a restaurant. That's all I'm referring to. You sure you got enough sleep to be using the dangerous weapons in here? Like the serving spoons and butter knives?"

He winked, and the rush of anger that had struck waned to be instantly replaced with blushing guilt. "Damn it, I'm sorry. I'm still wound up, and just assumed."

Gabe caught her by the shoulders and tugged her close, squeezing so tight she could barely breathe. The embrace offered security and acceptance, and was so totally non-sexual nothing stopped her from soaking in the comfort he offered.

Then as quick as he'd begun, he released her, patted her shoulder and directed her to one of the chairs. He settled on the opposite side of the table and opened the steaming Crock-Pot.

"Want a scoop?"

Allison held up her bowl as he ladled in the meaty concoction. He served himself about three times as much, buttered a couple slices of bread then started eating. She would have been more embarrassed about diving in without small talk if her stomach hadn't chosen that moment to grumble loudly.

Gabe laughed. "Your body's still complaining about you mistreating it the past couple days. Eat—there's plenty."

It felt like only a few minutes later before she was licking the sauce off her spoon to get at the final drops. "My compliments to the chef."

"High praise from someone who knows food. Thank you. I don't starve." His pleased expression faded rapidly into something unreadable.

"What's the extra seasoning you put in there? Can't be fresh thyme, not yet. Savoury? Basil?"

"Not completely sure—my ma makes these ice-cube things with the herbs when they're fresh. Mixes them in the blender with a little oil, then she shoves a Ziploc bag of them into my freezer. You'll have to ask her the secret ingredients. All I know is I toss one in the crock, or the soup pot, and suddenly I've got all my cousins clamouring for me to bring over my leftovers."

The setting and the conversation were comfortable and inconsequential. They both knew they were holding off the real discussion that needed to take place. Allison gathered her courage before it could escape again.

"Gabe?"

"Yeah?"

She stared at his face, gazing into his dark eyes, searching his expression for a hint of what his answer would be. "I've had a nap. I've thought it through some more. It might be the stupidest thing I've ever suggested, but I can't for the life of me see another way to do this."

Gabe sighed. "Then I won't try to convince you otherwise. Nothing I'd hate more than for you to carry regrets regarding your mom's final days."

Something inside her chest jerked, or maybe it was in her stomach. "You'll do it?"

He took her hand in his, strong fingers twisting around hers and holding on tight. "*We'll* do it. This entire crazy idea's got to be you and me together for it to work. Don't think for a minute that this is you alone, because that's not what I'm signing up for."

"You're signing up for the help I can give the ranch..."

The increased pressure on her fingers made the words trickle away. "I'll admit I'm damn hopeful your information can make a difference. But the ranch will be here for a long time. Your mom takes priority, you understand?"

The part of her that had worried how she would juggle everything eased a tiny bit. "Making sure my mom doesn't know it's a sham comes first. I swear I'll try not to drag this out any longer than we have to, but—"

His thumb rubbed over her knuckles soothingly. "You're getting yourself back into a flap. Slow down, we'll deal with that issue in a minute. There are a few big-picture things we need to discuss first."

She could have sworn he swallowed hard, but that wasn't the in-control and steady man she knew.

"Where are you planning on staying?"

Finally something she had an answer for. "I'll move back in with the family."

"Like hell."

She stiffened even though he'd said it softly. "Gabe?"

He shook his head. "No one is going to buy we're getting hitched if you do that. If you're all fired up about moving back to Rocky to be with me, tell me why you'd stay anywhere but in my place?"

Allison flushed. “Old-fashioned?”

He raised a brow but didn’t say anything.

“I don’t want to put you out more than necessary.”

“And I’m saying if you want this to work you’re moving in here. You’ll spend your days at the restaurant, and we’ll make sure you see as much of your mom and family as possible, but you sleep nights here. You and me need to keep in touch and...” Gabe sighed, reaching across the table to stroke her cheek softly. “And you’re going to need a place to hide out. This is it. What about when you have tough moments and need to cry, or scream, or to beat the hell out of something? You can’t do that at your mom’s house.”

The sheer magnitude of what they were undertaking started to register. “Do you think I’m wrong for doing this?”

Gabe shrugged. “That’s the kicker. I don’t know, which is why I ain’t trying to talk you out of it.”

They stared at each other, silent for a moment.

“So...what now? Do we go right away and talk to my mom?”

Gabe rubbed the back of his neck. “Unfortunately, I’ve already got plans I can’t cancel. I think we should give it one more evening before making any announcements. Once the word gets out, it’s going to spread like wildfire.”

Oh goodie. Part of Rocky that she really hadn’t missed. “You think they’ll use megaphones on Main Street or something?”

“Don’t go giving anybody ideas, because you know someone will do it. If not from town, one of my cousins, just to be a pain in the ass.”

His wide grin reassured her more than anything else. “Hey, Gabe?”

“Yeah?”

She let out a little of the tension she'd been holding inside, relaxing back into her chair. "Thanks for not throwing me out and telling me I'm crazy."

He raised his brows. "Fact is, I think we're both a trifle mad, but yeah—you're welcome."

Gabe rose to his feet, clearing his plate and hers to the counter. She helped by putting away what she could while he dealt with the dishes.

Outside the sky was changing to the most spectacular colours. Allison stared out the window. "There's going to be a beautiful sunset tonight, with the way the clouds are hanging on the horizon."

"I'll take you to a real pretty spot to watch from sometime. There's a comfy tree to lean on and everything." He tilted his head toward a side door. "I'll show you where you can put your stuff. I cleared out some space in the second bedroom while you were asleep. Rafe sleeps over occasionally, but I've kind of let the office stuff take it over. I'll bring in your bags and you can get settled while I'm out."

He pulled open the door to reveal a single bed shoved up against a wall, a small desk tucked beside it. A box on its surface overflowed with papers.

"I cleaned out a few drawers in the bathroom for you as well."

Suddenly her tongue wasn't working again. Finding the extra bed was a relief—she wouldn't have to sleep on the couch for the next however long. But there was only one bathroom.

She'd buy a robe tomorrow. Or give up showering, or something.

It took three trips for them to bring in her stuff. She put some of her things straight into the small shed off the back door. Extra lamps, rugs. She'd had a furnished apartment in Red Deer so she had less bits and pieces than usual, but an embarrassing amount still crowded the entranceway of his porch when her car was empty.

Gabe cleared his throat before tossing her that familiar *Angel Boy* grin she'd seen so often back in high school. The one that said mischief all over it. "Once you get settled, maybe you want to come up with the story of how we fell in love. If you figure it out, I'll play along. Easier if one of us does the setup."

Her pick for a helper couldn't have been better. This was beyond incredible. "You want to go over it in the morning?"

He nodded, seemingly lost in thought. "I'll rearrange my schedule so we can have some extra time. If we're ready, we can stop in at your mom's tomorrow night. However you feel works best."

Gabe pulled on a well-worn jean jacket and shoved his keys in the pocket. He opened the door, paused, then shut it with him still standing there, his back toward her.

Allison put down the suitcase she'd been ready to carry to the other room. "Gabe? What's wrong?"

He twisted gradually. "Just realized something."

One step forward brought him close enough to touch. One more, and she was ready to edge against the wall to get out of his way. That was her plan until he reached out and caught her, one hand snaking around the back of her neck, the other around her body so he could pull them tight together. He lowered his mouth over hers deliberately, slow enough she could have retreated if she'd wanted to.

She was too surprised to move. Or at least that was the excuse she gave herself.

His lips were firm but gentle. No tongue, just a meeting of mouths. Kisses, one after another followed as he controlled her position, not allowing her to squirm away. And when she opened her mouth to complain he took total advantage, deepening the kiss until she was ready to pass out for the second time that day.

Pass out, or she was about to wrap her arms around him and grind their bodies together, she was so excited. From kissing. From the feel of his long, hard body pressed up tight against hers.

He let her go, leaning away. Cool air and regret he hadn't done more than simply kiss her hit about the same time. Holy cow, what had she gotten herself into?

One corner of his mouth twitched before his wide smile reappeared. "Figured we'd better get used to each other a little—hate to have anyone call our bluff just because we ain't good at kissing."

The butterflies in her stomach didn't quite know what to think of his comment. The tenderness in his touch had seemed far more real than she'd expected.

Allison pulled herself together. "You're right. Totally right." She nodded briskly and snatched up a bag in either hand, turning her back to hide her flaming-hot face. "Have a good night."

She fled as unhurriedly as possible, but it was still an escape and he knew it. And she knew he knew because that wicked laugh of his followed her yellow-bellied retreat.

Allison stood on the porch in the dark and watched his taillights disappear down the long driveway leading to the main road.

Chapter Four

Loud music blared through the made-over barn, but it had been used long enough for its new purpose there was no dust or straw bits left in the rafters to shake loose and fall on those gathered beneath the bright lights.

The scent remained—nothing could remove that slightly sweet aroma of animals and feed that had permeated the wood itself from years of use. Layered in were the new scents of alcohol and cigarettes. Perfume and sweat.

Gabe watched the men fighting in the ring before him with only half his attention, the rest focused on his cousin who stood nearly motionless at his side.

Bullshit. Most of his attention was still back on the woman he'd left in his house. Wondering what Allison was doing, and questions of how they were going to pull this deception off, threaded through his brain like a snake holding its tail. An endless loop of unanswerable chaos.

Her taste lingered on his lips, and he gave himself a mental slap and refocused on the here and now.

Travis stared intently across the wide space of the room, his eyes almost glazed. It was always like this—the calm before the storm. His breathing slow and even, relaxed as if he were ready to fall asleep.

Deceptively dangerous.

It was nearly a year since Gabe had discovered what Travis did in some of his spare time, and insisted he be brought along as an emergency backup. Some nights he wasn't needed. Some nights, he was.

A roar of approval rose from the men gathered around the perimeter of the fighting area as one of the two in the ring landed a series of blows that dropped his opponent to his knees. Men with nothing more than wrapped fingers, stripped to the waist. Beating the hell out of each other because they wanted to. Because they could.

It wasn't Gabe's thing, but Travis sure the hell got something out of it, so who was he to judge? As long as his cousin got home in one piece, he figured the bruises and cuts would eventually heal.

The man teetering toward the floorboards was dragged to his feet by a couple of the watchers, raucous laughter and ribald comments flying through the air. Gabe ignored it all. He'd heard it before, seen it before. Shock value was gone.

Someone poked him in the arm and he jerked around.

Shit. "What the hell are you doing here?"

Tamara Coleman planted her fists on her hips and lowered her chin just enough to peer over the top of her glasses at him. "On-call medical. Don't tell me you're stupid enough to be participating in this free-for-all?"

Someone jostled her from behind, and Gabe automatically reached out to pull her closer to his side so he could protect her. "Not me."

The suddenly fucked-up situation got more and more convoluted, even though he'd expected this to happen eventually. In an area as small as theirs, it was inevitable that somewhere along the line someone in the family would find out.

He didn't expect it would be one of the Coleman cousins of the female variety.

He jerked his thumb over his shoulder.

Tamara leaned around him and swore lightly. "Travis Coleman, you're a bigger fool than I'd ever imagined."

Travis didn't even move his head. "Tamara. You slumming it tonight?"

"You lost whatever you had of your minuscule brains?" Tamara wormed past Gabe and got directly in front of Travis until he had to look at her. "You're an idiot, right? Your mama dropped you on your head when you were a baby."

Travis smirked. "She did, and I liked it. So if you'll excuse me..."

He was past them both and pushing through the bodies, climbing into the ring with the evil grin still on his face.

Tamara growled in frustration, arms folding in front of her across her flannel shirt. "When I volunteered to come stitch up the brainless twits who fight here, I didn't think I'd be working on family."

Gabe moved in closer, putting himself between her and the biggest of the men intently watching the ring. "Things can get a little iffy in the crowd too, so if you've got a safer place to watch from, let me take you there."

"I'm fine." She planted her feet wide, somehow echoing the stance Travis took as his fighting partner climbed through the ropes. "If I have to stitch him up? I'm not using any painkiller. Stupid ass."

In the ring, Travis and the wiry blond who'd joined him were already tossing experimental blows. Or the blond was swinging. Travis moved smoothly side to side, dodging and otherwise staying just out of reach.

"It ain't a dance party, Travis," someone catcalled.

"Take off his pretty head, Stan," another encouraged.

Stan lunged and shot out his fist, connecting with Travis's torso, high and hard. He followed with his left fist to ribs, the slam of knuckles against flesh loud even as voices rose. Gabe shifted to the side to see around the man in front of him, and in that single moment he missed Travis's first blow.

Stan was bent in two, his body doubled forward with Travis's fist still buried in his gut. Travis dragged his hand free, pounding a blow to Stan's face, then another. It was like watching an automaton, repetitious and consistent in motion. Travis had lost his smile, a concentrated glare replacing it. Drops of sweat beaded his brow, his muscles flexing as he worked around Stan. He backed up as if to allow the other man to straighten.

Stan drew in a deep breath, hands on his thighs to push himself vertical.

Travis stepped forward and swung, knuckles connecting with jaw. Stan's head snapped back, his entire body flipping in a wavelike motion as he collapsed to the floor.

Travis waited, arms bent in a ready position, as if eager for the man to get up and continue fighting. Gabe sighed, recognizing the energy still blistering out from his cousin.

"At least that's over," Tamara muttered. "Because while I have no objection to staring at half-naked men all night, including my cousin in that number kind of makes the thrill fade."

A snort escaped involuntarily. "Yeah, I can see how that could ruin the show. He's going to fight again," Gabe warned.

She turned to stare at him in shock. "But I thought once a night—"

"He gets like this. He's going to fight until someone takes him to the ground."

"That's insane." Concern and disgust warred on her face.

Gabe nodded. "Maybe. But if he doesn't get it in the ring, he'd be out at a bar picking a fight, and this is safer than getting cold-cocked by a dozen pissed-off hockey players he's managed to insult so bad they want to beat him until he's half-dead."

All her usual bluster vanished. "And you'd know this because that's not some random example you pulled out of thin air?"

"Nope. Been there, done that."

Travis was out of the ring and headed to the side of the room, so Gabe pulled Tamara after him, weaving through the crowd. Travis might be a grownup, but Gabe needed to keep an eye on him. Sometimes Travis got these notions into his head that something out of the norm would be great to try, and while Gabe had no trouble babysitting him here in organized chaos, he wasn't about to let his cousin go get beat up or killed in something even more free-for-all.

Tamara tugged his sleeve to get him to stop. "Is this habit something I should be worried about? Like more worried than not understanding why my cousin likes to get violent?"

Gabe dragged a hand through his hair and wondered how to explain this, then he realized he couldn't. "You have to ask him. As far as I know he gets something out of it, and he's not dead at the end of the night. That's it. That's my understanding. I like a good fight at times, as much as the average guy. Getting physical lets out the demons, and sometimes that means beating the hell out of something, and sometimes..."

He trickled to a stop and shook his head. Nope. Not a discussion he was willing to continue with her.

Tamara smirked. "You were going to add *fucking* to that list of physical things guys like, weren't you?"

Oh *sheesh.* "Not going there with you."

"You're such a girl."

Gabe laughed. "No, you're a girl, and my cousin, and I'm not talking sex with you."

He glanced around the wide-open space. Another fight had begun already, people crowded forward, some with beers in their hands. The few women in the crowd were held tightly, their guys keeping a close eye on them.

He took a quick peek at Tamara. She was far more covered than the other women in the room. Her jeans and flannel shirt were modest, her long hair pulled back into a simple ponytail. She wasn't going for the femme fatale look, but she was still an attractive woman. "You planning on putting in medical care often?"

She cocked out a hip, her head tilted to the side. "You thinking of becoming my keeper, Gabe? If you figure on following me, or otherwise trying to keep track of me, forget it. I'm a big girl. I can take care of myself. You're not responsible for making sure I get home in one piece."

Something twisted at her words, the echo of ones he'd heard so long ago, burning and painful. He stared her down, hoping he could keep what roiled inside from showing on his face.

The volume rose around them to a roar, someone shouted for a doctor. Tamara whipped away before he could react, elbowing her way through the crowd, ducking under arms. Gabe followed at a much slower pace, her smaller body wiggling easier through tight spaces. He was in time to see her snatch up a bag from the side of the platform then scramble through the ropes. She dragged on gloves before dropping to her knees to examine the downed fighter. Her orders rang out, and a couple of men stepped forward to lift the fallen off the mat. She worked efficiently, pressing a bandage to stem the blood pouring from a head cut.

It took so little time—one minute they were in the ring, the next Tamara had the man secluded to a small area off the side, bright light tilted to make it easier for her to see as she made an injection. Gabe moved in closer as she carefully stitched together the three-inch wound, seemingly oblivious to her surroundings.

The Whiskey Creek Colemans always came across as tough girls, somewhat inevitable as they'd had years of attempting to keep up with their multiple wild male cousins, but Gabe had never actually witnessed one of them in a setting like this before.

"I don't know why you're still hanging around, Gabe. I'm fine." Tamara let go of the fighter's cheek to slap his hand off her thigh. "And you. If you don't want me to stitch your eyelids shut, keep your bloody hands to yourself."

The fighter chuckled. "No harm in trying."

"I have a scalpel in my bag and an intimate knowledge of anatomy. You really want to get fresh with me?" Tamara was the one to laugh as the man sucked in a hiss of pain as she pulled the thread. "Yeah, poor baby. Concentrate on something other than your head."

"I was trying," the man complained.

Tamara didn't look up from her task. "Go away, Gabe."

"Going." But he wasn't leaving for good until he knew she was safely in her vehicle and headed home.

Gabe grabbed another beer as he casually followed Travis. They'd done this for long enough now he didn't have to put up with at least one cousin telling him to fuck off. Travis knew the story. Gabe wouldn't step in unless needed. And at the end of the night, after Travis had enough, Gabe would drag him to the truck and drive him home.

It wasn't typical, but it was what it was. Gabe didn't judge. Just did what had to be done.

He pulled himself onto the top of a platform area to the side and leaned on the wall. From here he could see the ring, see Travis clambering back through the ropes for round two of pain and punishment. Off to the right Tamara was finishing bandaging her fighter. Gabe took another pull from his drink and wondered if his life could possibly get any weirder.

He laughed at himself. Oh, yeah, it could. Because when his babysitting tonight was over, he would head home to a woman who planned on turning things upside down and sideways.

Kissing Allison—that had been both a good and a bad idea. Bad because it made him think of all the things he'd put aside over the past while. Trying to keep his family together, all the little bits he'd secretly been dealing with around the ranch.

Her lips were soft, almost innocent under his. Her body? Innocent miss she wasn't, not with those curves and the way she'd pressed into him. Pretending to be with her and not getting to have more than public tastes of her mouth was going to suck.

But perhaps...

Travis staggered for a moment in the ring, and Gabe held his breath. His cousin's right eye was swelling shut. Maybe there would be an earlier finish than usual to their evening.

Fists exploded out, rapid jabs flying like electric sparks from a welding gun. Travis's opponent reeled backward and collapsed onto the ropes.

Far more vertical than the other man, Travis raised a fist in the air in triumph. He headed back to the corner to snatch up his water bottle and press a towel to his face.

Gabe sighed. No reprieve. A long night loomed ahead of him.

After everything was over, after he'd helped Allison, and once the ranch was producing the money they needed to stay afloat, then he could approach Allison for real.

But for now, she was just another lost sheep to care for. His gaze moved carefully over Travis, over Tamara. Gabe leaned his head on the wall and watched.

It was after one, and Gabe still wasn't back. Allison pulled the packing tape off the bottom of the empty box and unfolded it, sliding the collapsed cardboard under her bed with the rest.

She looked around the room, trying to see if she'd spread out too much. There was surprisingly little when she'd actually decided what she needed to unpack. Clothes, her computer. Her ebook reader. The knickknacks and other parts of her stuff were stacked in the porch to be added to the items already stored in the shed. She didn't need them here, not for the while she'd be around, and the less she intruded, the better.

Who was she kidding? She'd totally come in and taken over his life. Just being in his house was bad enough.

Allison stepped back into the main living area and flicked on the kettle.

She was writing notes, sipping on a cup of tea, when floorboards outside creaked softly a second before the door opened.

Gabe hung up his jean jacket, turned silently toward the main room. He spotted her and shook his head.

"I thought you'd be asleep for a long time by now."

Allison hesitated. "I think napping so late threw me off. I'm tired, but I can't sleep."

"You're also worrying yourself to death, ain't you?"

She nodded. No reason to deny it.

Gabe stepped forward, long limbs eating up the distance between them so smoothly. He pulled out a chair and sat beside her at the table. "You settle in?"

"Feeling guilty the entire time. Not guilty enough to change my mind, though."

Gabe patted her hand. "I didn't think you would." He drew the paper toward him. "I take it this is what you've got planned for us."

"It's simple."

"That's always best." He read for a minute, nodding slowly. "You got it pretty much covered here, with the whole 'it's an engagement to see if it's gonna work'. That makes sense, with us supposedly dating long distance until now."

It would also help when they called it off down the road, after her—

Allison rushed ahead, refusing to let the thought fully form in her head. "Yeah, that's what I figured."

He leaned back in his chair. “So, tomorrow?”

She nodded. “I’m going to try to catch my mom in the morning, by herself. I think that would be the way to start. Maybe by some miracle she’ll confess what’s wrong before I begin the hoax...”

Surprise registered on his face. “I hadn’t even considered that. Hopefully she’ll see you and change her mind. It’s possible.”

She spotted blood on his fingers. She caught him by the wrist, turning his palm up to see where it had come from. “Did you cut yourself?”

Gabe withdrew his hand and went to the sink. “It’s not mine. Sorry about that, thought I’d washed it off. I was...helping a friend, and he got a bloody nose. That’s all.”

She deliberately didn’t ask. Just sat and took another drink. The tea was lukewarm, and she gave up. Even with the discomfort in her body and mind, she had to get to bed.

Allison took her cup to the sink and suddenly realized her mistake in staying up until he returned. A long hot shower would help relax her, but no way would she suggest she take one tonight. He’d have to wait to go bed until she was done.

Just, no way.

He cleared his throat. Must have clued in where her thoughts had headed. “I didn’t build this place very comfortably for two. The extra bathroom isn’t done yet, so you go ahead and get ready. I’ll take the things in the porch out to the shed, if that’s okay.”

They went in two different directions. Allison hurried through preparations for bed, pulling the door closed to the guest room and crawling under the cold quilts. It seemed to take forever for her body heat to make the room warmer. She gave up and grabbed a pair of thick socks from the suitcase she’d propped on the desk. Crawling back into bed with the fuzzy softness on her feet, and a toque on her head might not have been a fashion statement, but it made her warmer and it worked enough that she finally fell into a restless sleep.

Restless enough that when she woke her eyes were filled with sand and she couldn't stop yawning. The clock radio said six a.m. and she yawned again in protest.

The knock on the door was followed by Gabe's soft question. "Awake enough for coffee?"

"Yes. A gallon, please."

She'd have to give him money for groceries, or pick up some to replace what she'd be eating. All of her thoughts so mundane. Unimportant. Tiny little details of the morning that would all fade away once she got where she actually was going.

Allison squared her shoulders and got out of bed to face the start of the deception.

Chapter Five

Her mother's face lit up for a moment before concern crowded in. "Hey. What are you doing here?"

Allison stepped into the familiar kitchen and wrapped her arms around Maisey, tucking her chin against her mom's neck and breathing deeply.

The scent of family. The scent of home.

"I'm not allowed to stop in to say hi?"

"You didn't even tell me you were coming." Maisey squeezed one last time before releasing her and stepping back. Her gaze darted over Allison, probably noting the blue jeans and cotton shirt instead of her normal more businesslike clothing. "Look at you. You're in town to visit one of your organic suppliers, aren't you?"

Allison forced a grin. "Well, kind of. I have a ton to tell you. Are you headed into the restaurant this morning, or do you have time to talk?"

"Paul and Elle are working early today. I'll go in for dinner and shut down." Maisey pointed to the table and the coffee carafe. "And I always have time for you."

Maintaining an excited, happy expression was difficult, but Allison thought she managed, sneaking peeks at her mother as she prepared a coffee. The drink was more to have something to do with her hands than because she was thirsty.

Maisey had grown thinner. The lines on her face were deep this morning, and the shoulder-length hair she usually kept dyed brown was streaked with the grey that had set in during her husband's long illness.

Allison's doubts eased even as her concern grew. Returning to Rocky was more than a whim—her mom needed her.

Maisey sat and raised a brow. "So, talk."

Allison waited for a minute, hoping against hope her mother would be the first to crack. "Anything new in Rocky? How are all of you doing?"

Her mom paused then shrugged. "Paul was complaining about the tax forms, and Elle's been seeing one of the newspaper reporters. New fellow to town. He's nice enough, I suppose."

Even wound up like a spring, Allison couldn't stop the laugh from bursting out. "But he's not from around here, is that it?"

Maisey looked guilty. "I did say he was nice."

Allison pressed on. "And you? How have you been doing? It was a miserable winter."

Her mom turned her gaze out the window and stared for a moment.

Was she going to spill the beans? *Come on, Mom, tell me. Share.*

All her meager hope slipped away as Maisey did no more than sigh heavily then point at the tree outside. "It was a terrible winter. The last snowfall came after the tree was already budding out, and we lost a few limbs. Your father and I were married under that willow, you know. Sad to see it in such rough shape."

Allison made a mental note to get a tree-pruner in to save the tree if possible. "And you? What's new?"

Maisey waved off her attempt. "Now you, stop it. Tell me why you're here on a workday."

It was no use. The plan had to kick into gear, and now. She smiled as hard as she could, hoping her expression didn't look as fake as it felt. "I have good news. I'm coming back to Rocky."

Her mother stuttered to a stop with the coffee cup halfway to her lips. Her jaw dropped slightly. "No. I thought the company said there wasn't enough business yet to set up a second office, especially not out this way."

Allison shook her head. "It's not for work, Mom. I'm moving back, because, well, I've been seeing someone, and we're getting married."

Coffee sloshed over the edge of Maisey's cup as she placed it back on the table. "Married? I didn't even know you were dating, and you're getting married? What on earth?"

"Oh, Mom. I just...wait, I said that wrong. We're engaged. We're going to get married, only not this minute. At least, we think we want to get married, but it's been tough, since he lives here, and with me working in Red Deer. So I decided since he can't move, and I can, I'd come back to Rocky. While we double-check to make sure it's what we want. The getting-married, I mean."

Could she possibly do a worse job of this?

A small smile tickled the corner of her mom's mouth, though. "You're giddy. Who's got you so flustered you can't even tell me straight out that you've fallen in love?"

Allison flushed. She felt the instant heat on her cheeks and figured she must be beet red. "Gabe. Gabe Coleman."

Maisey full-out grinned as she lifted a finger and shook it in her daughter's face. "I told you he had a crush on you back in high school, but you never let on. You said it was nothing."

And it had been. But hey, if her mom wanted to think this was destiny finishing its work? Allison set loose the reins and let the idea run.

"Well, it's something now, enough I've come back."

"Well, we'll just have to find you a spot, then. Elle took over your old room when you left, but there's always the guest room."

The heat in her face continued to rage, but damn it, she was a grown woman. "I'm planning on moving in with Gabe."

Maisey's brow lifted, and Allison prepared for a lecture. When her dad had been alive such a thing would never have been considered appropriate.

She was tempted to return to the family home, but Gabe had made a valid point. She could spend as much time as she wanted to with her mom without him complaining, but staying nights at his place made their ruse more plausible without putting him out by always having to be with her.

"Well, you're old enough to know your own mind, Allison. But you're always welcome here."

It was what she needed to hear, but her mouth must have been hanging open in shock because her mom laughed.

"Oh, sweetie, I know. It's not what you expected, is it? But..." Maisey's gaze darted out the window for a moment before coming back to land on her daughter, the touch soft as a hug. "Life's too short. If you love Gabe and want to see if this is right for you, then you do what you have to. Only until you're sure? Please don't get pregnant."

"Mom!"

"Well, that happens, you know. When you're sharing a bed with someone you love."

Allison covered her face with her hands. "I'm not having this conversation. It's not happening."

Maisey stroked her fingers lightly, laughter still clear in her voice. "I'll shut up now. But I'm very happy for you." She rose and snuck around the table, and Allison savoured every second of her mother's hug. Just soaked in the acceptance and the warmth.

They separated, and Allison had one more second to enjoy the peace before a look of horror crossed her mom's face.

"What? Why are you looking like that?"

"Oh, Allison. The Colemans? There's no room here to have them all over for an engagement party. We'll use the restaurant. I can shut it down on—"

No way. She was cutting that one off at the pass. "Gabe and I talked about a party. Not now. Give us time, okay? We'll do dinner with you, Elle and Paul, and I'll visit with his family, but nothing big. Not until..."

Her mom slowed slightly. "Until you're sure. Honey, do you love him?"

Allison wondered if breaking into a coughing fit in the middle of her confession would be suspicious, but she didn't want to outright lie. She pulled out all the drama classes she remembered from high school and let the most fool-hearted sensation rise up. She was a romance heroine confessing her love for her suitor.

"He's...Gabe."

Even in her ears it sounded lovesick and dreamy. Now she had to concentrate on not bursting out giggling as her mother clasped her hands together with happiness.

"Then that's all I need to know. Oh, I'm so happy for you."

One more power hug later, Allison managed to escape with the promise that she and her fiancé would join the others for dinner Saturday evening.

"And I won't say a word to Elle or Paul. You and Gabe can tell them the good news yourself."

Oh joy.

"They're going to be so surprised," Maisey continued. Allison agreed, but managed to avoid snorting in response.

They worked together to clear the table, and fortunately, when her mother turned, it was for another reason altogether.

"If you're here, are you still able to keep your job?"

Allison shook her head. "That's the other thing I wanted to ask you. Is it possible for me to pick up hours at the restaurant? I don't want you to fire anyone, but if there's room for me..."

Her mom beamed. "We can always use your help. In fact, we were getting ready to make changes to the menu again—you know springtime is when your father liked to shake things up."

She went on for a while about improvements they had in mind. It hit Allison that she was fortunate she'd be able to honour the promises she'd made to Gabe. Even though she hadn't physically been working at the family restaurant, she'd always been involved in the supply and ordering end. One less thing to worry about.

There was no reason to rush away, so Allison pulled out paper and worked on ideas for menu changes with her mom. They opened up the laptop and poured over recipes. It was like in the old days, before she'd moved away, and it was so good.

Maisey looked tired, though, her skin slightly more yellow than usual in the bright sunshine coming through the window.

Allison put on the kettle and made tea. While there was still time, she was going to enjoy every second as much as possible.

Gabe waited as she pulled into the driveway. He'd called his ma and asked if she'd be home in the afternoon. News would spread quickly once the word got out, and he didn't want her to be the last one to hear. Even if this was a ruse, she'd kick his butt for not sharing.

Allison's face was red, tear streaks marking her cheeks as she came to a stop. She wiped a hand over her eyes and popped open the door. "I know I'm late. I'm a mess. Give me five minutes to wash my face."

"Take ten. You're not that late." He twisted his shoulders to allow her to pass him as she bolted toward the back of the house.

Following her would probably make her feel worse, so instead he slipped into the kitchen and poured them both drinks. The water ran in the background, and the soft sound of her voice.

"What you need?" he asked, but there was no response. The murmuring continued, low and steady, and his curiosity dragged him to the door of his bedroom.

The closer he got, the easier it was to recognize her words. A steady stream of them escaped her lips as she stared into the mirror and gave herself a pep talk. Gabe took a deep breath and stepped back before she could spot him.

Damn determined to do this, no matter what it cost her. Her stubborn resolution impressed him. Made something inside him kind of proud that she'd picked him as a partner in her wild hair of an idea.

He sipped his juice and resisted peeking at his watch.

"Ready."

Gabe checked her over quickly. Her eyes were still bright, her cheeks flushed but clean. She'd switched tops in the past two minutes and pulled on a white shirt that looked fancier than anything he'd seen her in before.

"You look good."

She shrugged. "Wasn't sure how dressed up to get, but I still want to look nice. I don't want to make your mom uncomfortable, but I don't want her to think that I'm not trying to impress her. But I don't want her to think I'm trying to impress her and..."

Gabe let his amusement bubble out in his laughter.

"You know how to tangle yourself in more knots than anyone I've ever met. My ma likes you. You don't need to impress her."

"I like her too."

This funny expression twisted her face and she peeked in his direction. She was checking him out, clearly wanting to ask him something.

"What's got you now?"

Allison shrugged. "You are a good man, Gabe. That's all."

Which was an answer, but not much of one. "Thanks."

He held out his hand and she eyed him with suspicion.

"Get used to it. I'm a romantic son of a gun, or so I've been told. If we're not holding hands or cuddling up, people will wonder."

She stuck her fingers into his, still warm from the washing. He ignored everything else and tugged her after him.

When she would have walked to her car, he changed her direction, bringing her to the driver side of his truck.

"I can drive, Gabe."

"I noticed. Get in." He opened the door and stood motionless as she stared at him.

"You going to be this bossy the entire time?"

"What? I'm opening the door like a gentleman. Nothing bossy about that."

Allison rolled her eyes before she followed his order and crawled up, shuffling past the steering wheel to the passenger seat.

He did up his seat belt without saying anything, but he didn't put the truck into gear. Just sat there. Waited.

She was a smart thing. He was sure he didn't need to give her any more directions.

"Gabe, you planning on heading over there soon? Your mom must be waiting for us."

"She'll be busy around the house, don't you worry."

Allison leaned on the side door, opened her mouth to say something else. Her gaze dropped to the empty space between them. The groan that escaped her was damn amusing.

She unclipped and slid to the center seat, her thigh nice and warm where it rested alongside his. "Like I said, bossy."

Gabe slipped the truck into gear and backed out of his parking spot. "Just making sure we don't do anything stupid to spill the beans. It's not as if sitting beside me is going to give you cooties or something."

She leaned back and sighed. "Nope. And you're right. The only time couples sit on the opposite side of the cab is when they've had a fight."

He laughed. "We used to tease the guys about how much action they were going to get based on how close their girls sat after a night out on the town. My cousin Steve got the worst ragging after he bought a truck with bucket seats in the front. He could never win after that."

"You Coleman crew can be nasty."

"Not even counting the stick-shift jokes." The burst of laughter from her made Gabe smile. That's what he wanted to hear. Get her mind off what she was doing for a while, because even though they were pulling a fast one, it didn't mean they had to live like some kind of robots for the next however many months.

Allison was going to need some laughter in her life.

The short trip to his parents' house they talked about the other Coleman cousins—who was doing what and who was still in the area. She'd known the entire clan, so it wasn't difficult to get her caught up.

"You don't have to see the lot of them until July first. Coleman Canada Day picnic. We'll hit Traders Pub to meet the cousins before then, though."

Allison nodded, but her attention was focused on the house as they pulled up front. “It looks pretty much the same as I remember.”

He stopped her when she would have slid over and crawled out the passenger door, instead pulling her after him. “When have you been here?”

“Outside? A few times when there was some sporting event and we came over to give Michael a ride…”

They both froze. Just for a second before Gabe pushed the memories aside and tugged her from the cab. “Right. Paul and Michael played basketball together. Or one of those sports, right?”

She was on the ground, right up close to him, but his body was so tight that she could have been anyone. Didn’t matter that she still smelt like apple blossoms, or that they were damn near hugging.

Michael’s grinning face flashed before his eyes, his younger brother’s cocky and devil-may-care expression imprinted on Gabe’s very soul.

A pair of soft hands cupped his cheeks as Allison tilted his head down and their eyes met. “I’m sorry. I didn’t mean to remind you.”

A million things reminded him of his missing brother, if he’d let the pain come. A million things, and his father. “It’s okay. We’re just fine.”

He pulled himself together, pulled on the façade and wrapped his pain up tight where it couldn’t sneak out. “Nothing to be sorry for. I don’t want you watching what you say around me. I’m not some china doll you have to worry about breaking.”

He started them toward the house, concentrating hard on not letting it show how much he hurt. It was Allison who slipped her fingers into his, squeezing tight.

God, if she apologized again he was going to be walking into his mama’s house while bawling like a damn baby.

"When does Rafe get home?" she asked instead, and a bit of his tension drained away.

"Usually around four if he takes the bus. Should just be my ma right now."

She nodded. They paused on the top of the steps, the wobbly fourth board pissing him off. He'd offered to repair it, but he'd been stupid enough to make the suggestion in front of Ben. Now he was forced to wait for the man to get around to fixing the problem so that his ma wouldn't take the brunt of his father's complaining.

Allison looked a little flustered. "Do we knock?"

He laughed. "She'd have my ears if we get all formal on her."

Gabe opened the door and leaned his head in. "Ma, we're here."

They stepped into the entranceway. The long line of hooks on the wall was so familiar, the worn linoleum underfoot. Inside was his mother's domain, as much as it could be, and everything sparkled. Scrubbed and cleaned within an inch of its life. Dana Coleman didn't tolerate her bit of the world to be messy.

He was hanging up Allison's coat when his ma came into view.

She wiped her hands on a towel, gaze skimming over him to land on Allison. She pulled to a stop, her polite visitor's smile leaping into place. "Allison Parker. You have grown up now, haven't you?"

"Mrs. Coleman." Allison held out a hand and his ma shook it firmly, her gaze darting over Allison's shoulder to meet his own. She raised both eyebrows high, as if asking what the heck was going on.

Gabe's unease shifted into something far different. "You need help with anything, Ma?"

She shook her head and led them into the house. "No, I've got a pot of tea on, and some fresh-baked cookies. Everything is in the back, though. Just let me grab it and bring it out here."

"Don't make more work for yourself. I don't mind sitting in the kitchen." Allison followed hard on Dana's heels.

"She's right, the kitchen is nice. Smells like heaven."

His ma paused in the doorway, obviously fighting her compulsion to seat guests in the living room. She frowned at him, and he smiled, ready to reassure her.

Allison's gasp distracted them both, as did her long *awww* as she pressed past Dana and headed straight for the box tucked up against the wall.

"Looks like we're sitting in the kitchen, Ma."

"Looks like it." Dana smiled but her questioning gaze continued to bounce between him and Allison.

The woman had apparently forgotten to feel shy around his mother. All her attention was focused on the swirling mass of furry kittens tucked inside the cardboard shelter. "They're adorable. Can I touch them?"

"Ma?"

Dana bustled about, setting another cup on the table and pulling out a few more baked goodies. "Go ahead. The mother died, and I found the little things just yesterday. Almost starved. They seem to have recovered nicely, though."

Allison needed no additional coaxing. She dropped to the floor and crossed her legs. In no time flat she had one of the dark brown bodies cradled against her cheek. "Oh, she's so soft. How old are they?"

"Just over a month I guess. They were nearly weaned, from what I can tell."

Gabe pulled out a chair and sat, smiling as Allison plopped one kitten into the hollow of her lap and picked up another. Watching her tenderly handle the tiny creatures made something inside of him happy.

He was glad she could find stuff to enjoy.

“Is tea good? Or you want some coffee?” Dana asked.

His ma held out the cookies and he willingly accepted a couple. “Tea is fine.”

He let her fuss for another minute since Allison was still distracted with the kittens. Distracted, but obviously watching enough that when Dana sat, Allison gently returned the tiny furballs to the box.

She rose and slipped to the sink to wash her hands. “They’re beautiful.”

Dana nodded. “That batch are pretty little things. I’m tempted to keep one of them in the house, but inside is not the place for barn cats.”

“My mom always says the same.”

Allison paused at the edge of the counter. Gabe answered her dilemma before her hesitation became any clearer. He pulled out the chair beside him and patted the seat.

He’d managed to twist the sturdy wooden thing to be right in line with his so when she sat, his arm along the backrest lightly touched her shoulders. She was as close to being held in his embrace as they could be while sitting in different chairs.

His mom’s eyes widened before she caught herself and poured Allison’s cup full. “You visiting your family, Allison?”

Allison fidgeted with her plate. “A bit.”

“She’s here to visit me too,” Gabe cut in.

His ma smiled, the touch of a smirk disappearing behind her cup. When she lowered the dainty thing, her expression still showed amusement. “Really? That’s nice.”

Allison twisted to glance at him. “Yes, Gabe and I…”

He covered her fidgeting fingers with his own. Dana’s gaze snapped to the linked hands, and her smile got bigger.

Gabe cleared his throat. Time to get this thing rolling. “We’re engaged.”

There was a moment's pause, but his ma pretty much did what he expected. She shot to her feet and was around the table and hugging them both without another word.

It was a bit of a tangle of arms and heads, and Gabe laughed. "I take it that's mom code for congrats."

Dana pulled back. "You two are the sneakiest people I ever met. I knew something was up, but damn if I could figure it out. Yes, congratulations. And, Allison, if this young man gives you any grief, you let me know. I'll tell you all the ways to make him behave."

Allison settled back in her chair as his ma returned to the other side of the table. "Thank you. I'm glad you're not..."

"More surprised? Girl, I am completely surprised. But at the same time, I knew something was up. Didn't think it was that you two were running around on the sly. How long has this been going on?"

Gabe dropped his arm along the back of the chair again. It was kind of nice to have Allison relaxing against him. "What do you mean you knew something was up?"

His ma stared him down. "You aren't the most talkative of creatures, Gabe Coleman, but the past couple years you've been awfully quiet, even for you. At the start I thought you were planning on moving out of the area again, but once you built your cabin I knew it couldn't be that."

Damn. Maybe his secret projects hadn't been so secret after all. This excuse of having been seeing Allison on the side was a good thing to cover his tracks. "I'm not planning on leaving anytime soon, Ma. I told you that when I came back to town."

Dana folded her hands in front of her. "Well, I'm glad to hear it. Are you working at the restaurant again, Allison?"

The conversation drifted into safe, easy territory, and Gabe listened without having to add much to the discussion as Allison and his ma chatted about the community. The side flap of the box came loose and one of the kittens got caught, hips falling through the crack. He leaned over to grab the little creature. So small and defenceless. He rested the tiny beast in his lap and stroked it carefully.

"You want an engagement party?" Dana asked.

Allison shook her head. "My mom asked the same thing, but if you don't mind, we don't really want one. I'll be busy getting settled in the new job and everything."

"No problem. I bet your mom is thrilled you're going to be so close by. I know I missed Gabe terribly when he moved out of Rocky."

Moved out because if he had stayed he would have gone mad. "Well, we're all back now. And I should get to work. We just wanted to let you know our plans."

"Did you—" Dana broke off then nodded briskly. "I'll let your father know. And Rafe, if you want."

Allison had tightened at the mention of Ben. Great, seemed she liked his father as much as pretty well everyone else in town. "I'll see Rafe when he's doing chores. Let him razz me about getting hitched on his own."

They rose and made their goodbyes, Dana promising to call Allison to chat when she could. It was all far simpler than he'd thought it would be. Once things got a little more settled in the next couple days, they could make a list of what he needed to do to get the ranch started on the road to recovery.

It was all working out just fine.

Chapter Six

Rafe's jaw hung open for about ten seconds before he burst out laughing. "You're shitting me."

"I don't shit." Gabe deliberately drawled the words.

His deadpan joke only made his brother laugh louder. "Yeah, right, that makes you full of shit. Who you engaged to?"

"Allison Parker. You know her."

Rafe wrinkled his nose. "She left here years ago. Did you date her while you were living away from Rocky?"

"No."

"Did you date her in high school?"

"No."

Rafe dug the shovel in deep before standing back and crossing his arms in front of him. "Then why you getting married?"

"We're getting engaged." Gabe snatched up the shovel and tossed another scoop of manure into the wheelbarrow.

"Which means you're going to get married, you idiot. Oh hell—" Rafe cussed a few more times then kicked the wheel in front of him. "I guess I can't come stay at your place this summer now, can I?"

"Well, you hadn't asked me in the first place, but you're right. You can't."

"Bastard."

Rafe snatched up the long wooden handles of the wheelbarrow and forcibly shoved himself and his burden down the narrow path leading toward the garden.

"What's that look for?" Gabe called after him. "Because I won't let you move into my house without asking?"

"Because I figured you knew I wanted to move in with you. I didn't think I had to ask." Rafe shouted the words over his shoulder before he disappeared between the row of trees separating the compost and manure piles from the new stretch of garden Gabe had turned.

Well, assumptions had a way of kicking a person's ass. If this was the first occasion Rafe learned that lesson, it was about time.

Gabe turned back and headed into the barn until Rafe returned. He took a quick check to see what was in the storeroom, and noted how little his father had actually listened to him in terms of needed supplies. There was a distinctive lack of a number of items, what looked to be overstock of others, and he closed his eyes and fought his frustration.

It was no use trying to take control of this area of the ranch. Not yet, not until he got Ben at least moderately onside.

He went back outside in time to catch his brother returning from another trip with the wheelbarrow. Rafe had already stripped off his shirt, the hard muscles from heavy labour beginning to show on his young body. The kid was growing up, and it was time to acknowledge that.

Didn't mean Gabe was going to let Rafe walk all over him.

"You ask Ma if you can move into the room over the garage?"

Rafe sighed. "No, because I thought I could move in with you and get away from—get to be out on my own."

"Moving in with me is not being on your own." Gabe dropped a hand on his brother's shoulder. Damn, he hadn't meant to block one of the refuges for the kid. "Check with her. I bet she'd have no issue with it. And Ben won't care as long as you're up and ready for chores without him having to haul your ass out of bed in the mornings."

The silence from Rafe stretched on until Gabe figured it was time to ignore it. If his kid brother wanted to pout, that was his business.

He headed over to the tractor instead, getting ready to transfer bales. A few minutes later a smack on the window next to him jerked him upright, and he turned off the engine and cracked open the door.

Rafe hopped down out of his way so the door could fully open.

"Can I come over later this week?"

Shit. "Allison's—"

"I'm not asking to stay over. Can I come over on Friday or something to meet her? Or are you bringing her over for a family dinner?"

Rafe's serious expression twisted something inside him. "No, we already talked to Ma. If you want to have dinner with us, Friday works. You usually go out with your friends then, don't you?"

"You're talking about getting married, and I've never even met the woman, I mean not really. I think I can skip hanging out with my friends for one night."

Gabe stared in mock horror. "Who the hell are you, and what did you do with my immature kid brother?"

Rafe grinned sheepishly. "Fuck off."

"Just saying. Let's make it Thursday, that might work better for everyone."

"You wait. I'll ask her all kinds of terrible questions to make up for being so mature right now. Does that make you happier?"

The tension that had rushed through when he'd shared his news with Rafe smoothed away. He was a good kid, and he was trying. "Remember whatever you do will come back to haunt you. I'm going to be around for a long time, and I have a great memory. Someday you'll find a girl you seriously like and it'll be payback."

Rafe walked backward, his huge grin not giving any sign he was returning to the dirty task of hauling manure. "It could still be fun in the short term."

Gabe pulled the door shut and went back to work. He had a couple hours before he had to get cleaned up and head out with Allison for the next round of family inquisitions. Maybe after tonight things would settle down.

It certainly couldn't get any worse.

Dead silence greeted her announcement.

Actually, that wasn't true. Music played, and the murmur of other people conversing carried in the background. Normal restaurant sounds that should have made Parker's Timberline Grill the perfect setting for them to proclaim to yet another set of shocked people the news about her and Gabe's engagement.

Maybe they should have had a party and gotten it all over at one time. The jolt would have been greater but less prolonged.

Paul and Elle exchanged long stares before Elle turned back and blinked hard.

"Congratulations. I'm... That's... How interesting."

Everything about her response was obviously a sham, but at least she attempted to smile instead of the near-violent frown that marred her brother's expression.

"Why the hell would you marry him?" Paul blurted out, and Allison's heart fell. She hadn't expected it to be all smooth sailing, but downright rudeness?

"Paul!" Their mother's hushed whisper carried volumes of disapproval.

He had the grace to look uncomfortable, but he didn't back down. "It's a bit of a shock. What did you expect me to say?"

Allison readied to defend herself, but it was Gabe who leaned forward. "I'd expect you to act like someone who gives a damn about your sister. You have questions, you go ahead and we can discuss them politely, but maybe first you stick out your hand and at least pretend you're happy."

Gabe settled back, draping his arm around her shoulders as he squeezed reassuringly. Allison leaned into him, grateful for his warmth and his support.

Paul eyed Gabe slowly then nodded. "I do have questions, but you're right, this isn't the place. Allison, I'm glad you're back in town. We've missed you."

Gabe chuckled. "See? It's always possible to find something to not lie about."

Allison bit her lip to stop from laughing. The tension between the two men was reminiscent of bulls vying for dominance. Somehow she had to defuse the situation before someone said something that made things worse.

It was their mom who smoothed matters over, at least temporarily. Her soft laughter trickled over Allison. "I swear, sometimes you children—it's as if you've reverted to being teens again, all poking each other and trying to get on each other's nerves. I'm so pleased. Allison and Gabe are obviously happy. There's nothing a mother wants more for her children than that."

Her beaming face said she wasn't faking it, and Allison smiled back. The heat from Gabe's body encircled her and held her up as well, and if Paul's scowl only eased a tiny bit, well, she'd just have to give him time. It was a shock, but the pleasure her mom showed made it all worthwhile.

Elle passed the breadbasket to Gabe. "Are you planning on coming to work for the restaurant as well?"

Gabe snorted before turning the sound into a cough. "No. Allison working here is enough. I've got the ranch to keep me busy."

Paul's lips twitched, but he didn't say anything.

Elle brought forward the topic of menus, and Allison got involved with her mom and sis in the usual brainstorming for new ideas. Their chef was good, but also loved the hands-on direction they gave, and together the combination had always been something to be proud of.

It was only after their meals had been delivered she realized the guys weren't doing a lot of talking. Gabe was listening in on her conversation, but Paul seemed too busy glaring daggers at Gabe to contribute much of anything.

Just what she needed, grief from her younger brother. *Not.* If this hadn't been a sham, his actions would have pissed her off even more. The jerk should know better than to stick in his oar that far.

Allison made sure to pull Gabe back into the rest of the discussion as best she could, but by the time they were done eating, she'd had enough.

"I'll grab the truck and bring it to the door." Gabe pressed a quick kiss on her cheek then rose. He nodded politely to her mother, winked at Elle who responded with a reluctant grin.

He tipped his hat forward and stared Paul down for a second before leaving without another word.

Allison sighed, ignoring the tingling where he'd touched his lips against her cheek. Good old family togetherness. She'd thrown a lot at them tonight, so she wasn't about to push it.

Paul escorted her to the door, though, something obviously on his mind.

She held back far enough Elle and their mom were out the door and out of hearing range before turning and raising her brows. "What's your problem?"

"Why him?"

She knew it. “So it’s Gabe in particular you have an issue with?” Maybe if she let him voice his concerns he’d relax. “Does he have a woman on the side I don’t know about? You don’t think he’s good enough for me? What?”

His nostrils flared as he drew a long breath. “Maybe it sounds stupid. And yeah, you surprised me with your announcement. But the Angel Colemans? I don’t have issues with Gabe himself. He’s been given the raw end of the deal in many ways as far as I know, but—”

His disapproval had simmered down and showed now as sheer frustration.

“I’m listening.” Allison finished buttoning her coat and waited as patiently as she could.

“If you really care about him, fine. But I heard they’re having money troubles lately, and all of a sudden he’s engaged to you? Face it, Ally, we are one of the wealthier families in town. Sorry if it makes warning signs go off, but I don’t like it.”

Allison wrapped her arms around his neck and squeezed tight, the laughter escaping her completely real and relieved. “Is that what you’re worried about? That he’s marrying me for money? Oh, Paul, trust me, that is not at all in the picture.”

Maybe it was the fact she wasn’t lying that helped her sound extra convincing, but his shoulders eased slightly, and he smirked. “It does sound a little cloak and dagger when I say it out loud, but come on, I’m your only brother. If I don’t guard you from the dragons of the world, who will?”

She stepped back and nodded. “I can probably slay them on my own, but I understand better why you were grumpy. It’s fine. Gabe’s okay. Give it some time, and you’ll see. He’s so not about the money thing I can’t even begin to explain it.”

The door opened and Gabe’s smiling face appeared, the dark brown of his cowboy hat contrasting with his blond hair. She moved forward automatically to take his hand.

"Give me a call," Paul suggested. "We can get together for..."

Allison peeked over her shoulder to discover her brother wasn't talking to her, but staring directly at the cowboy at her side.

Paul cleared his throat. "We could have a beer or something. Catch up a little."

Gabe blinked in surprise, but managed to pull it together quickly. "Sure."

Allison pressed her shoulder against Gabe's and they headed out. Elle had already taken their mom home, and it was quiet on the street as Gabe led her to the truck.

He helped her in on his side, and this time she didn't even think to protest. Just stopped in the middle, buckled up and then closed her eyes and wondered what in the world they'd gotten themselves into.

They were halfway home before Gabe broke the silence. "That was a particular sort of hell I don't want to have to do all over again. Shit."

Allison laughed. "Don't you mean 'What the hell were we thinking?'"

"That too. Hell of a night. Hell of a day."

Allison leaned her head on his shoulder and let the laughter take her. "Oh my God, did you see Paul's face? I thought he was going to blow a blood vessel. And you know why?"

"Figured you'd gotten the reason for the stick up his ass. That invitation to join him for a beer was not what I expected. Did you kick him in the balls while I was gone and tell him to behave?"

"No, he explained he was worried you were marrying me for my bank account. *Idiot.* If he knew I was the one who had harassed you..."

Oh Lord. It had been a long day, but at least the worst was over. She could concentrate on getting back into the swing of things at the restaurant and being there for Mom.

Somehow try to secretly prepare the family for having their heart torn away.

Chapter Seven

Gabe splashed cold water on his face before soaking a washcloth and applying it to the back of his neck. Allison's toothbrush rested in a glass, and a neat little fancy black case sat on the side of the counter. After a couple days of seeing them there, his eyes didn't jerk to the side in shock as much. Now it was more in amusement.

Subtle signs they were sharing the house showed up everywhere.

A damp towel hanging where usually only his would be. Extra footwear stacked by the bench on the porch, and how anyone could possibly need that many shoes, he had no idea.

Still, she was trying damn hard to not spread out and take over. There was way less of a mess than his brother usually managed to produce after he'd been around for no more than a single night.

Gabe hurried through his cleanup and back into the bedroom to get dressed. The biggest issue was morning and a single bathroom. He tried to be done and into the kitchen before she crawled out of bed. The schedule wasn't perfect, but it was working.

He knocked briskly on her closed door before calling out cheerfully. "Your turn."

A low groan was the only response.

Gabe chuckled all the way to the kitchen area as he got the coffee going.

He was in the middle of breaking eggs into a bowl when the door at the edge of the room finally cracked open and Allison shuffled out, pale green robe wrapped tightly around her.

"You can stop the whistling now. I'm awake. You evil, inhuman person."

"Hate to see you sleeping away your morning off, is all."

She held up one strategic finger a second before disappearing into the master bedroom. Gabe went back to making breakfast without worrying too much.

Morning and Allison didn't get along. Less than a week waking up in the same house, and he'd already figured that out.

Maybe he should have let her sleep in a little, but he was too excited to wait. She'd been gone to the restaurant and doing things at her mom's for the past two days, but she'd promised to spend the morning with him, taking a look over the land.

Finally he was going to find out if his dream of making this section viable for organic ranching was possible.

Loaded coffee mugs on the table, a stack of pancakes at the ready. Allison dropped into her chair and reached for the steaming liquid without a word.

Gabe kept quiet even though what he really wanted to do was pepper her with a million questions. He had all the information she'd given him way back when, but trying to figure out how to apply it had been tough. Rules change, situations change.

He took another pancake and tried not to look at his watch again.

Allison held out her cup and shook it slightly to get his attention. "Are we driving or riding?"

"I thought we'd ride." He filled her cup then drained the rest into his own before setting the thermos aside. "You need me to take along anything? I'll have the saddle bags, so collection bottles, soil samples, anything we need..."

"You are way too energetic. Stop it. No being bouncy before noon."

Gabe snorted. "Bouncy?"

"Like one of those teeny tiny rubber balls."

He wasn't sure if this was an insult or a compliment. "You're calling me bouncy."

She narrowed her gaze. "Drop it, Gabe."

Something evil twisted inside. "Like a bouncy ball?"

"Arghhh." Allison hid behind her mug and ignored him.

He was done well before she was ready, horses saddled and seemingly as eager as him to head out into the fresh morning sunshine. Allison finally joined them, her hair pulled back into a ponytail, big sunglasses covering her eyes. She plopped her cowboy hat on and tilted it back, and the cream-colour edges set off her face like a picture frame.

"I didn't have a key to lock the door," she apologized.

He passed over Patches's reins. "Don't need one. You're not living in Red Deer right now."

He stayed close enough he could give her a hand if needed, but she was up and in the saddle effortlessly.

"Right. Unlocked doors. You wouldn't believe how long it took to break myself of that habit."

Gabe settled in comfortably. The familiar leather of his saddle was age worn and totally a part of his life on the ranch. He led the way out of the corral, the dogs racing around in crazy excited circles. Allison's mount moved through the shuffling, yipping mass of canine excitement without a qualm, so he turned his attention upward to see how the rider was doing.

She was in the middle of a huge yawn, her hand rising from the reins to cover her mouth at the last second. She sat easily, body rocking gently as they took the trail to follow the extreme east boundary of the Angel land.

"You ride pretty good for a city slicker," he teased.

She stuck out her tongue for a second then grinned. "I've been riding out in Red Deer. Not Patches—I didn't want to haul the old girl too far from home, but there's a couple great places that board horses and were always looking for help in exercising them. I got out at least a couple times a week."

The trail narrowed, and he pulled in front to take her around the narrow gorge to the shallowest part of the creek. "We haven't had a lot of runoff this year. The water table's about as low as it's been in the past ten years. Last year's crops were lean because of the drought."

"It wasn't much better over most of the province. A few pockets got too much moisture—go figure—but it was a bad year all round." She drew in a deep breath. "It's hard to think of that right now, isn't it? When there's that smell of everything bursting out with new growth?"

She closed her eyes and the faintest hint of a smile teased her mouth. Gabe watched as a butterfly rose from the tall grasses to their left, its pale yellow wings barely visible against the deeper yellow of the old strawlike stalks. The little thing flitted up and past her face, circling and coming to land on the raised pommel of her saddle.

"Don't move," he said softly. "Open your eyes and look down."

Her smile unfurled into full bloom as the butterfly took wing and escaped forward, dusting past Patches's ears.

She turned to grin at him. "Nice. They're a good sign, butterflies. Plus the frogs I hear going nuts at night outside your cabin."

Gabe took her carefully through the rough terrain on the far side of the creek. "Right. If the ecosystem is in balance, there will be more butterflies. I remember reading that."

"Is this part of the Angel land?"

He pointed to the side. "Everything on the west is ours. The creek is the dividing point on this side. It's not a straight line, but when you're splitting up land for the family, you don't have to get out a ruler and set things in stone."

"Who got this section?"

They topped the hill and he figured he probably didn't need to answer.

Allison pulled to a stop beside him and sighed in admiration. "The Whiskey Creek clan do love their horses, don't they?"

"Uncle George has got the touch when it comes to breeding. He's not moving too fast, but he's already managed to get a couple of their animals noticed in the stockyards."

"Any studs?"

Gabe shook his head. "They need another generation, I think. It's not an area I've been studying on—well, I've been working on the genetics part, but horses are outside my price range. My cousin Karen is the one who seems to be able to get them to do anything for her—she's the magician around here."

"I used to ride with her sometimes. She is good."

He took her along the eastern boundary, talking comfortably the entire time. They stopped and took samples when she asked, but it wasn't often.

"I thought we'd be doing a lot more testing," he admitted.

They stopped at the end of the coulee at a small watering hole to refresh the horses, a place to sit and lean back and stare out into the blue spring sky.

Allison pulled off her hat and dropped it beside her, loosening off her ponytail holder and running her fingers through her hair to fluff it out. "It's early testing, Gabe. And honestly? I don't need to test often at this point. The uncomfortable truth is unless you and the Whiskey Creek side stopped using banned fertilizers a few years ago, chances are a lot of your fields around this side will be contaminated. You're too close to other spreads as well."

He nodded slowly. "I did think of that. And that's why I thought this and the backside of the land are the most important to see first and take off the list. Our west boundary is up against crown land—if anything is going to meet standards, that will be it."

"I'm glad to hear you've anticipated a few of the troubles. I didn't want to be the one to have to burst your bubble."

She looked so nervous he couldn't stand it. Gabe leaned forward and caught her hand. "You're not wrecking anything by telling me the truth. I am going to find a way to make this happen, but there are a ton of options at this point. You knocking a few of the blocks out from under me is helping, not hindering. Got it?"

"I still worry."

"Ha." He squeezed her fingers. "You were born worrying. Just saying you don't have to tread carefully around me. You've got enough of that to deal with every day."

She nodded. "Thanks."

"How's it going with your mom? You want to talk about it?"

She pulled back her hand—he hadn't even realized he was still holding it—and dragged her fingers through her hair again. The act left the long tresses in a wild scramble around her shoulders and something shot hard into his gut.

"Things are good. My mom is thrilled to have me back. She doesn't suspect why. I've managed to convince her to not show up any day before noon."

"Your mom is taking time off?"

"I know. It's like a mini miracle. She asked if I'd come to the house this weekend and help her with some boxes." Allison smiled at him. "It's right to be here. Thank you so much for making it possible."

"No problem."

She was in the middle of pulling her hair back and fastening it with an elastic when her bracelet got caught. "Shit. Gabe?"

He laughed and shifted forward, reaching around her to loosen off the bit that was caught in the tiny clasp.

She smelt good. Clean and fresh with that hint of flowers. He was kneeling at her side, one knee tucked between her legs where they extended in front of her. He tried his best to not pull as he worked, but he was getting distracted. The softness of the hair under his fingers, and the flannel of her shirt as it brushed his arm caused all sorts of wrong reactions.

"You having troubles?" Her wrist jiggled and pulled, and she hissed in pain.

He trapped her in place. "Hold still. What kind of unsolvable puzzle do you have on this damn bracelet?"

"Ouch. I'm not sure, but you're scalping me."

He couldn't work the thing one handed. "This may seem strange, but don't argue, okay?" He twisted her hand and placed it palm down on the top of her head.

Allison giggled. "I need to rub my tummy at the same time, right? To test my coordination?"

"Or walk and chew gum as we'd tease the twins. Hold still, I think I can get it now."

He had to lean in even closer, but with something to brace on, she kept her arm steady and he had her loose from the tiny trap. He smoothed back the long strand of hair he'd freed, the silken softness a caress against his fingers, and suddenly he was aware of how close they were to each other. That he was damn near straddling her. Her breath brushing across his chest.

He retreated as carefully as he could, hoping she wouldn't move and crash them together, because if they fell to the ground in a tangle there was little doubt in his mind he'd end up doing something other than try to get free.

He was brushing the dirt off his knees and looking for what he could pick up. Anything to distract him. That's when he heard it. Small, but definitely there.

"Are you laughing at me, Allison Parker?"

She jammed on her hat and pulled the front brim low, effectively hiding her face. "Course not."

One twirl took her away from him, but her shoulders continued to shake suspiciously.

"What?" He followed after her.

She stuffed her water bottle back in the saddlebag and obviously refused to face him. "Nothing. Ready to show me more of the land?"

She was still laughing.

Gabe stepped in close and tugged on her shoulder. He pulled hard enough she spun around, her full grin right there for him to see. "I knew it. Why you laughing, woman?"

She planted her fists on her hips, head tilted to the side a tiny bit.

She looked damn adorable. More than adorable, she looked edible and fuckable...

And that wasn't appropriate for him to be thinking.

"There." She snapped up a finger and pointed at his face. "You did it again."

"Did what?" He would have stepped back, but she snatched up a fist full of his shirt, and he froze.

The images of wrapping his arms around her and dropping her to the ground and taking her right there were not a part of this deal.

"Gabe Coleman, are you scared of me?"

What the...? "What kind of shit question is that?"

She didn't let go. Her right hand stayed fisted around a good chunk of his shirtfront, but her left hand snuck under his chin and her soft fingers cupped his face. "Not trying to tease, but damn it, Gabe, you should have seen how you scrambled away from me. It was like you'd seen a snake. And just now?

When I kind of gave you that flirty look the girls do? You were ready to bolt."

"Was not."

"Bullshit." The hand at his chest let go, only to thump down with the side of her fist. "You kissed me that first night—said we didn't want to be caught because we couldn't even get through a little kiss. But you've been shying away from me all day. What's going to happen if you do that when we're around family?"

"There's no problem," Gabe insisted. Damn it all. Last thing he wanted to admit was he'd been too ready to take things further than they needed for the deception to work. "And I wasn't scared. Just didn't see any need to make you uncomfortable."

"You can't mess up like that in public, Gabe."

"I won't. I didn't."

Her fingers left his cheek. Before he figured out what she planned, she'd slipped off his cowboy hat and run her fingers through his hair.

His instant response was to trap her wrist and not let her continue the caress.

She raised a brow. "You have something in your hair."

"I noticed. Your fingers."

"You're overreacting."

He was getting far too turned on by her touch for them to still be standing this close together. "I think I need to show you the pigpens and chicken coops now."

She had this expression that didn't make any sense. "You need to relax."

He needed to go jump in the creek. "You had enough fun yet, Allison? Because we really should be going."

"Not yet."

Dammit if she didn't press against him, her soft body warm and curved in all the right spots. The hand that had stroked through his hair was at the back of his neck, playing and teasing him until goose bumps rose. She slid her other hand across his chest and upward until they met, then she tugged on his neck. Hard enough that he would have had to act like a scarecrow to resist her, so he let her guide him.

Just far enough down she could tilt her head back and join their mouths together.

She'd meant it as a taunt. A bit of a payback for the mind-numbing impact of his kiss a couple days earlier.

But when their lips touched, joking was off the agenda. Now? She just wanted.

This habit she had of jumping in with two feet had gotten her in trouble before, and maybe this time it would as well, but with her fingers tangled in his hair she didn't care.

She traced his lips with her tongue, tasting him slowly. He wasn't moving. Not toward her, not away, so she leaned in a little harder and dipped a little deeper. Mmm, something about kissing him in the outdoors made it that much better. It was right, mixing the scents of the country with the taste of him, his firm lips moving against hers.

He must have finally given in, because his hands were on her hips. Not dragging her tighter, but at least not pushing her away. The gentle squeeze of pressure proved he was there willingly, and she concentrated on enjoying the kiss more.

She was up on tiptoe, breathing through her nose. The masculine scent of his soap and skin filled her head. His tongue brushed hers. A far cry from the passionate and overwhelming exchange they'd had at the start of the week. Somehow, it was just as perfect. Allison tugged him closer yet and he followed her lead. Bending over her, and allowing her to rest on her heels instead of straining to reach him.

His hands hadn't moved.

The kisses stayed soft. Exploratory. When she would have offered more, an extraordinary sound escaped from him, and this time he did pull back. Not far, only enough to rest his head on her shoulder and take a shaky breath.

She ran her fingers through his hair, the thick texture soft and yet firm against her palms.

It was reassuring and peaceful. The edge of sexual attraction there but dim enough all she felt was his presence. A comfort and an anchor.

"You trying to drive me crazy?" Gabe wouldn't lift his head, so she had no idea what kind of expression he wore. Only the edge of tension in his voice—damn. She hadn't meant to hurt him.

Allison tried to step away. "I'm sorry. I didn't mean—"

"Shhh. Just give me a hug. You crazy woman."

She slipped her arms around his torso and squeezed him tight. "I only wanted to tease you."

Gabe patted her on the back, his touch nicely platonic, and she breathed a sigh of relief that she hadn't mucked things up between them with that impulsive move.

He stooped to recover his hat. They were still close when the buzz of an engine rose into hearing. Gabe groaned and twisted to face the open field on their right, a narrow dust trail rising to show the approach of someone drawing nearer.

"You expecting anyone?" Allison asked.

"No, but that doesn't mean anything." His tone was so dry she glanced up to see what had caused it. He shook his head as the quad came into sight. "One of the twins. Figures. I haven't put out a fire for them in nearly two weeks."

Allison would have moved farther away, but he caught her fingers in his and tugged her against his side.

She laughed. "You really plan to pull out all the stops, don't you?"

"If it's Joel, or better yet, Jesse, we got ourselves the nearest thing to that megaphone on Main Street we were talking about."

He tucked his fingers under her chin and lifted her face toward him.

"Gabe..."

"Stop talking and kiss me, woman. He's watching."

It felt different this time. More like pretend, even with the heat of his mouth touching hers. Allison was distracted, wanting to find out what their visitor was up to.

The motor on the quad cut out and Gabe released her.

"Don't stop on my account." Jesse tipped back his hat and grinned, blue eyes shining bright, huge grin plastered across his face as he swung his leg over the seat and jumped to the ground.

"Morning, Jesse."

"Gabe." Jesse turned all his attention on Allison, and damn if she didn't feel her cheeks rush with heat. "And Allison Parker. You sure you want this old man? If you're in the market, there are younger Colemans available who have way more energy."

Talk about a tease. "I thought about that, but Rafe isn't ready for a steady girlfriend yet."

Gabe chortled as Jesse mocked being kicked in the gut. "Low blow. Well played. Good to see you back in the area."

He wrapped her in a bear hug and planted a huge kiss on her. Allison was too surprised to stop him.

Gabe wasn't. "Bastard. That's enough." Allison found herself tucked back tight against his side, one arm possessively holding her close.

Jesse's grin didn't budge. "I've heard the phrase *kissing cousins* for years, and never thought how much fun it could be."

"What do you want, Jesse?" Gabe all but snarled the words.

Allison hid her amusement as Jesse deliberately leered in her direction.

"Is that an open-ended question?" Jesse backed away as Gabe advanced. "Kidding. Man, you two are going to be a blast to rag on. I've never seen him with such a short fuse. Well done, Allison, you've managed to rile up the good kid on the block."

Gabe tightened at that jibe, and suddenly the teasing wasn't as funny anymore.

"What *do* you want, Jesse?" she asked. The sensation of possessiveness and wanting to protect—it wasn't unfamiliar, but she hadn't expected to feel it for Gabe.

All Jesse's mockery vanished. "Gabe, favour to ask. Lend me your truck."

"Oh God, again? Use Joel's."

Jesse pretty near scuffed his feet in the leaves underfoot like a little kid. "Can't."

"Can't? Did the two of you both bust up your vehicles the same day? I don't believe that. What's happening?"

Jesse dropped his mouth open and widened his eyes innocently. "Nothing, I need to get to Drayton Valley tonight, and I don't want Joel to know. Come on, I'll make sure it's full when I bring it back."

"What the hell you up to?" Gabe poked him in the chest. "Keeping secrets from your twin just screams you're pulling a fast one."

Jesse continued to bullshit for a while, not saying much of anything, while Gabe did his best to cajole the information out of him.

Listening to the cousins ramble back and forth was another wonderful addition to her already great morning.

Returning to Rocky for her mom's sake had been impulsive. Total fly-by-the-seat-of-her-pants move, and only now was she aware of other positive effects. Being around familiar people who all had the same kind of goals as her—there was something energizing about it.

Coming home for her mom had meant coming home for herself far more than she'd imagined, and she'd noticed it, even in just a few days.

Gabe still had his arm around her, and he reluctantly released her to dig in his pocket. "Fine. Stop whining like a little girl and get out of here. Only no using purple fuel in her."

Jesse snorted. "Did you hear? Cousin Anna caught Steve with a tankful."

"Oh sheesh. Really? Buttbrain."

"Yeah, she wrote him up too."

"She ticketed her own brother? God, I love that woman."

Allison laughed with them. Seems there was always someone trying to get away with using the cheaper ranch-supply gas. And someone was always getting caught. Purple dye was hard to explain away.

Gabe tossed over his keys. Jesse snatched them in midair and retreated, flicking a finger to his hat at Allison. "I'll see you guys on Friday at Traders?"

Gabe nodded. "We'll be there."

Jesse rode off in a cloud of dust as Allison and Gabe gathered their things and got back in the saddle.

"Ready for more exploring?" he asked.

She nodded and kicked Patches lightly, urging the horse up and back into the wide-open spaces of the fields. The scenery around them bursting with energy, the man riding beside her comfortable and everything at peace. A brief moment of respite in the middle of the whirl of life.

Allison soaked in the sensation as a buffer against the tough moments she knew had to be coming.

She nudged Patches alongside Hurricane, and Gabe looked up expectantly. “Okay, let’s talk about long-term plans for your ranch.”

He grinned, and the rest of the morning fell away in easy companionship.

Chapter Eight

Gabe pulled up to his parents' house and hopped out of his truck. Thursday morning had vanished before he knew it, and he still wanted to track down his father before the day was over.

Damn man seemed to be hiding, which normally wouldn't be an issue. Keeping lots of distance between the two of them was usually a good thing. But now that he needed to talk, Ben was nowhere to be found.

Gabe shoved open the front door, calling as he burst in. "Ma, you seen Ben this afternoon?"

No answer from his ma. The kitchen smelt wonderful as usual, and the oven was hot, crowded with pots for dinner. But there was no sign of either parent.

He stepped out the door off the kitchen and spotted a patch of bright colour over in the garden. His boots left imprints in the soft new grass as he shortcut across to where his ma was working a hoe.

She smiled at him as she leaned on the tall wooden handle. An oversized set of gloves on her hands and a huge pair of rubber boots on her feet, she looked like any of a hundred other ranch women out planting their gardens. It was such a familiar sight.

He had to make sure they didn't lose the land. No matter how much work it was. This was home.

"You seen Ben lately?"

She pushed a loose hair out from in front of her eyes, frowning for a minute. "I guess I did. He came out of the house about fifteen minutes ago and headed that way."

She pointed toward the back of the barns, and he waved and took off. He had no more time to waste. Practicing on the donkey—those days were done. Now that he'd had a chance to brainstorm with Allison, there were things they needed to start doing right now. Getting Ben on board was the only way to keep the momentum going.

After Allison's inspiration? He was ready to take on anyone. There was no way that Ben could dismiss these ideas.

Five minutes later he discovered Ben standing on the edge of the dugout beyond the barn.

He forced the words past his suddenly dry throat. "Got some interesting information for you."

Ben turned, his brows furrowed together. "What you doing here?"

"Wanted to talk. You got a few minutes?"

His father grunted.

"I took Allison out for a ride the other day, to show her the land."

Ben scowled harder. "You really marrying that woman?"

"We're engaged."

"You knock her up?"

Not only was his father an ass, he had yet to catch up with the twenty-first century. "No. That's not a reason people get married anymore."

"Well, she sure the hell must have some excuse to be willing to get tied to a loser like you."

Gabe pulled in his temper. "This isn't a discussion about Allison and my relationship. I wanted to let you know she had some great ideas for the ranch—you do remember that she works in the industry. She's a highly respected consultant."

Ben crossed his arms. "If she's willing to get hooked up with you, I'm not sure how highly respected the woman could be. Doesn't get any from me."

Gabe chose to ignore the stupid comments and press ahead. "We can make a few changes and start increasing our profits. Aren't you at least interested in what she had to say about that?"

His father stepped closer. "I'm not interested in a woman coming and telling me how to run my place. I don't care to hear any ideas from some high-strung pup who can't keep his responsibilities in line and has to go chasing a skirt to find a way to become important. Is that why you hooked up with her? So people in this town might finally respect you? It's not going to happen." Ben spat to the side. "The only reason I don't kick you out is you at least have the guts to halfway do your job on a daily basis."

Gabe held in the words he wanted to scream. To tell his father to shove the ranch up his ass, and that Gabe was leaving and never coming back.

The same thing tied his hands as had made him return years ago.

Dana. And Rafe.

Ben reached down and grabbed something from the tall grass before walking away without another word.

Gabe stared after the man, the sense of lost opportunities and lost hope slowly crowded out as he realized what was in his father's hand.

Dammit. The cardboard box from the kitchen.

Rage exploded like a long-set mine. He pictured the expression on his ma's face, on Allison's, as they'd cooed over the tiny kittens.

It might have made no sense, but his limbs were already moving. He threw his hat to the side and raced to the end of the dugout. The water was murky with springtime runoff, but the ditch wasn't that wide. He stepped forward and leaned over, hands reaching for the bottom. Hoping that whatever Ben had used could be found quickly.

He ended up with his head under the dirty water, hands grasping at weeds and rotting straw that had blown and settled in the waterhole. He rose and sucked in a breath, diving again and moving farther toward the middle. He was nearly out of air when his fingers caught on the edge of a rough sack.

Feet to the bottom to propel himself upward, Gabe pulled the burlap free, lifting it over his head. He scrambled one-handed up the narrow embankment, mud coating his clothes. The chill of the water not even registering as his anger burned.

Yes, at times the farm cats got out of control, but they didn't have too many right now. No need to go and drown the little things.

His fingers felt like wooden sticks as he tore at the knot. A heavy rock pinned the sack to the ground, motionless lumps lying next to it.

A beam of sunshine hit the ground to his left, spotlighting the sad little creatures he pulled one at a time from the open bag. Motionless, their soft fur matted and clumped to their lifeless bodies. Gabe fought the tears that a grown man shouldn't shed, but damn it all, this was part and parcel of how fucked up his life had become.

He wasn't dead, but at times it seemed being dead would be easier. And it was his father who had tied the sack tight and thrown him in.

Regret at having been too late tore through him, and he growled in frustration. Tiny bodies lay in accusation that what he had done was too late and too little.

That it would always be too late and too little.

Gabe jammed on his hat and sat back on his heels. Soaking wet, mud covered from head to toe. Staring down, his heart breaking over a bunch of useless, insignificant kittens.

The urge to give up was so damn strong right then. To become bitter and cold like his father would be preferable to the pain eating him inside.

He moved the kittens back to the sack to carry them to be buried somewhere. One after another he lay them gently next to each other, swear words filling his mind along with the frustration and confusion.

One twitched.

He paused, lifting the soggy black body and placing it carefully in his palm. He gently rubbed up the creature's chest and neck, like he would a newborn lamb to remove the mucus after it was born. He didn't dare let the flicker of hope inside grow too fast.

It was like watching a candle on a gusty windowsill quivering to stay lit. The kitten's chest moved again, and when its tiny mouth opened in a pitiful meow, Gabe bit his lip to stop from shouting out loud.

He tucked the little thing inside his shirt against his body, close enough that even with him soaking wet there was heat. It cuddled in and planted its paws on his skin, needle-sharp claws popping out to poke him, and he didn't give a shit that he was being used as a pincushion.

It was a hell of a lot harder to one-handed finish the grisly task of caring for the kittens who hadn't made it, but he was too grateful and too spent to care how long it took or how awkward it was. The tiny creature nestled against his ribs was like a miniature spot of hope.

Fuck his father. The man had told him again and again he was worthless. Why Gabe continued to try had always been for his own reasons. For his ma and brother. For his own soul—to keep alive the good things he knew about himself in spite of whatever Ben said.

He wouldn't let the bitterness Ben kept dumping on him leach into his soul anymore.

There with the sunshine coming down like in some great cathedral, Gabe had his own revelation. He was done fighting

Ben's way. He was going to win this damn war between them, and he was going to use his own methods to get there.

And heaven help Ben if he wasn't able to accept that.

Allison wasn't exactly fussing—it was a teenager joining them for dinner for Pete's sake. But she knew that of all the people who might see through what she and Gabe were doing, his kid brother was the most likely.

So she'd made sure she stopped working at the restaurant with enough time to get back to Gabe's cabin to double-check things before Rafe arrived.

Kissing her mom goodbye for the night and seeing her bright smile was encouraging and lightened Allison's spirits. So far Maisey seemed to be healthy enough. There were no signs of the disease sweeping through her body, but the expected deterioration could begin at anytime, and Allison snatched up every good moment for all she was worth.

There wasn't much to do to get ready once she did get home—and wasn't that a strange way to start thinking of Gabe's place? It was a safe spot, though, after not even a week.

She finished setting the table then suddenly realized something.

She slipped into her bedroom and nabbed her things. It was a little weird to waltz into Gabe's room and deliberately put her clothes there. It wasn't as if she had to shove her nightclothes under the pillow, but her robe hung on the hook next to the bathroom, and she dropped her makeup kit on the dresser top.

She had to grab her pillow from the spare room and place it at the head of the bed, and this unexpected sensation snuck over her.

Kissing him the other day wasn't something she should be remembering in such minute detail. The firmness of his lips, the pressure of his hands on her hips.

They were getting along fine, and she had been mean to tease him so hard. And mean to tease herself because with things working out with Mom, at least temporarily, there was a whole bunch too much time to think about how hot and achy Gabe made her.

She lay on the bed and stared at the ceiling. After their talk the other day, she felt she could offer the Coleman ranch advice. That alone made it easier to keep going. The ploy wasn't her taking from him selfishly, she would contribute.

She closed her eyes for a moment to relax until either of the guys arrived.

"Allison."

Gabe's shout brought her to her feet with a start. No way did she want to be caught sprawled in his bed. "In the back," she called.

"I need help." His voice was terse, the words clipped.

She raced from the bedroom and met him at the front door.

"Gabe, what happened?" He was soaked and filthy, from his boots on up.

"I'll explain later. Here, help me. Take the little thing."

He opened his shirt, one hand on the outside of the fabric cradling something. She leaned in closer and slipped her fingers along his abdomen, catching hold of a small warmish bundle of fur.

"Why…never mind, I've got it." She pulled out a tiny kitten, and it meowed plaintively. "You need help with your boots?"

"There's a bootjack outside. Go grab some towels to wrap that thing in. I'm going to make a mess across the floor in a minute."

She was already on the way to the kitchen. "Strip outside and leave your stuff there if you want."

She snatched a towel out of the drawer and gently deposited the kitten in it, wrapping the warm cloth tightly. Gabe's earlier solution sprang to mind, and she headed into the bedroom to nab an old hoodie. She pulled it on and tightened the bottom tie strap, creating a snug basket. She slipped the kitten under the layers and petted it carefully. Her fingers met mud and bits of straw, and she pulled them aside, all the time caressing the little thing as it shook.

She stepped out of her bedroom the exact second Gabe strode past. Naked.

Their eyes met, but there was too much tension in his expression for it to be sexual or even embarrassing. He was furious, and she paused in the doorway to let him stomp through his bedroom and into the bath area.

If she happened to stare at the way the muscles in his ass flexed as he moved, she wasn't going to tell him.

"You okay, Gabe?"

Nothing answered but the sound of running water. She made sure she kept her back to the open arch of the bathroom to give him privacy, but still stepped into the room. "Gabe? You need me to do anything?"

He sighed. "I'll be fine. How's the kitten?"

She touched her fingers lightly to its head, and it pressed against her palm. Something inside her went soft. "Warming up."

Asking what had happened didn't seem like a great idea.

He was quiet for another moment, then spoke. "Good. I guess I should ask if you'd like a pet."

The out-of-the-blue suggestion made her heart flutter. "Pet? I can keep it inside?"

"You seemed to like them. If you want, you can name it. And when you leave, you can take the kitten with you. If that doesn't work for you, I'll keep it here."

It was nearly enough to make her forget she was studiously avoiding looking in his direction. Cats were never inside pets. "Really?"

His fingers appeared along the edge of the glass as he grasped on tight. When he stuck his head around the corner he was still dripping wet, but the mud covering his forehead had washed away. The hard tension in his face softened although his nostrils flared for a moment. A slow smile came onto his expression, almost reluctantly, as if he was forced to let it show. "You look like a kangaroo."

She cuddled her burden, feeling a little silly but still curious as all get out. "Body heat is probably good for him."

Gabe nodded. "I hadn't even checked to see what he was. Tough little guy, and yeah, I'm serious. If he was too stubborn to die, I'm not going to toss him to the wolves. If you can't keep him, I'll take him on."

He was pulling back and Allison impulsively reached out and laid her fingers over his, trapping him. "I take it something bad happened."

He shrugged. "Something typical happened, but I'm not going to let *typical* run my life."

Which made no sense, but she wasn't about to ask for more explanations. Not as she realized only that narrow glass barrier stood between her and him. Naked him.

Their eyes met again, and this time she was even more aware of where they were. His strong hand under hers, skin slick with moisture. She snuck her hand back as if she'd touched the stove.

The lazy smile expanded until it was hundred percent Angel Coleman who she remembered from years ago. "You planning on scrubbing my back?" he asked. "I'm feeling extra dirty right now."

She paused, shocked at his suggestion. "Gabe, what are—?"

A cough sounded behind her, and she spun to find Rafe standing in the doorway, grinning at them both.

"I...well, I didn't knock, but I did call a couple of times. You guys need me to get anything ready for dinner? Or you want me to come back in a few hours?"

Allison's cheeks were burning hot, but she kept her chin up. Behind her Gabe's bright laugh boomed out. "Get out of here, you ass."

Rafe winked and retreated.

Allison's heart was still pounding.

Gabe's suggestive comment—he'd known Rafe was there all the time.

She was torn between being even more embarrassed and being angry. Didn't matter that their cover was now firmly established with Rafe—the situation was wholly believable—she was still pissed.

Because I wish he'd really been talking to me.

The truth made her bold. She wanted to somehow get back a bit of her own power in the situation. Maybe it wasn't smart, maybe it was the stupidest thing she'd ever done.

Gabe had retreated behind the glass barrier, Rafe gone the opposite direction. Allison squared her shoulders, supported the kitten in place and stepped into the opening of the shower.

This time she didn't keep her eyes locked at head level. She let herself enjoy seeing him naked in the middle of the spray. He was facing away from her, and that perfect backside was center stage, his muscular ass flexing as he shifted his weight. Soap bubbles escaped from where he rubbed his hands over his shoulders, the liquid splashing up as he lifted his face into the direct line of the water.

Wet, his blond hair was darker. He grabbed the soap from the wall dish and his hands moved quickly. Over his chest, his abdomen. Lower still as he twisted to rinse the soap from his back.

Which gave her the best view possible of his front. Of his hands rubbing over his cock and balls.

"Fuck."

The word surprised her into looking up, all his body gone tight again. Hands crossing to cover his groin.

"Allison?" Confusion in the word, a frown on his face.

She opened her eyes innocently. "I thought you needed me to scrub your back?"

A short pause was followed by a hearty snort. "You're as much trouble as my brother. Go on."

She tilted her head to the side and looked him over once more before turning as casually as possible and retreating.

Retreating because, hot damn, the man was fine. And if she'd stayed there a moment longer, she'd have forgotten everything—their visitor in the living room, the kitten in her pocket and maintaining deceptions. She'd have stripped down and pressed herself against him and not left until she'd found out exactly how heavenly this Angel Boy could make her feel.

Chapter Nine

Dinner with Rafe was a different affair than Gabe expected—he was shocked how much the tiny package of fur he'd rescued impacted, well, everything.

Rafe seemed equally fascinated and scandalized by the kitten's presence. Gabe played down the details of what had happened, just tucked the warm bundle into his brother's hands and watched the results. Allison called the vet to find out if the kitten would need special attention.

They all hovered.

He made a mash for the creature that, miraculously, seemed none the worse for its experience. Conversation during the meal went back to ordinary topics except they all constantly checked to make sure the cat was okay.

After dinner Allison sat on the floor, Rafe squatted by her side, both of them totally into discussing names.

"Blackie?" Allison suggested.

"Boring." Rafe grinned. "Midnight is better, or Starbender."

Allison snorted. "Those are better names?"

"Cobalt. Black Lightning." Rafe was way more into this than Gabe had anticipated. Allison glanced up, and he winked at her, content for a little bit of normality to finish his day.

The kitten stepped all the way into the cookie sheet Gabe had spread the mash in, instantly coating all four paws with white goop.

"Oh no." Allison grabbed him around the middle and reached for a towel.

"Don't," Gabe warned. "It's okay—he'll lick the mash off his paws and eat it. It's a good way to get some food into him."

"Really? Okay, but it looks like he's wearing rubber boots with the white on his black fur."

Rafe laughed. "Puss in Boots."

"There you go." Gabe scratched the kitten's head. "There's a good name for him."

Allison nodded. "I like it. What do you think, Rafe?"

His kid brother shrugged. "Sure, I mean, whatever, it's just a cat, you know." He jumped to his feet and pretended to be busy clearing the table.

Allison and Gabe shared a secret smile—Rafe's embarrassment was the final bit of tension lifter they needed.

At the end of the evening when Gabe grabbed his keys to drive his brother home, Rafe reluctantly passed a sleeping Puss in Boots back to Allison. "Hey, you guys headed to Traders tomorrow night for the Coleman gathering?"

Gabe wasn't sure. "Why? You want a ride?"

Rafe fussed with his jean-jacket lapel. "Just thinking, you guys should probably go, right? If you'd like, I could come over to make sure the cat's okay. Just, if it would help."

The urge to tease his brother was tempered by the sense of relief in his own gut. Damn, he wasn't going to leave the little thing alone until he knew it was going to be okay.

He was as tenderhearted as his brother…

Allison finished tucking Puss into the box they'd turned into a bed, and came over to wrap her arms around his brother. "You are a genius. Thank you so much for offering, that would be wonderful."

Rafe's surprised expression switched to happiness. "No problem. I'll come over after we eat."

Allison let him free. "Why don't you come for dinner again? Whenever you're done chores."

Her welcoming his brother back made Gabe strangely content.

By the time dinner was done on Friday, he was doubly glad of Rafe's suggestion. Not because he was worried about the kitten as much anymore—Puss in Boots seemed to have made a complete recovery, even playing with Gabe's sock-covered feet under the dinner table while they ate.

It was good to have the kid around, though. Made things a little less awkward as he and Allison prepared to head out. Rafe even walked outside with them, chatting nonstop to Allison the entire time.

"We shouldn't be too late," Gabe managed to cut in. He worried for a minute that Rafe would suggest sleeping over, but the kid was totally wrapped up in the cat he held against his chest.

"No worries. I'm going to watch TV."

When Gabe opened his truck door and pressed his palm against her lower back, guiding her forward, Allison rolled her eyes. "I could use the other side."

Rafe laughed. "Gabe told me once he's a lazy gentleman. Saves him having to come around the truck if he takes you in and out his side."

"Whatever. Shut up, Rafe." Gabe helped her in and tried not to stare at her ass as she settled into the center seat.

She didn't protest snuggling up tight in the cab. Maybe having Rafe standing outside the door waving them off made it easier to pretend there was an excuse for her to be pressed close to Gabe. He wasn't going to complain, that was for damn sure. After everything, including dealing with the kitten, having a touch of physical distraction was a good thing.

They were only halfway down the driveway when Allison spoke.

"You sure you want to go out?"

He wanted it, for more reasons than to keep his mind off his father and his worries. "Friday night at Traders is like the Coleman blood bond. It's as good a place as any to do the final round of introducing you as part of the group."

She leaned back and sighed. "I'm ready for the telling-people part to be over. It's taken way more energy than I expected."

A comfortable silence surrounded them. The road into town passed quickly, the warmth of her thigh against his helping him relax. He did need tonight. They both did, for many reasons.

He parked next to one of the Coleman trucks, glancing around to see exactly who was going to be on the inquisition squad for the evening. "Shit, we got a crowd."

"What do you mean?" Allison peered out the window, obviously trying to figure out what he'd noticed.

He pointed. "We got a full showing of the family. There's a good dozen trucks, and they've probably doubled up to get here. You ready to run the gauntlet?"

The tension that had haunted her since their reunion had faded over the last week. The acceptance of her mom to Allison's return, and a few good nights' sleep seemed to have done wonders in helping her recover her spirit. The woman who accepted his hand as he helped her out of the truck was closer to the one he recalled from so long ago.

He remembered liking her. Liking her a lot.

She grinned and tilted her head again, the flirty look she pulled on so easily appearing. "Your family is fun. And I want to dance. I don't have to be over at Mom's until around ten o'clock tomorrow, so let's get some Friday night relaxing in."

He twined his fingers with hers and led her through the doors.

Something was different tonight. Less like deception, more as if this was a real date.

Only he had to watch out for that—she hadn't said anything about changing the status quo. Sure, they'd shared a couple kisses, and damn if seeing her staring at him in the shower yesterday hadn't made his heart skip a beat or two.

But Allison had always had that streak of mischief. He squeezed her fingers and pulled her toward the back of the bar, pleased things were going well enough she was able to relax and be herself.

It wasn't anything to do with him. He had to remember that.

A cheer rose as they stepped into view of the clan's usual section. Allison's grasp in his tightened before she slipped her arm around his waist and glanced up. "Holy. Shit."

"I warned you."

She blew out a quick breath before shaking her head slightly. "Into the lair I go..."

He laughed, holding her close as he led them to one of the tables and pulled out chairs.

"Oh no, she's not sitting way over there." The girl cousins at the next table overrode his seating decisions and surrounded Allison like a swarm of puppies with a new toy. Allison stared over her shoulder at him, her expression filled with laughter as she was led to the side and plopped down with great ceremony in the middle of a group of six ladies.

"You may as well give up all thoughts of getting any time with her tonight." Joel passed over a beer and motioned to the empty chair in front of him. "Congrats, by the way."

Gabe dipped his chin. "What's happening tonight? Anything special on the agenda?"

His younger cousin leaned back his chair and gestured with his bottle as he spoke. "Pool table—Travis is grinding everyone into the ground. Don't know how he can see straight with that shiner he's got, but he's already won over fifty bucks each from Steve and Trevor. My big brothers have been shanghaied to the dance floor by their women. Jesse isn't back from his trip to Red Deer yet—he called to say he's still about thirty minutes out. Other than that, it looks as if Karen and Tamara are determined to interrogate your woman. You will have no secrets left whatsoever by the end of the evening."

Gabe leaned back to catch Allison's eye, just to make sure she was still comfortable. The brief glimpse he got showed her smiling widely, laughing at something someone said. She looked as if she was handling his kin no problem.

Relaxing back in his chair was exactly what he needed for a while. The area around them was filled with cousins and friends. Wild, noisy and perfect.

He'd missed this when he'd left.

"That's a very serious face for someone with a bottle in their hand," Joel teased.

Gabe considered. Out of all the boisterous lot, Daniel and Joel from the Six Pack side were the closest to him in temperament. Daniel was happily married now, and usually too busy running after his adopted boys to spend tons of time with Gabe anymore. Even at eight years younger Joel would probably understand.

"Thinking about the time I lived away from Rocky. I worked hard and met some nice folks, but in the five years something was always missing. This whole nosy, noisy clan gets under your skin, and it was tough being away, no matter how annoying everyone can be."

"I hear you. At college, Jesse and me would sit and shoot the breeze with people from all over the province, but they only understood part of the picture. There's a feel to family, isn't there?" Joel twirled a bottle cap in his fingers, staring over the room slowly as if thinking it through. "Still, there's something to be said about looking a little farther from home when it comes to dating."

"You seeing someone?" Gabe refrained from asking if Jesse was seeing her as well. It wasn't his place to poke, not when he had a few threesomes in his sexual history. Although, his few previous experimentations and the twin's typical two-on-one reputation were very different things.

Joel glanced around cautiously. "Just started. Don't want to talk about her."

A loud roar sounded from behind them, and Gabe stood to get a better look at what was making the girls so rowdy.

"Oh hell, you're in for it," Joel warned. "They're doing shots."

Gabe snuck his chair back and made his way over to the section the ladies had taken control of. A surprising amount of teeny glasses littered the table considering they'd only just gotten there.

Allison was very red in the face. He stepped behind her chair and leaned over to whisper in her ear. "You okay?"

Karen Coleman shook her finger. "Oh no, you don't. No interference from the guys allowed."

"Maybe he's here for the—"

Tamara got cut off, a hand slapped over her mouth by her little sister, Lisa. "Don't say it!"

Feminine laughter rang out again.

"I think you should allow us guys to join your party," Gabe suggested, squatting beside Allison's chair.

For some reason, that only made the laughter get louder.

A huge tray was lowered to the table, small shooter glasses covering its surface. Karen looked around at the other ladies. Universal headshakes were the instant reaction. She shrugged. "Sorry, Gabe. Looks like you've been voted off the island."

Now he was more curious than before. "I'll just stay and watch then."

"No," Allison shouted.

More laughter ensued.

"Oh boy." She covered her cheeks with her hands before glancing at him. "It's okay. You go have fun."

Tamara giggled. "He's gonna..."

Allison held her finger to her lips before giving up and grinning. "You are so bad."

"Which is why you like me. Go on, pick another shot."

Allison eyed the tray as if it might explode.

"Let Gabe pick one for you," Karen suggested.

That suggestion was greeted with a lot more enthusiasm. Whatever the hell they were up to, Gabe would go along with it if he could keep an eye on Allison. He reached forward for a creamy brown shooter.

"No, not that one," Allison gasped.

Gabe jerked his hand back. "Why not?"

She flushed so red. "Already had one of those."

"Oh yeah, she did."

He shook his head and ignored the jokes and nudges going on. Instead he picked up a nearly white drink with whipped cream on the top and handed it to Allison. "You let them know if you want to stop, okay?"

She nodded. "I'm fine. This is fun."

Across the table Lisa tipped back a shot, swallowed, then slammed the glass upside down in front of her. All the women leaned forward. Lisa covered her face as her friend nabbed the small piece of paper stuck to the bottom and read it out loud. "Passed Out Naked on the Bathroom Floor."

Oh jeez. Now Gabe knew what they were doing. "Dirty shots?"

"Aren't most of them dirty?" Karen asked. "Go on, pick one. If you dare."

He glanced at Allison, wondering which shot she'd had that put that blush on her cheeks. It was mostly harmless fun, though. "What the hell."

Gabe selected one and tossed it back, hoping he had managed to pick something not too terrible. The alcohol went down smoothly, too many fruit juices along with it for his taste. He tipped the glass over.

"Read it," the chorus demanded.

"Really? Fine." He leaned over and checked the shot name. *Ah shit.* "Sex on My Face."

It took a while for the laughter to slow. He took the teasing with a grin. "Here I thought the male Colemans were the dirty perverts of the group, but I can tell I was wrong."

When he went to stand, Allison caught at his hand. "Don't forget you promised to take me dancing."

Loud protests greeted her suggestion. Gabe raised his hands in submission. "Tell you what, I'll come back in a bit."

"She's got to have the shot you picked for her before you go," Tamara warned.

Allison gave Tamara a dirty look. "You know something."

Tamara opened her eyes wide. "Me? I'm truly innocent."

"Right—you were the one to order the drinks." Karen poked her sister good-naturedly.

Allison shook her head, but she took the shot, passing the empty glass to Gabe. He turned it over.

Angel's Kiss.

He glanced at his cousin to discover Tamara grinning from ear to ear. She waggled her brows suggestively, tilting her head toward Allison.

"That was a setup. I don't know how you did it, but that was a total setup."

"Hey, be happy you didn't pull the Suck, Bang and Blow."

"Troublemaker." Gabe cupped Allison's chin carefully and pressed his lips to hers. He meant to make it a quick, easy kiss, nothing too showy for the group of rowdies watching keenly.

Only she slipped her arms around his neck, and her mouth edged open, and next thing he knew his tongue had slipped in to taste the sweet remainder of her shot. Or maybe it wasn't the shot. Maybe it was just her. She tangled her fingers in his hair, and he could have happily sat there on his knees kissing her for the rest of the evening.

The taunting when he did pull away was to be expected. He ignored them all and stared into Allison's eyes. "You have fun. I'll come get you in a bit to dance."

After Gabe left, her third and final shot had been one with the unfortunate name of *Bull Rider*. Still, it had to be the alcohol dancing in her veins that made her face feel so heated when Gabe returned to claim her and take her out on the dance floor. The slow music was exactly what she needed so she could catch her breath.

Except being in his arms, swaying slowly, was making it tough to breathe for all sorts of other reasons.

She rested her cheek on his chest and gave in to the urge to relax as she let him lead. "I think I'm more tired than I knew."

Gabe chuckled. "I think you're more drunk than you know."

"Three shots, that's all I had," she protested.

"Fine. It's not the alcohol. It's all the stress from the past week. Taking an evening off and relaxing—you're feeling it."

They moved together easily and she had to agree. "Kind of like after exams when everyone succumbs to the flu."

"Right. Don't worry, I'll get you home okay."

A yawn snuck out and she barely covered her mouth in time. "I think my plans for kicking up my heels for a few hours of dancing needs to be revised."

"We can head out anytime you'd like. There's someone here most Fridays, and if you don't have things happening with your mom, I don't mind bringing you."

She bit her lip for a second. "It feels wrong. Laughing and dancing knowing that..."

"Allison, don't." He stopped right in the middle of the dance floor and lifted her chin until she had to look in his eyes. "Don't do that to yourself. Your mom is so happy you are here, and she's not going to begrudge you enjoying yourself and having a few laughs."

"I guess, only—"

"No only. It's true." He tugged her off of the main floor, bringing her back into his arms more like a hug of reassurance than actual dancing. He spoke softly. "You came to give to Maisey, to help her. You need to stay healthy so you can be there for her. Don't sacrifice your happiness thinking that's what she wants. Because it's not true."

Allison squeezed him tight, nodding her agreement. "You're right."

They danced for a few minutes, the music pouring over them gently, others moving around in an easy rhythm.

The room was a little blurry through her tears and she wiped them away as discreetly as she could.

"Gabe?"

"Yeah?" He pulled back and gazed over her face, concern in his expression.

"Thank you."

He tweaked her nose and motioned toward the door. "Come on. Let's go home."

Chapter Ten

Gabe squeezed Allison's shoulder before leaning over to grab her plate, stacking it with his and making tracks for the clean-up area. The laughter of the Coleman Canada Day gathering that surrounded him was part of why he'd worked so damn hard to come back. To make things work for his family—so they could continue to be a part of the extended family. He scraped the dishes and brought them around the corner to where a makeshift kitchen had been established for washing.

The Six Pack twins were elbow deep in clean up. "Did you lose a bet?" Gabe asked.

"Shut up," Jesse snapped.

Gabe snorted. "You did. You must have, or you two would be so long gone by now we wouldn't even see your dust."

Joel kept drying but jerked his head toward his twin. "This one had the bright idea to gamble with the girls. Offered both our services without even asking me."

"Well, that part is nothing new. Who'd you bet with?"

Jesse didn't answer, just groaned as their cousin Karen carried in another huge armload and deposited the mess to the side. She blew them a kiss and sauntered off.

Joel raised his brows and stared in disgust at the never-ending pile of plates and utensils. "Dammit, Jesse, I'll say it again. If you're going to make a wager, at least don't make it a stupid one. Horses? You're brainless enough to include horses in a bet with Karen involved?"

"She wasn't there when I made the bet. It's the rest of the girls who pulled a fast one on me," Jesse complained. "How was I to know she was around the corner?"

Joel snapped his towel and Jesse shouted as he dodged. Gabe walked toward the barns still laughing at their antics and feeling good about the entire day.

This evening they would spend time with Maisey—he'd promised to do the heavy lifting for a couple of clean-up projects. After there would be fireworks and more time to sit and be with Allison.

He pushed open the barn door and ambled cautiously toward the stalls. His Uncle Mike had a couple of new animals he wanted to see.

After about a month around each other, he and Allison had fallen into a comfortable routine. They'd had no further little misadventures in terms of naked surprises, or kissing, or dirty shots for that matter, and he should have been happy.

The deception was going well. Why did it feel as if something was missing?

The horses nickered softly at his approach, and he slowed his steps. They'd been purchased for a good price, and had the potential to be fine animals one day, but it would take time to train and gentle them along.

He paused far enough away the horses stopped their rambling, and instead looked him over with curiosity.

"You are a pretty girl." Gabe smiled as the filly on the right dipped her head as if in response. "Oh, you like being sweet-talked, don't you?"

The stallion in the next stall snorted, wanting attention, and Gabe took a step closer, still moving smoothly. Keeping himself confident and strong, sending out all the positive vibes he could.

Horses were the mind readers of the animal world at times like this.

"They are beautiful animals, aren't they?"

Gabe twisted his head slowly to see his Uncle Mike approach from the back of the barn.

"You found yourself some wonderful additions to the ranch," Gabe admitted, speaking softly. "I'm a little jealous."

Mike nodded. "I think the Whiskey Creek side are a touch green with envy right now as well. But once these two are settled in, I've no objection to helping you strengthen your herd."

Gabe grinned. "Hopefully by that time I'll be able to afford it."

Mike winked, picked up one of the buckets and slipped down the barn toward the feed rooms.

Gabe took his time, one small pace after another, until he was beside the mare. He didn't move, just let her sniff him, her wide nostrils flaring as she leaned down and finally nudged his shoulder.

He pressed a palm to her nose, the heat of her breath shooting out and hitting his chest.

A low hiss sounded behind him. Ben snarled, "You get your fool hands off that animal. You want to fuck up something else?"

Gabe's tension shot skyward. Way to make a family event special—his father was such a ray of sunshine. Remembering his promise to himself, though, he stayed where he was and concentrated on not letting his anger show and further upset the pretty mare that had frozen in place at the new visitor.

"Lower your voice," Gabe ordered.

A swear exploded from his father, and Gabe sighed. He carefully backed away from the horses. He had barely cleared four feet when a hand grabbed his shoulder and spun him.

It was obvious his father had been drinking. Figured.

The man looked him up and down with fury in his eyes. "Don't you ever think you can start ordering me around."

Gabe pushed past him without a word. Or he tried to. Ben grabbed his arm and locked him in position.

Gabe jerked his arm forward but it wasn't enough to break free. "Let go."

Ben shook his arm violently. "You want to call the shots, you try it with that woman you hooked up with. At least until she realizes what a loser you are. She's far too good for the likes of you."

"She is amazing, isn't she?" Gabe ignored the insults and broke free. "Smart as well. Far smarter than you, old man."

Ben spat to the side. "She chose you. Means she's too stupid to know much. Maybe I should go and tell her exactly what kind of fucked-up bastard you are, before it's too late and you screw up her life as well."

"Leave Allison out of this."

"Not satisfied to crawl off like you should." Ben moved in closer, the scent of the liquor on his breath making Gabe gasp and turn away. Ben jabbed him in the arm to get his attention. "Where the hell you get off trying to tell me what to do? I'm your father, and you damn well treat me with respect."

"I'll treat you the way you deserve, and right now, that's like a drunken ass."

Gabe regretted the words as soon as they were out of his mouth. Not that they weren't true, but this wasn't making his own decisions, this was stooping to his father's level.

Ben's punch came amazingly quickly for a man too tipsy to stand without swaying. Gabe twisted aside at the last second, and the fist grazed his jaw instead of landing squarely.

The urge to swing back and lay the man out flat was incredible. He wanted to punish and hurt the way Ben had managed to wound him over the years. The way he'd torn up the family and negated all their hopes.

The image of the kittens both tightened his fists, then made him lower them. He would not join this battle. He would not move farther down the road his father walked.

Ben didn't show the same restraint. He waded forward, fists flying. Gabe was forced to grab hold of his father's forearms to stop from being hit. Ben's voice rose, and in the background, the horses grew more agitated, crashing against their stalls in response to the anger and noise.

Suddenly Mike was there. Grabbing hold and pulling them apart. Gabe went willingly, his father not so much.

"Enough, Ben, calm yourself." Mike spoke firmly, dragging his brother out of viewing range of the horses.

"His fault. Should never have come back. Nothing is right because of him."

Gabe was still struggling for words when his uncle defended him.

"You're not thinking straight. Gabe works as hard as you do to keep things going on the ranch." Mike glanced at Gabe, as if willing him to step back. "You need to stop this fighting."

"Works hard? Only at what pleases him." Ben tore himself free from his brother's grasp and turned to glare at Gabe. "You think you're so smart? You have all kinds of wild ideas about improving the place? You just want to tell me I'm wrong with nothing to back it up. So, shut up. You couldn't do any more than I have. Tear the family apart, turn us out on our asses—"

"I could run the place a damn sight better than you do," Gabe blurted out.

His father laughed. "You'd like to think so. You and that woman, and your fairy-tale ideas of making money magically appear. It doesn't happen like that. It's impossible."

"It's not possible because you're clinging to old-fashioned ways that are going to get us tossed out. You stubborn fool."

"Enough." Uncle Mike's command cut through the tension for all of a second before the volume rose again.

"Fine—prove it," Ben shouted. "You think you can do better than me, it's on your head. Payments are due end of the summer. Find a way to make your pot of gold appear in time to stop us from losing everything."

"With you blocking me at every turn?" Gabe kept his voice low, but it didn't stop his anger from coming through. "You'd hang me without a reason, and then blame your own incompetence on me."

"Run the show. Do all the stupid changes you've been itching to try. I won't stop you. I'll do my part in keeping the work done, but when we have to beg for an extension come September, you admit you're the cause and get the hell out of my life for good."

"*Jesus*, Ben. Think about what you're saying," Mike warned. "Gabe's done nothing wrong, and that's not a fair challenge. No way in hell can he turn things around in that short a time, not even if his ideas are good."

"I accept."

The words burst from him like a bullet. His father had no idea what Gabe wanted to try. Ben had no ideas, period, and that was the trouble. Working hard at losing propositions still meant you lost.

Uncle Mike shook his head. "Gabe, don't."

There was little chance he could win the challenge, but it was his only choice.

"I accept," Gabe repeated. He stuck out his hand, not really expecting his father to take it.

The man hadn't touched him in years except in anger.

Ben glanced glassy-eyed between his son and brother then walked out without another word, his boots hitting the barn floorboards with a muffled click like the ticking of a time bomb.

Gabe took a deep breath and let it out slowly. He thought through all the reasons he had for doing this, shoving aside the desire to stick it to his father. Instead he concentrated on his ma, and on Rafe. On the feeling of riding over the land in all the different conditions—sunshine and rain, cutting cold and sweltering heat. It was worth fighting for.

He opened his eyes to see Mike staring, concern written on his uncle's face.

"Your father is drunk. You don't have to do this."

It was an out if he wanted it, but Gabe had secrets Ben had no idea about. All his planning and working behind the scenes? It might not be as far a reach as his father hoped to make the payments, at least if they could get moving. "I have to do this."

"It's not possible." Mike stepped closer until his firm hand rested lightly on Gabe's shoulder. "This isn't about you, it's his ghosts. His...hurts."

"It doesn't really matter why, does it? The truth is we need to change or die. He's willing to lie down. I'm not. The challenge stands. You're a witness if I need it once he's sober."

Mike didn't say anything for the longest time, then nodded.

Gabe glanced back toward the horses. "You've done a lot of things differently over the years. You're seeing the benefit of it now. Maybe I can't catch us up in the short time, but if I can get us on the right track, it will be worth it."

Mike sighed. "He's not the man he used to be. Not an excuse, just a statement of fact."

They stood in silence for another moment before Gabe dipped his head and strode from the barn.

They didn't need to talk about it anymore—it was well known to everyone when Ben had changed.

Only Gabe knew exactly why.

Chapter Eleven

The silence stretched between them. At first Allison hadn't really noticed, just accepted his hand, said her goodbyes and let him lead her to his truck. They had already spoken that morning about stopping at her mom's for dinner. She leaned back on the seat and into his side and relaxed after the chaos of the Coleman gathering.

The lot of them made a ton of noise when together, and the quiet in the truck cab was soothing.

Only there was tension in his body. Pressed against his side, she finally noticed it and wondered if she'd done something wrong.

Allison thought through the afternoon, but in terms of their deception, nothing had gone south. It was well accepted she and Gabe were together. Not that she forgot this was temporary—although thinking about what exactly would happen over the coming year was something she deliberately avoided.

Moving ahead with her life meant losing Mom. How could she even begin to prepare for that event?

But something was definitely going on in Gabe's head. She didn't have the right to ask what had upset him. Walking the line between friends and a more intimate relationship—they were only people passing each other for this short time. He could tell her what was wrong if he wanted to.

She ignored the tiny part inside that was saddened by that realization.

"You enjoy the picnic?" Gabe asked.

"Mostly." Allison stretched her arms forward and rotated her neck to loosen up. "The food was great, and the conversations—well, your Uncle George trapped me and told me a long story about a cold cellar that I never quite understood the punch line."

Gabe nodded absently, staring at the road ahead of them.

Allison sat forward and looked into his face. Now for sure she knew something was wrong. Normally he would have laughed. Told his own story about his uncle. Gabe always did what he could to make her comfortable.

All he did was flick a glance her direction. "What?"

She couldn't ask. She leaned back. "Nothing."

The silence stretched uncomfortably. She had to work to keep from squirming in her seat.

Five more minutes and they'd be at her mom's house, and the business of helping, and hiding her concern, would distract her from the worry she currently felt for Gabe.

He pulled off to the side of the road, down a narrow lane that didn't lead anywhere close to her mom's house.

"Where we going?"

Silence answered.

A moment later they stopped, truck bumper tight against a guardrail that was the only thing between the end of the road and the bend of the river. Gabe got out and didn't wait for her, just stepped up to the edge of the embankment and stood there, arms folded, staring down the ten-foot drop.

His face in profile was expressionless.

Shit.

Allison slid over and out the door. She stood, hanging on to the solid metal, using it like an anchor. Gabe didn't move, and her worry increased.

Screw it if this wasn't her business.

She followed him, pacing forward warily. The same way she would have approached a strange animal in someone's field. Gabe didn't acknowledge her. Not when she stood right next to him. She threw caution to the wind and slipped an arm around his waist. Rested her head against him and looked into the swirling water below, searching for a clue of what to do.

He sighed. A chest-raising, body-moving motion. Then he dropped his arm around her shoulder and brought her forward, hugging her tight. Squeezing her to him, his face buried in her neck.

Allison held on, letting him cling. Her arms were free so she stroked his back, petting him. Soothing as best she could.

How long they stood there, she wasn't sure, but slowly the tension faded from his torso, and suddenly she found herself airborne as he scooped her up in his arms.

"Gabe, good Lord, what...?"

He'd lifted her then dropped himself to sit on the grass with her still cradled in his embrace. "I'm a fool. And you're in the wrong spot at the wrong time and too damn cuddly for your own good."

"What's wrong? What happened?"

It might not be her place to ask, but she needed to know. She cupped his face. Sitting in his lap, his strong arms around her—it was strangely nonsexual. She just wanted to know what had managed to upset this man she had been spending so much time with.

Her friend—at least she hoped they were becoming better friends.

He caught her hand and pulled it from his face. He didn't let go, though, keeping her fingers trapped in his. "Had a fight with Ben. Nothing unusual about that. Only—"

He tugged her against him again and swore lightly.

"I know you two don't get along." Allison hugged him, trying to give him whatever it was that he needed. Tough, when he wasn't giving her many clues.

"Understatement of the year. Ben and I have a mutual 'ignore' policy."

Allison nodded. "But you wish things were different."

He finally made a sound that was kind of like a laugh. "I don't know what I wish."

"You're a guy. This is emotional stuff. It's tough for you to talk about it, right?"

This time he did laugh. He also let her go, and she scrambled off his lap to kneel on the grass beside him.

"It's in the rules. I can't talk about emotions," Gabe deadpanned.

"Right. I forgot. You want me to talk about them for you? Like call out a list, and you check off one by one what you can't say but you're feeling?"

There was a flicker in his eyes—something sad and haunted—before he shook his head. "I didn't mean to dump on you. Just didn't want to go to your mom's place all tensed up. I'm okay now."

"Liar." Allison bit her lip at his expression. "Well, you are lying about being fine. And I get that you don't want to talk about what's upset you. But tense I can help with. Give me a second."

She scrambled to her feet and raced back to the truck, reaching behind the seat for the blanket she'd tucked there earlier.

He gave her a confused look. "What are you doing?"

She shook out the sturdy picnic cloth, placing the cushiony fabric on the grass beside where he sat. "You're still tense. Take off your shirt and I can at least massage out a few of the knots."

Gabe eyed the blanket warily, then nodded, rising on his knees to strip off his shirt and undershirt.

Allison pulled a small bottle of hand cream from her purse triumphantly. She dropped the bag to the side and turned to deal with Gabe.

Oh damn. He'd laid himself out on the blanket like she'd asked, resting his head on his hands. The position showed off his muscles beautifully—shoulders, biceps, and the firm bands that wrapped around his torso down along his waist.

A slick of sexual tension stroked her spine. A massage might help get rid of his tension, but it was going to increase hers.

"You ready?" *Gack*. Her voice sounded far too high-pitched and unnatural.

"Yeah, I guess."

She knelt at his side and warmed up the cream before putting her hands on his shoulders.

For the next fifteen minutes Allison's mind raced as she worked her hands over Gabe's back. Her thumbs along his spine, fingertips digging into the hard bulges that slowly relaxed. She slipped lower, wondering why she was doing this to herself. What had started as an offer from a friend to another was making all kinds of more-than-friends ideas pop into her head.

No. They'd made it clear that this was about helping each other. The little bits of teasing they'd done at the start of their time together—she'd made sure that was put aside. Just ignored any of the sexual attraction she felt for the man.

But right now? Good Lord, she was getting turned on.

She'd straddled him shortly after she began, and now she sat on his legs, the edge of his jeans the barrier line for "go no farther". Only she wanted to. Wanted to pull down the fabric and let her hands wander all over his warm skin. Wanted to press hard into his ass muscles and curl her fingers around his naked flesh.

Wanted what she shouldn't want.

She swallowed and tried to ignore the lust. Focus instead on the sights and sounds around them.

Only the rush of the river and the nearby trees weren't nearly as mesmerizing as his body. She smoothed her palms all the way up to his shoulders, wishing she were brave enough to lean down and set her teeth to his skin.

Suddenly she was no longer sitting on his thighs, but lying on her back as he loomed over her.

It was the little noises she made that finally broke his control.

He'd been riding hard on his frustrations as much as possible, not wanting to punish her for what Ben had stroked to a high pitch. Holding on to her and accepting her comfort had seemed like an innocent thing. Until she put her hands on him and all that adrenaline was directed away from anger at his impossible life. Now the fervour was firmly centered on his cock, and she was the reason for the change of locations.

He held her trapped, her dark hair spread out on the blanket as he examined her face for a sign he was about to get rejected. Little puffs of air escaped her lips, her chest rising and falling way too fast for someone who'd simply been giving a chaste rubdown.

She stared up, pupils dark and wide. Their bodies tight together, his groin solid to hers in a way that couldn't possibly let her fail to recognize the state he was in.

She licked her lips, and this time he was the one who groaned in frustration. In need.

"Tell me no," he whispered.

She caught his head in her hands, fingers threaded through his hair to hold him in place. "No."

Then she dragged him toward her and lifted her lips.

The connection between his brain and his body shut down for the second time that day. He took the kiss she offered. Took her mouth and lips, their teeth knocking for a moment as they both went a little wild. Frustration, fire from whatever source, they both took and gave and god*dammit* if it wasn't exactly what he had to have right then.

Allison squirmed, opening her thighs wider to let him settle tighter between her legs. He matched his hips and his tongue, pulsing slower now, making firm enough contact to tease them both. She dragged her hands through his hair and down his back, fingernails scraping over the territory she'd been rubbing so enthusiastically earlier.

When she clutched his ass, planted her feet on the ground and rose to meet him, he was caught wanting to take this way further than it should go.

He rolled them slightly, breaking their kiss. Keeping her against his body but pressing his lips to her face, to the hollow of her neck. "I should stop."

"We should stop. Oh God, yes, Gabe...*ahhh...*" She held on too tight for her words to push him away. He sucked on her neck again, and she jerked as if he'd put a brand to her skin.

He smiled before licking the sensitive spot. "I found a hot button."

She had thrown a leg over his thigh, keeping their groins in contact. "I think my entire body is a hot button right now."

Somehow he found the strength to stop. Well, not stop, but slow down. He leaned up on an elbow and stroked his knuckles over her cheek. "I feel like I should apologize, but I'm not sure that's the right thing to do."

"You didn't do anything to be sorry for."

"I want to."

Her eyes widened for a second then lowered until she was looking at him from under her lashes. "Me too."

As if they'd talked it through, they both relaxed down from high alert. Gabe lay back, head resting on his arm. Allison leaned away slightly, a narrow gap opening between them.

He kept touching her, though, trailing his fingers along her arm, over the dip of her waistline. "We're a couple of fools. Or I should just speak for myself."

She shook her head. "I don't know if it's foolish, but...Gabe?" She lifted her chin and smiled. "We're grownups. We're allowed to—"

When she didn't continue but flushed bright red, he had to stop from laughing and embarrassing her worse. "We're allowed to go from me being mad at Ben to damn near fucking each other in an open field?"

She poked him in the chest. "You telling me you were touching me just because you're mad at your father? I call bullshit."

She was a smart one. He'd told Ben that, and here was more proof. "I'm touching you because you're a beautiful woman. And you've been living under my roof for a month, and seeing you wander around in that thin bathrobe is driving me crazy."

Allison's mouth fell open. "Thin?"

"See through. Completely. Damn, when you stand in the kitchen getting coffee in the mornings? The light shines right through the window, and I can see every curve and hell if I don't want to go back and take another shower. Cold, to make me stop from thinking about peeling the fabric off you and—"

Her hand covered his mouth. "You should have told me."

He licked her palm, and she smiled, the smile turning to a gasp as he slid his hand over her ass and cupped her butt cheek. "You would have turned even redder than you are now."

She nodded, pulling her hand down his chest, her gaze following her fingers. "So...what're we going to do about this?"

"Buy you a thicker robe?"

Allison stuck out her tongue, and he had to hold himself back from wanting to lean in and catch it with his mouth. Start kissing her all over again, maybe remove a few of her layers.

Lay her out in the full sunshine and examine every single part of her in minute detail, preferably with his mouth.

She exhaled slowly. “We shouldn’t strip and have sex right now, should we?”

“We shouldn’t.”

“But we want to, right? Both of us?” Her bravado slipped for a minute before the mischievous smile returned. “Well, I’ll speak for myself. Right now I’m fairly certain I’d be fine with the sex-in-the-meadow thing.”

Oh God. “Oh, we’re both on board, but we can’t. Shouldn’t.”

She shook her head. “We’re both crazy.”

Gabe gave up and rolled to his back, staring up at the sky. His body ached, but his mind was strangely clear. A lot more clear than he’d been while driving away from the picnic.

Allison leaned over him, her dark hair falling past her shoulder and brushing his chest. “Gabe?”

He kept his hands pinned where they were to stop himself from grabbing her and starting all over again. “Yeah?”

She wrinkled her nose. “We should get over to my mom’s. She’s going to wonder where we are.”

Somewhere deep inside the amusement started. It had just been that kind of fucked-up day, and there was nowhere else for this to go. From contentment to envy to anger to lust. And back to contentment—and the start and finish were because of Allison. “I’d say you were right about that.”

When she would have pulled away, he caught her, hand gentle but firm around the back of her neck. Her lashes fluttered as she stared at him questioningly.

“We’re not done this conversation,” he warned.

“We were talking?”

"With our bodies. Yeah, a loud conversation. Nearly shouting."

Allison nodded. "I think we should…finish the discussion later. Sometime. If you'd like."

His cock, which had begun to relax, kicked back up a notch. "Maybe later tonight?"

That tongue of hers slipped out again, just briefly, and he bit back a moan of frustration.

He kissed her. Briefly. Intensely. Then let her go and they both found their feet. Gabe had to adjust his cock, attempting to do it discreetly, but when he glanced at her, Allison was grinning and trying not to show it.

The crazy mixed-up sexual tension between them was somehow cathartic. All his frustrations with Ben, and the impossible task before him, had morphed into the single thought of taking Allison into his bed. Focusing on finding out what made her squirm even more than sucking on that sweet spot on her neck.

She scooped up the blanket and shook it out, waiting for him to join her.

Wasn't much that he could think of to say. Thank you? That was stupid—and yet it was somehow right as well.

She'd saved his sanity, if only for a moment. He'd take sexual frustration any day for that.

Chapter Twelve

"I need those three boxes as well, please, Gabe."

Allison stopped in her unpacking of one of the earlier totes he'd brought to watch the organized chaos taking place before her. Like some miniature commander in chief, her mother was having a great time ordering Gabe around. He'd carried everything she'd asked for from under the storage section of the garage. Then he'd been sent to the shed for all the boxes marked *Christmas Ornaments.* Now he was climbing up and down a ladder to pull out a stash that had been hidden in the attic space.

"Mom, what on earth was Dad doing putting stuff up there?"

Maisey lifted her shoulders briefly, one hand fluttering up to brush back the hair that had fallen across her forehead. "He loved to save junk. A bit of a packrat, you know. I've been slowly cleaning through things, but since you two volunteered, I thought this was a good time to do another chunk of the work. No sense in having this stuff all over the place taking up room if no one is going to use it."

Allison focused on the box before her a little more firmly. She didn't want to think about how her mom was probably doing this so that once she was gone, they wouldn't have to.

Gabe placed another box on the stack against the wall before coming around the table to where she stood. He leaned into her, wrapping his arms tight for a moment and hugging her. His lips skimmed her ear. "You okay?"

She shivered involuntarily even as she nodded.

The goose bumps that rose on her arms—how could she be getting turned on at the same time she was worried sick over her mom?

"You two—" Maisey turned from the kitchen sink with an empty garbage bag in her hand and a smile on her face. "I swear. It's good to see you so much in love."

Allison wasn't sure if she was red or not, but Gabe let her go after a kiss on the cheek. The deception was working better than ever, although now there was the added distraction of wondering exactly what kind of *discussion* they were going to have once they left her mom's house that night.

Sex could confuse things. Could mess things up, and yet she didn't want to deny either of them what they both seemed to want.

Her mom pulled out a chair and sat, her face gone white, pinched with pain.

"Mom?"

Allison was around the table and at her mom's side as fast as possible.

Maisey waved a hand. "It's nothing. Indigestion. Those leftovers from the restaurant were too spicy for me."

Allison turned to grab a glass of water only to discover Gabe standing right there, holding one out. His expression showed his concern, but there was no trace of it in his voice as he spoke.

"You sit and relax. If you'd like, I'll go take care of those trees you asked me about, and Allison can help you sort here at the table." He leaned in and gestured toward the pile Allison had been working on. "You keep an eye on her. I think I saw her sneaking some papers out of that one. If she's hiding old love letters or something, I need you to catch her for me."

Allison's mom sipped the water, lightness around her eyes that hadn't been there a moment before. She put the glass down and patted Gabe's hand lightly. "You go on. I'll watch her for you."

"Mom!"

Gabe squeezed Allison around the waist as he headed to his task, and a wave of something far more than gratitude swept over her.

He knew when she needed a touch. Not just the physical touch, but the emotional. How many nights had he sat and listened to her talk about the restaurant? Let her go on about the things that were happening, the changes she'd seen in her mom.

So damn patient.

"Now that's what I like to see." Maisey tugged on her sleeve and dragged Allison's attention to the fact she'd been staring after Gabe's back as he walked out the door.

She twisted to look at her mother. "What do you like to see?"

"You. In love."

Allison got herself busy digging into the nearest box and lifting things onto the table. The flutter inside pointed out maybe being in love and being very much in lust looked somewhat similar. She wasn't going to let the bad moment pass, either. "What did you eat that's upset you so much?"

Maisey took the pile of paper from the table in front of them and started flipping through them. She returned a few to the pile on the left, dropping the rest into the garbage can at her side. "Just a rich sauce. I'm feeling better already."

The house fell silent for a moment, only the soft noises of her mom going through the old receipts and bills. The gentle ticking of the ancient family cuckoo clock in the living room—a sound that had been a part of all her growing-up years.

For a second she imaged it as a stopwatch, an eerie hourglass ticking down the moments of her mother's life.

The pain inside grew too large to contain, and she carefully came to her mother's side. Knelt by her chair and wrapped her arms around Maisey and held on tight.

Her mom stiffened slightly, then sighed and returned the embrace. "You're a little old for crawling into my lap now, aren't you?"

Allison didn't speak. Couldn't speak. Her throat had closed up at the realization these moments were fading. At some point she'd reach out to hug her mother and the woman would be gone forever.

"I love you, Mom." Cracking, barely understandable.

"Oh, sweetie." Maisey sniffed and squeezed even harder. "You going to be okay?"

"No." Allison pulled back so she could look at her mom directly in the eye. "Mom, I know."

"Know what?"

Allison gestured, even though her flailing probably made no sense. Nothing more than a whirl of her hands, but holding back the motion was impossible. "About you. About what's wrong."

Maisey's face tightened, her lips pressed together. She blinked hard and then nodded once. A sharp, sudden jerk. "I wondered if you did."

Allison held her peace about how she'd found out. If her mom asked, she'd consider telling, but who spilt the beans was less important than everything else right now. "I'm here for you, okay?"

Maisey stared out the window. "I didn't want you to have to worry. Do Paul and Elle know as well?"

"Not yet, but you should tell them—"

"No," Maisey blurted out. "Allison, no. And promise me you won't tell them either. After everything that happened last time with your father, I don't want to see them hurting because of me."

"There's nothing you can do?"

Maisey shook her head. "Nothing. It's cancer, sweetie. Pancreatic. And taking experimental drugs in the hopes of prolonging my life just to make it to Christmas? I can't—" Her voice broke, and she sucked back a gasp. "I can't watch you all go through that again. It's better if it's quick."

Listening to her mom list all the reasons Allison had thought of was confirmation, but it also gave her the chance to add her plea. "We're not children anymore, Mom. Telling them is the right thing to do. Give them time to say goodbye."

Maisey's lips pressed together tight as she avoided Alison's gaze.

Stubborn as always. Allison readied herself to argue some more. Maisey broke down crying, and suddenly she was neck deep in tears and having to be strong for her mom. It took a while before the torrent passed, both of them using the box of Kleenex at an alarming rate.

Maisey finally nodded. "I'll think about it. Don't say anything yet, will you?"

Allison hesitated before giving in. "But don't wait too long. I'll help you. We'll all want to be here for you."

Maisey clutched her hands. "In a way, I'm glad you know. And I'm ever so glad you have Gabe right now."

And with that one comment, any chance she had of confessing that she and Gabe weren't really a couple slipped away. It was terrible, and it was probably wrong, but Allison felt the same way. "Do you want anything? Can I get you anything?"

Maisey shook her head.

They both sat back, the clicking clock in the background now just the familiar noise that had been part of life forever. Maisey played with the papers a little, then straightened. "Well, enough moping. I want to get this cleaned up so we can enjoy some supper and then maybe we can just talk for a bit. If you don't mind staying and visiting for a while?"

Allison squeezed her mom quickly, not trusting herself to give a full-out hug without breaking into tears. Then she returned to the other side of the table and continued her part of the job.

"You want me to..." No better way than to just say it straight, now that the truth was out. "You want me to divvy up pictures between us kids? Or do you have things around the house you want given to friends? We don't need to talk about it now, but you should think about it."

Her mom nodded. "I will. Not that I really care who gets the hurricane lanterns, but I sure don't want you kids throwing out something that's actually valuable."

"Oh, Mom."

"Well, you remember Paul was snitching coins from your father's coin collection to buy candy at the corner store."

Allison groaned on her brother's behalf. "He was ten years old. One mistake and you're never going to let him forget it."

Maisey moved the box in front of her to the side and started on the next one. "It was rather memorable because he was using real silver dollars. If Mrs. Fortney hadn't told me, he would have gone through the entire set."

They continued their task. Allison let her mom ramble about all kinds of things and words poured out—every topic under the sun. She listened and soaked it in. At the same time, a part of her wondered where Gabe was. When he'd get back, and how he would react to discovering Mom's secret was out.

Would he stick with the plan or try to convince her the deception could be finished?

Worry prodded her uncomfortably.

She should have saved her concern. He pulled open the back door, the screen sticking slightly, and before anything could be said, Maisey was up and across the room, squeezing Gabe in a huge bear hug. Considering how frail she had become, the contrast in size between the huge cowboy and her mom was extreme.

Gabe hesitated for a second before bringing his hands around to pat Maisey's back. His gaze snapped to Allison's, questions in his eyes.

"I'm so glad you're in my Allison's life," Maisey said. "It makes it easier knowing she's not alone, and that she's got a good man around to care for her when I'm gone."

A flash of panic crossed Gabe's face, then resignation. Allison's heart tightened. Was he regretting this more now? The tumble outside earlier, and the lying in the first place?

What in the hell had happened?

He'd gone out to do some simple yard work, and the kitchen looked like there'd been a bomb dropped. Not just the paper and clutter scattered all over the table and floor, but the tear streaks still visible on both women's faces.

Something had gone down, only he wasn't one hundred percent sure what.

He moved cautiously, patting Maisey's back gently. "You bet I'll take care of Allison."

Across the room, Allison nodded. "I told her I know. We've had a good cry, and we're going to move forward now," she shared.

Okay, that was what he needed to know. He acknowledged Allison and gave an extra squeeze to Maisey before breaking her hold and leading her back to the chair she'd claimed earlier.

"I'm glad it's not a secret anymore. So now I can tell you to make sure you call us anytime you need anything, understand? Night or day, we can come. Do you have my cell phone number?"

Maisey touched his arm gently. "You are a darling. And yes, Allison gave it to me, but I'll be fine."

The conversation continued as they cleaned up and worked together to bring out dinner. Spent the meal and the hours afterward talking about old memories. Gabe watched the two women as they moved easily around each other, their love and caring so clear.

For a moment he was jealous.

That someone was so willing to turn their life upside down for another. To sacrifice and suffer to try to ease the pain for another—it wasn't that he'd never witnessed that in his life. His ma lived it daily. But the burden of it seemed less for Allison and her mom. As if they'd found a way to share the pain and hold it together. And that together the burden was lighter.

A part inside him hated Ben just a little bit more.

He and Allison were headed home before he realized they were returning to a whole different situation. Not the fact that Maisey's secret was partway out, but the earlier tangle in the field.

It was a knot of dilemma.

Allison shifted position at his side. Rested her head on his shoulder. She slipped her hand under his arm and held on tight. "Thank you."

Wasn't what he expected. "For what?"

"For not spilling the beans. For sticking to our commitment. Not that I didn't think you weren't going to, but it's a huge thing you're doing, and I don't want you to think I'm unappreciative."

"You're welcome." He slowed to take the back route toward the cabin. The twisting road would take a little longer. Maybe by the time they got home he'd have figured out what to do.

Allison squeezed his arm again. "You were wonderful with my mom."

"She's a great lady. I'm sorry she's going through this. Sorry you are as well."

They fell silent, and Gabe tried to concentrate on the future. On which projects he had to get rolling immediately to meet the challenge his father had set.

All he could think about was the sensation of Allison's fingers on his arm, and the heat of her body next to his.

"Oh look—" Allison pointed to the side. In the middle of the field three deer were feeding. One lifted its head as they approached, wary and alert. When they slowed but drove past, the animals didn't move from where they were enjoying their dusk dinner of new summer's grass.

Suddenly all three heads shot up, and tails flashed white as they took off into the trees, spooked by something,

A brilliant burst of light rose over the treetops, the shimmering circle of fireworks displayed in the darkening sky.

"I'd forgotten about the fireworks tonight," Allison said.

Totally slipped his mind as well, with all the rest of the chaos. "You want to go back to town to watch?"

"No." But she leaned forward like a kid, checking the heavens for more.

"Come on, I'll take you to another spot." He eased the truck off the road and up the narrow lane to the private access. The rise of the land was enough they wouldn't see the lights of town, but the higher bursts should still be visible.

Chapter Thirteen

He pulled over and parked, adjusting the wheel to give himself more room. When he opened the window, the loud snap of another cracker sounded—loud enough for them to hear even at this distance.

The air was warm and he leaned back, trying to relax.

Allison loosened off her seat belt so she could perch on the edge of the seat. A few more single bursts rose before the actual fireworks display took off. He found himself observing carefully, more to see her reaction than to watch the fireworks. She was pensive at first. It took a while for her to relax, to start to smile at the colour changes. The first time she gasped at a more brilliant explosion, it twisted something inside him.

She'd had to deal with a horrible situation this evening, and he was glad she could put aside her sadness for a moment.

He was a bastard that her childlike responses of delight also made him react in a totally adult way.

The noises she made went straight from his ears to his cock. It wasn't as if she was watching a light show, she was in the middle of the best damn orgasm of her life and the happy sounds made him twitch with need.

Lights were still going off when she turned toward him, her face finally relaxed and at peace. She stared at him, and the longer she looked, the more her expression changed.

"Gabe?"

Low. Sultry. Sex-laden and hot. Of course, maybe that was his imagination, but damn if he didn't hope she was thinking even a fraction of what he was.

She climbed up on the seat next to him, her boots abandoned on the floorboards. She pressed her hand to his chest, eyes locked on his.

Under her fingers, his heart was pounding.

"You said we'd…talk…later," she reminded him.

"It's been a long day."

Fuck.

That wasn't what he wanted to say. What he wanted was to order her to strip naked and crawl on top of him. Once he'd managed to do the naked thing as well, of course. Then he'd find other things to do, including tasting every inch of her skin and fucking her until she saw more fireworks.

Allison wrinkled her nose. "If you're too tired to talk, then maybe I should do all the…discussing."

She leaned forward and their mouths met, and damn, he was glad she wasn't the kind to just give up. He curled a hand around her waist, the other around her neck, and kissed her for dear life.

Her taste rolled over him, pleasure increasing. Her tongue teased his tentatively at first, then bolder as they tangled themselves up. Breaths mingling, bodies closer. Somehow she crawled into his lap, and he had her shirt tugged free of her jeans.

He slipped his palms up her torso, soaking in the warmth, the silky smoothness of her skin. She groaned into his mouth as he undid the clasp on her bra and snuck his hands forward, warm full globes of her breasts filling his hands.

Her nipples were hard against his palms as he rubbed slowly, loving the weight of her breasts, wanting more than to touch, but first, dammit, he was going to enjoy touching.

He remembered something from earlier in the day, a good memory, and he left her mouth to press his lips to her throat.

She sat up like he'd electrocuted her.

"Hmm, nice." He nibbled on her neck while playing with her nipples, tiny pinches and tugs that made her volume increase and her squirming ratchet up a notch.

Her bra was in the way, and the fabric of her shirt, so he grabbed them both and lifted, Allison helping until she was naked from the waist up. He stared down, and that electric cattle prod zapped along his spine.

"Sweet Jesus, woman."

She had a tattoo. And a belly ring. He traced the edges of the butterfly with his finger, the single wing he could see just poking out from the edge of her jeans.

She grabbed his hands and pulled them back to her breasts. "More. I'll show you my tatts later."

More? Gabe's brain went into overload. "Allison, this isn't the place, but damn if I don't want you."

She knelt and offered him her breasts, and thinking about putting the truck into drive and getting them home where there was a bed slipped away like the ashes of the fireworks blowing on the wind.

He licked her nipple, twice, just because he loved the sound she made the first time he did it. Then he switched to the other side and sucked.

He got lost for a while in touching and tasting. Coming back to her mouth again and again even as he couldn't keep his hands off her.

When she popped the top button on his jeans, he finally found the strength to grab her wrists. "No room. Let's take it home so I can make this good for you."

She lifted a brow. "First, let me make it good for you."

Nope. Not doing it. He still had enough of his brains, barely, to back the truck up, Allison squealing with laughter as he snagged her with one arm up against his side.

She kissed his neck, dragged her fingernails over his shoulder. Pressed her fingertips down his chest and played with his abs until he was ready to explode.

The truck skidded a little as they pulled into the parking space next to her car. He was parked twisted sideways and he didn't give a damn. He had them out of the truck and into the cabin without stopping, without thinking. He carried her, leaving her boots abandoned behind them, shirt as well. All the way into the bedroom where he tossed her on the mattress and crawled over her, unwilling to take a break from making physical contact.

"Condoms?" Allison gasped when he finally sat up to strip off his shirt.

"Side table."

She scrambled away as he jerked off his boots and peeled down his jeans. A pair of arms came around from the back, warm breasts pressed to his naked skin, her fingers flicking his nipples.

"Damn it, woman. I can't think... Fuck—"

She'd slipped one hand all the way down and grasped his cock over his boxers, fingers wrapped tight. "Yes. Fuck. I want to. Need to."

Maybe he should have stopped them, but that point had passed, and now there was no getting the horses back in the corral without letting them have a good hard ride.

He clasped her wrist and held on tight, turning to discover not only was she naked from the waist up, heavy breasts right at mouth level, her jeans were gone. The only thing remaining was a tiny triangle of sheer fabric over her mound. Dark curls showed through the material, and the head rush he felt nearly knocked him to the bed.

Which wasn't a bad idea.

"Come here," he ordered, tugging her downward. Allison collapsed willingly, hair around her shoulders, limbs at rest.

Gabe leaned up and kissed her, one hand cupping her breast. Thumb sliding back and forth over the tip. When she gave him one of those sexy moans, he changed his tack, licking and sucking on her neck, moving his fingers lower until he covered her pussy.

"Oh God, yes." Allison clutched his head, and he smiled all the way to her nipples. He pressed his fingers along the edges of her labia, the thin fabric of her panties slipping between her folds. The hard point of her clitoris sat up as if eager for his touch.

"Not enough." Not enough time to do everything he wanted to. Not with the way his cock ached, wetness already marking where the tip pressed into the fabric.

Gabe kissed his way down her stomach, stopping to lick her belly button and tug lightly on the ring looped there.

He didn't pause to take off her panties. Just covered her with his mouth and licked, hard pressure on the sensitive nub at the top.

Allison breathed erratically, chest heaving. She pulled up her thighs, knees falling aside to reveal herself, as much as she could with the material still between them.

He slipped a finger under the fabric, lightly tracing her opening. Again and again until she lifted her hips toward him, begging him for more.

He thrust in the finger at the same moment he made contact with her clit, and Allison jerked hard. "Finally. Holy shit—more."

"You say that a lot." He paused for long enough to tease her with his words, then bent intently to his task. Adding another finger, working her with his tongue and teeth until her passage tightened around him and she gasped out her pleasure.

She clutched his shoulders, trying to pull him over her.

"Condom." The bit of his brain that still functioned kicked out the word.

Allison swore, and they pulled apart for a second, him to cover himself, her to strip off the sopping-wet underwear. Then he kissed her and pressed them together. His cock nudged her hip, bumped her thigh. Centered over her warmth, wetness and heat guiding him.

As the tip of his cock slipped in Gabe lifted his head to look into her face. He wanted to see what was revealed there—what speed she wanted, how hard, how soft.

Allison panted lightly, pleasure lighting her eyes and shaking her limbs. She wrapped her thighs around him and arched upward, impaling herself on his cock.

He'd never had anyone do that before. Not while they stared at him with mischief and urgency, and something halfway between pain and pleasure in their eyes.

She relaxed her upper body and threw her hands over her head, grabbing on to the sturdy wooden posts of the headboard.

Gabe tilted his hips and rocked slowly, and her smile got bigger. He did it again, dragging back an inch at a time and then pressing into her. Her sheath was tight around his cock, squeezing and holding him perfectly.

He kissed her again, and suddenly going slow was for the birds. The next motion forward became an actual thrust. His bed was too sturdy to squeak. Too heavy to move. But by the time he'd pumped five or six times, Allison was calling out his name and digging her heels into his ass like she was determined to last a full eight seconds, more than once.

Eight seconds was about all he had left.

He snuck a hand between them and caught hold of her clit, and her eyes that had gone half-lidded with pleasure, popped open. Her lips quivered as she called out.

Her orgasm wrenched his own from him, the sweat on the superheated flesh of his back cooling in the air. Balls emptying, arms shaking as he fought to keep from crushing her.

Allison relaxed, her legs falling away, heart pounding so hard he felt it against his forehead when he rested his head on her to catch his breath.

"Holy. Fucking. Hell." She gasped the words out, one after another.

Gabe collapsed beside her, his cock slipping from her warmth. Rolled to his back and managed to drop the condom to the floor, and that sucked dry all the energy he had left.

Allison curled up against him, resting her head on his chest. Her hair curtained over them, and he lifted a hand to run his fingers through the soft mass.

They were both quiet for a long time. Quiet, except for the occasional gasp.

He finally had enough strength to do more than let the blood return to his extremities. Gabe leaned over and kissed her forehead.

"Thank you."

Allison traced circles on his chest. "I wanted it too."

"Needed it."

She leaned up on her elbow to look at him. "I like you. I'm glad we're friends. And tonight…I needed this so bad. It's like—"

Allison stopped.

Gabe was more up on the psychobabble than she'd probably expect.

"We needed to feel alive."

She thought through his words before nodding.

He'd wanted her too. He wasn't going to let her offer excuses. Or feel bad about having sought comfort.

"I wanted to give you pleasure. I needed it myself. And there's nothing wrong with that."

She rested her head on him again, and he couldn't see her face.

"You're right. And it was. Pleasurable, I mean."

"*Holy fucking hell* I think you said," Gabe teased.

Allison laughed, and they curled up together. Just being. Holding each other.

Usually at night Gabe planned the chores he had to complete around the ranch the next day, but tonight somehow it was easier to put that aside for a bit. Label it tasks to be dealt with tomorrow. Right now? He had something else that was a far higher priority.

Feeling that way was pretty much as special as it was confusing.

Chapter Fourteen

The changes were subtle, but there. Over the next week as Allison went through her day it was disconcerting how often she was distracted from the task at hand. More and more she found herself thinking about Gabe. Longing for the time when she could get back to the cabin and they could curl up together.

Curl up. What a bunch of crock. She meant so they could strip naked for another round of sweaty, satisfying sex.

After that first frantic night, the next time wasn't as desperate but just as needed. Something about tangling with him let her forget her worries and fears for a moment.

She was still going to lose her mom. They still had to tell her siblings and deal with the fallout of that. But the body-shaking pleasure helped numb the hovering pain. Somehow made her able to get up in the morning and head into her day.

She stirred the sausage in the pan as she planned what she needed to accomplish that day. Friday. Time off from the restaurant opened up her agenda. Her mom had suggested coming over in the afternoon—Maisey was doing the morning shift at the Timberline and had promised she'd be home early after that.

There had also been talk of letting Paul and Elle know the truth soon. Maybe even this coming week. Allison wasn't holding her breath, but while keeping the secret was hard, having it still secret meant she didn't have to worry about dealing with their reactions either.

A meow brought her attention to the floor just as Puss in Boots wrapped himself around her ankles, looking for attention. Allison stooped and picked the kitten up, nestling him against her chest and cuddling him. Scratching his tiny chin the way she'd learned he liked.

Puss had made himself at home in the cabin, claiming an old T-shirt of Gabe's and turning it into a nest. With Gabe in and out during the day, and Rafe offering to stop in to take care of him, it seemed the little creature had both made a full recovery and found a home.

Taking him with her when she eventually left seemed cruel, but the idea of leaving without him didn't sit right either.

She was so deep in thought she never heard Gabe step behind her.

His greeting wrapped around her the same moment his hands slipped over her belly. "Good morning."

He pressed his lips to the back of her neck, and goose bumps rose. A delicious shiver somewhere between anticipation and the ready knowledge of the pleasure he could put her body through.

"You're lazy today," she teased.

Gabe lifted his hand a little higher to pet the kitten, smoothing his fingers over its head gently. "Someone wore me out last night."

Allison snickered, pulling the pan off the heat and turning off the burner. "I slept without moving for ten hours. I'm not sure who wore out who."

He turned her, the kitten supported between them as Gabe lifted her chin. His toothpaste-fresh mouth woke desires inside she really didn't feel comfortable with. Sex in the evening when it was about giving each other comfort? Sex in the morning when it was sheer physical pleasure? She could handle those situations.

This seemed far more intimate, and damn if she didn't like it. Liking it was a bad thing.

Reluctantly, she pulled away, patting his chest for a second. "Breakfast is ready. If you grab the coffee, I'll serve up."

Gabe didn't let her go. Instead, he stared down with a touch of something in his expression that looked strangely like fear before it vanished, and she wondered if she'd seen it at all.

He followed her orders, taking food to the table. Sitting easily.

Allison lowered Puss to the floor by his bowl, leaving the kitten with a final pet. She had to resist running her hands along Gabe's shoulders as she made her way past him back to the sink to wash her hands. Addicted, that's what she was fast becoming. Addicted to his touch. Since this wasn't about anything permanent, she needed to nip those impulses right now before they got her in trouble. Bad enough she'd messed up his life with her crazy demands—last thing he needed was for her to fall in love with him.

Gabe pushed the sugar pot toward her. "I went over the reports you got back from the lab. Doesn't look like I'll be to be able to use the south fields for organic grain this time around."

Another blow. She hated to be the bearer of bad news, but he'd told her to be upfront about the truth. "No. They'll have to be in transition the three years. I guess the positive is that gives you time to talk to your neighbour. To convince him to stop spraying so close to the line. I'm sorry."

He shrugged. "That section was the least likely to work. I'm okay with it."

Only she could tell he was still disappointed. She hurried to the good news, hoping to put the smile back on his face.

"The vegetables from your mom's plot are working out wonderfully with the new menu we put together. Is Dana okay with the orders we put in?"

"She's happier than I've seen her in a while. Swear that woman never sleeps. Every time I go over there she's found something new she wants me to ask you about. Latest is she wants to know if you'd like her to plant a second crop of spinach—seems she found a shady spot she thinks will work to stop the plants from going to seed too soon."

Allison smiled, thinking the last time she'd stopped in at the house and got to listen to Gabe's mom enthuse about the new crops. "Yes, we can use the spinach. If there's a bit of excess, I'll ask the chef to create some specials to use it up. People love that we're using more local produce. The whole 100 Mile Diet craze is making them more aware."

Gabe laughed. "Remind me to thank my cousin Blake's wife for that one."

Allison paused. "Jaxi? What'd she do?"

"The usual. Interfered in all the right ways. I found out she's involved with the reading club at the library and added that book to the reading list. She organized a challenge for the summer, daring people to try to meet the 100-mile goal."

The Coleman clan—through thick or thin. "You think she did that to help you out?"

He raised a brow. "Helps them out as well—she's selling farm-fresh eggs like crazy. I've set up with my Uncle Mike for us to butcher some of the sheep privately come the fall. The profit per animal is way higher than taking them to market, especially the ones that I've been keeping aside and following the organic rules on. I've got the turkeys as well."

"I can get you in touch with a few more sellers out in Red Deer—people who work the farmer's markets and that kind of thing. That organic meat is going to be like gold, you know."

His grin lit the room.

It was comfortable and peaceful, sitting and talking through the plans for the Coleman land. By necessity things were slow to change, but Gabe seemed content not to rush, and some of her burdens fell aside.

The sexual frustrations and longings? They stayed right up at high.

There was also the part of her that wondered why she wasn't more focused on getting back to her life in Red Deer. This was supposed to be a temporary gig, living in Rocky, being there for her mom. Thoughts of wanting to see what Gabe could make of the land in the next five years had no place in her long-term plans, and the thought itched her the wrong way.

She really didn't want to think about why.

Gabe was stacking their plates when loud knocking hit the door.

He sighed. "Bet it's Rafe pretending to need something, but really here to visit the cat."

Allison smiled. His kid brother had been coming over often, but he wasn't bad company. "I don't mind, and neither does Puss. And hey, at least Rafe's knocking now."

"Afraid to catch us fooling around on the kitchen table, or something."

Her gaze darted to the solid wood planks still covered with the dirty dishes from breakfast, and the thought of having Gabe bend her over the surface made the most delicious shiver go through her.

She turned to the door instead of being brave enough to meet his eyes, just in case he could read the insta-lust that notion created.

It wasn't Rafe on the other side. It was Travis, face bloody, clothing torn up. He was supporting another young man who hung limply at his side.

Allison gasped, "Oh, shit. Gabe, help."

She swung the door open wide, and Gabe rushed out, catching hold on the opposite side and assisting Travis in bringing the staggering blond into the cabin. Puss in Boots vanished into the back bedroom, tail down.

"I couldn't think of where else to go." Travis's voice rattled out, faint and rough like he'd been shouting for hours and had barely anything left. “Too many people around my place with the twins moved home.”

“Just get him inside.”

While they manhandled the stranger into the living area, Allison raced for some water and a washcloth. She didn’t recognize the stranger, which didn’t mean much since she’d been gone for years.

Gabe and Travis were speaking in low voices when she returned.

“I didn’t break my promise. I wasn’t fighting. That’s why I didn’t call.” Travis accepted the washcloth and applied it to the man’s forehead where a large cut had bled profusely, dripping across his face and into his hair.

Gabe glanced at Allison. “You want to make Travis something to drink?”

He was trying to get rid of her, which made sense. She didn’t need to know the details. “You want anything, Travis?” she asked.

Travis closed his eyes for a moment, frustration screaming out in his every move. “I’m not thirsty, dammit. Gabe’s trying to keep a secret for me, but since you two are getting hitched, I guess I’m just going to have to trust you as well, aren’t I?”

Oh God. Allison wasn’t sure how to stop this. “I don’t need to know anything you don’t want to tell.”

The man on the couch groaned loudly, and Gabe swore. “Travis, if he needs more than a place to sleep it off, this isn’t it.”

“Cassidy is fine.”

Gabe grabbed Travis’s hand and stopped it in midair. “He’s covered in blood and barely conscious. Not to call bullshit on you, but I don’t want a man dying on my couch just because you’ve got some screwy idea of keeping secrets and not going to the hospital.”

"Fuck it. I'm not dying." Cassidy opened one eye a crack. "My head is killing me, but don't start digging a hole to hide my carcass or some crap."

"See? He's alive. He's also an asshole and an idiot, but chances are he'll continue to be an asshole and an idiot for a long time." Travis pressed the cloth against the man's head, the blood slowly cleaning up.

"Takes one to know one."

She should leave, but that was impossible. Allison waited, hovering on the perimeter like a forgotten puppy.

Gabe leaned in to examine Cassidy's face. "Great. Not dying, but you still look like shit."

"Nice place you got," Cassidy forced out, blinking hard as he looked around. "Not that I can see much though the blurred vision."

"Be quiet," Travis ordered. "Gabe, I'm sorry. I didn't want to be traipsing around town looking like we'd done murder. We'll clean him up and get out of your hair."

Gabe's response was a low growl. "You've already involved me. Stupid to stop now. Just tell me—either of you got the RCMP or anyone like that looking for you?"

The laughter that escaped Cassidy's lips died off in a groan of pain. "Nice cousin you got there, T. Thinks the best of you and your friends, doesn't he?"

"Shut up. He's got every right to wonder, with you looking like you escaped from the pen or something." Travis lifted his gaze to Gabe's. "Nothing illegal. No one died."

"That we know of—"

"God*dammit*, can you shut the fuck up for five minutes so I can explain this?" Travis dragged a hand through his hair, gaze snapping between Allison and Gabe.

The black circles under his eyes made her suspect whatever had happened had been going on all night long. She met Gabe's gaze, looking to him for a sign of what to do.

Cassidy passing out and nearly sliding off the couch gave them all something else to think about for a few minutes.

"Allison, go take the quilt off your—the guest bed," Gabe ordered. "Travis, pull off his boots. We can at least lay him flat while we argue about if we need to call an ambulance."

She hurried away to do as he asked. While she might have been sleeping in Gabe's bed for the past week, her stuff was still all over the place in the extra room. She barely had time to strip away the covers before the guys were there, gently depositing an unconscious Cassidy on the bare sheets.

"He got hit a few times that I saw, but I thought he was more dazed than anything."

Gabe unbuttoned Cassidy's shirt. "Not the fight club?"

Travis shook his head, gaze darting to Allison's then away. "We were kind of ambushed—they took us by surprise."

There was a world of things Travis wasn't saying, and she didn't want to know more than he was willing to give. "You guys need me to do anything?"

Gabe nodded, the bloody shirt tossed to the floor. "Call Tamara. Ask her to come out."

"Dammit, Gabe," Travis complained.

"No—" Gabe held up a hand. "It's the hospital or Tamara, you choose. Passing out isn't fine in my books, but you can decide. At least until Tamara gets here. If she says he needs medical attention, then he goes. If you have a problem with that, you picked the wrong place to come for help."

The tension rushed out of Travis so fast he folded, collapsing to the ground. Allison instinctively moved forward to help him, but he waved her off. "Do what he said and call Tamara. You're right, Gabe. You're right."

He leaned back on the wall, one leg pulled up, totally drained. Staring intently at the still body on the bed.

Getting hold of Tamara and asking her to quietly join them at the cabin only took a few minutes. Allison hurried and grabbed a cup of coffee for Travis—from the looks of it the man was barely staying vertical himself, and he probably wouldn't give in to reason and go take a rest without a huge protest. By the time she returned to the bedroom, though, Travis had vanished.

"Where…?"

Gabe nodded toward his bedroom. "Showering. Help me with Cassidy for a minute."

She put down the cup and joined Gabe. He'd been carefully washing the cut on the man's forehead, the edges already turning blue, bruises rising on his torso as well. Cassidy was powerfully built, his muscles visible even while totally relaxed.

"Must have been quite the crew to put that kind of hurt on someone this strong." Allison picked up a second washcloth and carefully wiped Cassidy's knuckles and hands.

Gabe didn't say anything for a minute. He peeked out the doorway, but the shower was still running. "Travis goes to a fight club every now and then. I go with him to make sure he comes home in one piece. Tamara is aware of Travis's little adventures because she's volunteered a few times now—just so you know."

Fight club. She'd never heard of it. "Maybe I'm too sheltered, but what is that. A boxing ring?"

He shook his head, pulling a light sheet over Cassidy and gesturing her out of the room. "More hardcore, less rules—bare-knuckle a lot of the time."

The mental image she'd had of boxers in the Olympics vanished to be replaced by street fighters. "Sounds dangerous. But Travis said they weren't fighting."

"I don't need to know the details, Allison. I just want Cassidy to walk out of here in one piece."

They were at the edge of the living room when he tugged her against him and held on tight. It was out of the blue, and slightly confusing, but being back in his arms? Whatever reason put her there, she was willing to take it. Pathetic as that made her if she thought about it.

So she didn't think. Just tucked her head under his chin and held on. Soaked in his warmth. Waited, taking every second she could until he decided to let her go.

Somewhere in the past seven days Gabe had lost track of exactly what he was trying to accomplish. Oh, he still knew his deadline was coming at the end of the summer, but even the burning need to provide for his family was less on his mind than Allison.

Sex had changed things. That was the best reason he could come up with, and yet it didn't seem to be the complete answer.

This morning when he'd woken and found her already out of his bed, the nudge of something missing had been more than just a physical need to take her all over.

He stared out the window and held her close, her warmth wrapping him up tighter than binder twine. The sweet scent of her body lotion drifted to his nostrils, combining with the images he had of licking her skin, and suddenly he wasn't thinking about the man who lay passed out in his guest room. He was plotting how soon he could get Allison alone and naked.

A bolt of remorse hit hard enough to shake his limbs.

Allison's head swung up, her gaze searching his face. "What's wrong? You okay?"

The demons of the past poked his gut with blazing-hot pitchforks. If he could have shouted out his frustration without scaring her half to death, he would have.

Instead, he caught her face in his hand. Stroked his thumb over her cheekbone. "I'm fine."

She raised a brow. "Interesting. You called bullshit on Travis for using that word a few minutes ago."

"Smarty-pants."

He couldn't stop himself. Leaned over and pressed their lips together for a brief, intense kiss.

When he stepped away, one corner of her mouth was turned up. She'd found her smile again, even though it was far more tense than usual. "You sure you're okay? Need me to do anything while we wait for Tamara?"

A number of suggestions sprang to mind. None of them he could voice, all of which increased his guilt. How he could have sex on the brain at a time like this was stupid. "I'm kind of lost right now as to what to do."

"If Travis is capable of staying on his feet, maybe we should head out for a bit."

"Leave?" That idea hadn't crossed his mind. "What if they need me?"

Allison's nose twitched, as if she were fighting to find the right way to say something. Finally she shrugged. "If you really think you should stay, you should. Only, you can't fix whatever is wrong, Gabe. It's great Travis felt comfortable coming to you for help, but either Cassidy needs a hospital or he needs to sleep. Neither of which you have to be here to supervise."

She was right, but actually walking away—he wasn't sure he could do that.

Allison reached up and brushed his arm. "Gabe, you decide for you, but maybe they'd like less people in their business. I think I'll go before Tamara gets here. I've already heard more secrets than I should have."

"Travis had no problems with it," Gabe pointed out.

She lowered her voice. "He thinks we're getting married."

Shit.

Gabe twisted to face the guest room. The shower had stopped, and Travis would probably be out in a few minutes. He'd left some clothes for his cousin to borrow to replace his torn and stained things.

Allison was right. He'd done what he could, and it wasn't his job to stick around longer. Even though everything in him screamed for him to stay, their deception was forgivable up until the point it started impacting other people.

Neither he nor Allison needed to know more secrets.

He turned back and caught her fingers in his, squeezing them tight. "You really are a smart one. How fast can you grab what you need to head out for the morning?"

"Five minutes."

He nodded, glancing back to see Travis emerge from the bedroom. "Go on—if you need the bathroom, it's free. I'll talk to Travis for a minute then meet you at the stable."

"Riding?"

He'd blow off his morning work and put in time later. A head's up to Rafe would be enough to let the kid know to start alone. "If that works for you."

"I'd like to ride. It's been a few days since I got out."

They separated, Allison stopping as she passed Travis to give him a quick hug.

His cousin stared after her for a minute before slipping into the guest room. "She's alright."

Gabe snorted slowly, trying not to disturb the man on the bed. "Thanks for your vote of approval. Tamara is on her way over, and Allison and I are going to head out."

Travis pulled the chair from under the desk and propped it beside the bed, straddling the seat and resting his arms on the rail back. "I'm a shit for bringing him here."

Gabe shook his head. "I don't mind. I mean that, and if he needs a place to crash for a few days, he's welcome. But only if he's healthy."

"Just got the crap beat out of him is all."

Gabe wasn't ready to try to figure out why Travis wasn't looking him in the eye. "Great. Because that's so much better than needing to sleep off a drunken bender or something."

Travis sprawled over the chair back and swore lightly. "Shit, that's not what I meant. Just trying to tell you he's not on drugs, or somehow dangerous. I never would have brought him here if he were, okay? I do have some sense."

"I didn't think you would. And you have tons of sense, when you use it. Fuckhead."

Travis grinned at the insult. "Yeah, this time, you're right."

"I'm always right." Gabe stood from where he'd been leaning on the doorpost. "I'll have my phone. Call me if you need to take him in, and we'll come back so I can give you a hand. If not, make yourself at home. We'll be out until around lunch. Oh, and don't let the cat out."

His cousin didn't answer, just checked to see that Cassidy was still breathing, then lowered his head to his forearms and let out a huge sigh.

Gabe snuck from the room, exiting the house to meet Allison by the horses.

Walking away was tough. Really tough. Only the thought of what he was walking toward kept his feet moving.

Chapter Fifteen

She worked efficiently, lifting the saddle in place. Securing the girth smoothly, her hands easing over Patches's belly.

He had to drag his gaze away and pay attention to Hurricane before his horse stomped him underfoot for trying to slip the bridle over his ass or something. Gabe hadn't been this distracted in a long time.

It was an uneasy sensation, and yet a twist of pleasure in it as well, and damn if he could figure out why.

Allison stepped from behind her horse and smiled at him. "You said riding, but where are we going? We don't need any more samples."

"Forget the tests. Let's ride along Whiskey Creek."

"Now I'm feeling doubly guilty."

He jerked to a stop. The guilt *he* was trying to ignore poked him, and he beat it down ruthlessly. "Why?"

She held Patches's reins in one hand, slipping her fingers along the strips of leather over and over. "Not only did I order you to get out of your own house, I'm keeping you from work. I have the morning off, but you don't. Do you want me to come help with your chores instead?"

Not if there was any chance of them running into his father. Ben's caustic comments had slowed, but the threat of the bitter sting from his tongue hovered over everything—like a loaded trap, ready to snap closed at the least little provocation.

No way was he taking her near the man. "I called Rafe. He knows I'll be around after lunch."

She swung into the saddle and tucked her hair behind her ears, adjusting her hat. Her smile was a little shaky. "I hope everything is okay with Cassidy."

"He'll be all right." Gabe put more confidence in the words than he felt. "Come on. Let's warm them up so we can run."

They followed the old trails across the sun-warmed fields, increasing pace slowly as the horses tossed their heads and stepped impatiently. Summertime heat and a total lack of breeze made the scents of the ground rise around them, earth baked and rich.

He glanced over his shoulder to make sure she was following. Allison's cheeks were flushed with colour, her bright eyes taking in the scenery around them as she swayed comfortably in the saddle. Her blouse clung to her breasts, and every time she rocked, the fabric drew taut over her curves.

Another jolt hit his gut. A hunger—and yet more.

They had slipped into the physical relationship partly as a coping strategy. Her to deal with the pain she saw coming, and him to deal with the pain he felt every fucking day.

The counsellor he'd seen back in the day would have been proud to know some of the lessons about ways people dealt with shit had actually sunk in.

Whatever their reasons for diving into bed, there was no reason to apologize for it. They were both consenting adults, and the time they spent shaking each other's bodies to the physical limits wasn't hurting anyone.

Only now he wasn't so sure that it was just about the rocking sex. The fact he couldn't keep his mind on what had to be the most important task in his life was making him stupid.

Over the past couple years, he'd learned a lot about goal setting. He'd managed to start a section of the land to be free range and totally organic without letting his father know. Got the turkeys in place, and begun work on breeding lines for the cattle—all of that he'd worked on in addition to his usual tasks without ever losing his concentration. If he'd been as mush-minded over the past two years as he'd been this week, even his cabin would have come to crap, a pile of ideas instead of a place for him, Allison and other strays to find refuge.

A few truths grew a little more apparent to one narrow-focused cowboy. Some of his strategies for revamping the ranch had been shot down over the past month. What had potential on paper wasn't possible in the here and now. Not with the current market, not with the land he had at his disposal. With every new revelation, he'd taken it in stride and moved forward as best he could, because he was positive what the final outcome had to be. Adjusting plans didn't mean abandoning them.

He allowed Allison to catch up with him. One thought circled back again and again. They'd begun this deception for two separate reasons—he'd been totally absorbed by what it meant for the ranch, especially now with a deadline hovering over him. Helping Allison get through a tough time had been a bonus, but not really anything other than lending a hand.

Maybe this plan could be adjusted as well.

They could become something more than a temporary alliance.

Why the hell not?

"Gabe, look."

He followed her pointing finger in time to see a covey of grouse fly into the trees, spooked by the ever-present ranch dogs that had followed them from his place.

"Should figure out how to breed them. Is there a market for wild birds?"

Allison laughed. "I didn't point them out so you can stick them in a cage."

"What about rabbits? Got way more of them than we need right now as well."

She moved in closer. “There is a market for everything if you find the right buyers.”

Patches and Hurricane bumped noses briefly before Gabe tugged the reins and made his horse mind his manners.

They rode forward in a comfortable silence for another ten minutes. He kept trying to find a few good reasons to shoot down the idea that had crept into his thoughts, and frankly, he was having a devil of time coming up with anything.

They were good together, and he didn’t mean just in bed, although, holy fuck, they were definitely compatible there. Even if they still hadn’t had sex at any speed other than frantic. Understandable, in a way, but he was looking forward to showing her a little more finesse.

Why was that suddenly such a high priority for him?

Their family had accepted them as a couple—other than Ben’s toxicity, but that was a given from the start. Nothing he did would ever please the man.

They paused at the edge of a field, grain swaying slightly in the breeze. Allison turned her face toward the sun, eyes closed, body relaxed as her breathing slowed.

He could have stared all day.

Right about then, he made a decision. Just like the other plans had been adjusted, this one was going to be as well. A little more attention to her, rather than to the plot. If he put in the effort, perhaps they’d be able to do more than help each other out over the upcoming months.

Maybe they could find something more than friendship.

His phone rang, dragging him back to the here and now.

“Gabe?”

Tamara. He clasped the reins a little tighter. At his side, Allison moved in to listen intently. “What’s up?”

"Cassidy should be okay. Nothing internal damaged that I can tell." She clicked her tongue in annoyance. "Of course, this would have been so much easier in a real examining room."

Travis muttered in the background, and Tamara swore at him, speaking to the side of the phone. "You're still an idiot, Travis. Now shut up while I talk to Gabe."

"He giving you trouble?" Gabe asked.

"Nahhh, he's just got more balls than brains at times. I've told him to wake Cassidy up at intervals to check for a concussion, but other than that, nothing."

"Lucky bastard."

"Agreed. Just wanted to let you know. I've got a shift starting in thirty minutes, so I'm heading out now. But if you need me again, call."

Gabe hung up, relief threading through him like a rush of chemicals. He hadn't realized how uptight he'd been.

Allison tugged on his sleeve.

Shit. "Sorry. Tamara gave the all clear—of sorts."

"Good." She patted his arm before drawing back to pick up the reins. "Now we can both stop feeling guilty for abandoning them, right?"

He nodded even as he examined her closely, as if this were the first time he'd seen her. Beautiful, caring—he longed to wash the sadness from her eyes.

She turned to face him, head tilting in question.

"What you thinking about?" he asked.

Allison gave him a smile. "Wondering how slow you are."

And she took off, heels to Patches's flanks, the old mare's tail flicking as she kicked up a trail of dust underfoot. Gabe wheeled Hurricane and raced after them, his own smile stretching his face.

It felt good. It felt as if it had been a long time since he'd just relaxed like this.

They slowed at the far edge of the meadow, cooling the horses before leading them down the ravine to walk beside the creek.

"I love how rivers don't flow in a straight line." Allison took a deep breath as she leaned her face toward the sky.

"Especially around these parts," Gabe teased. "We've got more bow curves and corners than most of the land east of here."

"It does make a huge impact. Plotting the dividing lines between the Coleman land must have driven the surveyors crazy." Allison prodded Patches forward, and Gabe followed her lead.

The narrow ravine opened into a wide half-moon, the river lapping at the gentle edge of the slope. He smiled at the familiar tree that leaned over the water, and wondered if he'd still find their swinging rope tucked off to one side.

He joined Allison on the ground as she slipped off Patches. He led the horses back and tethered them, turning in time to see Allison step into the thick mud at the edge of the swimming hole and lose her balance. She fell to the ground, sliding on her back to stop just shy of the water.

"Shit, you okay?" He hurried forward, more cautiously as he hit the slick section.

Allison sat up, mud coating her hands, boots and jeans. She looked around slowly, her face twisting for a moment before peals of laughter, one after another, escaped her. Gabe took the final wary steps to her side, looking down as she continued to laugh, her head tossed back in delight.

He joined in, offering a hand. "You crazy woman."

Her eye sparkled as she tucked her fingers into his. "Crazy, eh? Who's the crazy one?"

He should have expected it. He really should have, but when she grabbed on tight and threw all her weight backward, he wasn't prepared. He lost his footing and stumbled, falling to his knees. Momentum forced his body forward, his hat tumbling off. Suddenly he was over top of her, one hand either side of her body as she lay in the thick mud.

Allison gasped for air. “Oh God, your face.”

To hell with it, he was a mess. They both were. He crawled forward and trapped her between his thighs. “What’s wrong with my face?”

He spotted the sheer wicked mischief two seconds too late to stop her from grabbing his head and pulling him down to her lips.

The mud she smeared on his cheeks was warm from the sun, but he was more interested in the heat of her mouth. She slowly explored, slipping her tongue along his before drawing back to nibble his bottom lip.

“Minx.”

“Hmm. We’re a mess.”

He could think of a way to deal with that. “There’s water right here.”

But first he lowered himself on top of her and rocked his hips slowly. Lining up his cock with the vee of her thighs. Rubbing slowly, giving them both time to enjoy the rising sensation of lust. All the while they kissed. Dirty, but in the very best sense of the word.

She squirmed under him, lifting her hips to meet his thrusts.

His cock filled, urgency driving him again. This time he didn’t want to answer, not so fast. So he did the first thing that came to mind to cool them both off.

He grabbed hold of her, pinned their bodies together, and rolled.

The first thrill of being jerked over his rock-solid body was instantly doused by icy-cold water.

"Shit, Gabe, what the—*ahhh.*" She choked off her scream barely in time to slam her mouth shut and stop the water from pouring in. She squirmed in an attempt to get away, but his arms were iron bands gripping her. Instead, she caught hold of him, tightened her legs around his hips and clung to his neck until the tumbling stopped, and he rose to his feet.

"Oh, yeah, that's fresh," Gabe gasped.

"Fresh? Oh Lord—" Allison let out another involuntary squeal as he hoisted her, his hands under her butt.

Then his mouth was over hers and complaining about the cold wasn't nearly as important anymore. She rubbed her torso against his. Her nipples had gone tight, but were now tingling for more reasons than the temperature of the water around them.

She buried her fingers in his hair and held on, panting breaths escaping them as the kiss got wilder.

He tore his mouth free only to drag his lips along her jawline, taking small bites at her skin. "Why the hell can't I slow down with you? It's like touching you flips a switch, and all I can do is blast ahead full speed."

Allison didn't care, not one little bit. "Who said we had to go slow?"

She rocked against him, and he ground their hips together, the pace he'd begun lying flat out in the mud and muck heating up again in spite of the cool water around them. The sun had topped the tree line, filling the pool area with shadow and sunbeams. Turning the area into a stage. His hair where she'd mussed him stuck up, the blond tips reflecting light the same way the teeny ripples on the water's surface sparkled.

She was caught between dazzling sights and dazzling reactions as he pushed her closer to an orgasm with barely any effort. She felt as if she'd been on edge forever, longing for him to take her over.

He jerked her higher, somehow securing her on one arm. His teeth closed on her nipple at the same moment his hand landed between her legs.

Allison held on to him for dear life as he ground his thumb over her clit with just the right pressure, just the right speed.

"Gabe, oh God, yes. Yes..."

Her orgasm hit without any warning—not a burst of fireworks, or breaking her apart into a million pieces. Just intense pleasure that made her damn glad she was there and then shaking in his arms. Shaking so hard, in fact, if he hadn't been holding her in an iron-tight clasp she would have collapsed into the water. Satisfaction and pleasure rippled through her like the water rippled around them, lapping at the shore.

He lowered her slowly, letting her slip along his body, unapologetic as the prominent ridge of his cock pressed against her belly. His desire undeniable. She lowered her hands and covered him, palms tight to the bulge, rubbing intensely until he groaned.

"Stop." He latched on to her wrists and stilled the motion.

"Why?" She leaned against him, clothes soaking wet and clinging to her. "I want to. Want to make you feel good too."

He grinned, sexual desire streaking along her spine at the look in his eyes. "You will. And you do. Now take off your top."

He placed her on her feet and held her for a second until she caught her balance. Allison took hold of the bottom of her shirt, but instead of yanking it up and over her head in one motion, she inched it slowly, pivoting as she lifted. Turning back toward him in time to stare at his face and see the hunger there.

He'd cupped himself through the jeans, gaze locked on her body. Tracing the edge of her bra. His focus so intent she swore she felt it like a touch. A stroke over the line of her collarbone. The merest caress across the swell of her breast. Her nipples tightened and poked against the sheer and soaking-wet fabric of her bra.

She clutched her wet shirt, suddenly—not shy, not really, but feeling the passion between them with far less nonchalance than she expected. Maybe it was the stress of the morning with Travis and Cassidy, and everything else. She and Gabe had only been lovers for a week, and the difference this time was apparent. The intensity was certainly high. High enough for that look in his eyes to melt something inside.

She didn't want to think about what had changed. Or why she didn't want to think about it.

Gabe stepped closer and reached for her. She escaped his grasp with a grin. "Your turn."

One brow rose in question.

She pointed. "Your shirt. I'm all about the equal playing field."

He laughed and stripped off his T-shirt in one move. No teasing like she'd done. Just firm muscles suddenly revealed, the dusting of hair on his chest darker than usual with the moisture. The narrow trail that led downward toward the button of his jeans, and lower, irresistible. Allison closed the distance between them and pressed one palm to his chest.

And realized her fingers were still covered in mud, so now his chest was as well. "Shit."

She was pulling away when he caught her wrist and stilled her in place. "Don't go away."

"But I—"

He tugged her shirt from her other hand, wadded it together with his, and threw them toward the river's edge.

"Now, where were we?" Gabe caught her hands in his, putting them back on his chest. The warmth of his skin made her fingertips tingle.

The slick of the mud made her smile. "Finger painting."

Gabe touched his hand to her face. She couldn't figure out what he was doing until he placed his thumb against the base of her throat and stroked a line down her skin.

Leaving a trail of mud behind.

Her happiness rose as she copied him. Taking a small messy lump from one place and using it to decorate him. She stroked his ribs, traced around his nipples. Made a tribal tattoo of her very own design on his biceps.

He returned the favour. His touch light on her skin. Over her breasts, the length of her collarbone. Sometimes fingertips, sometimes he'd flip and use the back of his knuckles.

All the time, teasing. Caressing. Making her skin come to life and heat impossibly considering they were standing hip deep in the river, and the water wasn't that warm.

She reached for the button on his jeans, popping it open and loosening the top of the zipper.

"Allison, wait." He escaped before she could do anything else.

If it wasn't childish, she would have pouted. "But I don't want to."

Gabe laughed. Full out and full of life and energy. The sun shone on him and made his body, and the mud she'd traced on him, glow.

He shook his head. "I'm not stopping us. Just getting distracted. And as much fun as the mud is, it's not a part of the next portion of the day."

They both worked at stripping off their final layers, clothes abandoned along the river's edge. Allison had to sit in the mud to peel her jeans off, cowboy boots filled with water and abandoned with the rest.

She was down to her underwear and hesitating when a large palm slapped her butt, and she let out a scream.

"Get yourself naked, woman." Gabe trailed his hand over her hip and caught the edge of her panties in his fingertips. "Or do you need help?"

Allison snorted inelegantly. "Now you ask. Where were you two minutes ago when my boots were stuck?"

"Watching your ass wiggle."

"Gabe!"

"It's a fine ass. It needed watching."

He tugged lightly and the material slipped down her thigh, her heated core aching for more of what she'd gotten earlier. More of Gabe doing wonderful things to her. With her.

He'd already lost all his clothes, and his cock stood high and hard to his belly, moving as he did. She was tempted to reach for him. To stroke and tease, but her hands were still covered in muck. "Don't suppose you want me to finger paint anywhere else, now do you?"

Gabe knelt as he finished pulling her panties down. "No, thanks. Not my kinda kink."

"Hmmm, mud sex." Allison squirmed as she reached behind her to get rid of her bra.

His gaze darted over her body, admiration on his face as she dropped her bra and stepped out of her panties.

"Damn, woman, you're gorgeous." His lips made contact with her belly button. Well, just to the side where there was a clear patch of skin.

"That's going to be a tough task—sticking to the clear spots."

"Then we'd better get cleaned up." He whooped as he stood. Two strong arms wrapped around her, swinging her in the air before he strode back into the water.

Her bare butt hit the surface of the river and she gasped. "Oh God. It's colder than before."

Gabe snorted. “Stop complaining. You’re not the only one getting slammed in sensitive places.”

Allison tucked her head in tight and squealed as he deliberately fell, twisting to land on his back, soaking them both. They separated, floating apart, and she rubbed her hands together to remove the leftover mud.

She bobbed to the surface and was caught from behind in his embrace.

“That’s my job you’re doing.”

Allison lay against him. “Don’t let me stop you.”

The water was cold, but his hands still managed to heat her like crazy. He started at the top and worked his way down. Palms smoothing over her skin, brushing the mud loose, the clear running river carrying away the debris.

What didn’t leave was the tingling sensation that came well before his touch. He looped to the right, and her left side ached in longing. He stroked along her ribs, and she grew breathless in anticipation for him to move on to her breasts.

It was one long session of foreplay countered by the cold of the water and the heat of his body supporting hers. And by the time all traces of the mud were gone, she was both a quivering mass of expectancy and totally boneless from relaxation.

She rolled, slipping her hands around his neck. Her naked breasts pressed to his chest, nipples poking him lightly. “Skinny dipping. You sure know how to show a girl a good time.”

Gabe held her, his palm planted firmly in the center of her back to keep their bodies in tight contact. “Where else can you have good clean fun for this price?”

Allison cupped his cheek, wiping away the final bit of mud that clung to his skin. “Frugal and fun. Double win.”

She leaned down to press a kiss to his lips. Addictive. She was positive that she’d had enough and then she’d spot his mouth and need another taste all over.

Their torsos were touching, but his hips moved away from her as he supported them, kicking slowly across the smooth water of the swimming hole. She was too interested in nibbling on his lower lip to worry much about where they were going, at least until he changed their position and lifted her into his arms, stepping forward and out of the water.

She managed to break off the kiss. “Time to go?”

“Hell no. Only I’d have to have bionic body parts for the next part of the adventure to work.”

Allison wrapped her arms around his neck, looking where he was taking her. “Drat, why didn’t I see the grassy section earlier?”

“Because we needed a little mud bath. Don’t worry, this works out fine in my books.” Gabe twisted her to the side and lowered her. The warm surface of something dry and solid hit her backside, and she glanced down.

“Oh, nice tree. You have all the angles figured out, don’t you?”

Gabe settled her completely on the fallen tree trunk, the section where she sat smooth and time worn. It was as close to a bench as anything she’d seen, only far more rustic. And far sturdier, since it extended three times the distance of a regular bench.

“I think I have all the angles. Just let me see to be sure.”

He slid his hands up her thighs, pausing with his thumbs resting at the junction where leg met body, fingers extending around toward her butt. One more kiss. Still one more, as all the while he stroked her softly. The light breeze made her shiver, but with the sun full on them she dried quickly.

Gentle but firm Gabe slipped his hand along her thighs and pressed them to the side. Stared down at her, his breath gusting past her cheek. “Oh yeah, I think I got the angles figured out exactly right.”

He knelt and his mouth was level with her hips. He kissed the inside of her right leg, and the shiver that followed had nothing to do with the weather. Everything to do with the temperature in her core that was rapidly rising.

He traced his tongue along the inside of her leg until he was inches away from her mound. Allison wasn't sure this was the best idea ever or the worst. "What if someone comes?"

Gabe chuckled, his eyes shining as he looked up at her. "Well, I certainly hope someone comes."

"Turkey."

"Gobble, gobble, gobble."

She was laughing when his mouth covered her, and the slick of his tongue between her folds was enough to twist the sound into a moan. He brought his hand up and opened her, tracing her labia, following with his tongue. Teasing and testing, all the while avoiding direct contact with her clit until she was on edge and ready to hit him.

"Tormenter."

"Tell me what you want." He spoke against her core, the words vibrating and teasing even more.

"Fuck me with your fingers. Suck my clit."

He grinned. "You're sexy when you're all bossy like that."

He slid a finger into her, and she squeezed around him involuntarily. It felt so good, and yet not enough. Not nearly enough.

"More."

When he was too slow to move, she moved for him. Grabbed his head and tugged until he stopped the slow circle around where she wanted him most. Gabe hummed, the buzz of his mouth warning her a second before he finally, *finally* touched down on her clit.

He thrust again. This time the movement felt thicker, more pressure. He must have added a finger, or she was getting closer to exploding. The speed of his thrusts increased, the angle changed and—

“Oh my God, do that again.”

Whatever he was up to made it nearly impossible for her to catch her breath. Made her gasp for air as stars floated in front of her eyes. He caught hold of her clit with his tongue and flicked it again and again, and with his teasing touch deep inside she trembled on the edge of her climax.

It was raw, and slightly rough. Perched on the stump of a tree, sunshine all around them. The sound of the woods showcasing how wild they were, fully naked in the middle of the morning. She hadn’t felt this alive in forever, and when he sucked and stretched her on three fingers, she lost it. Waves of pleasure slammed into her, jerking her body. Taking her and tossing her so hard she had to cling to him to keep from sliding off into a puddle on the ground.

He slowed. Planted kisses on her sensitive flesh. Fingers moving slower until the last of the internal pulses died away.

Her head was spinning as Gabe rose before her, brushing his hand over his mouth. “You like the angles I worked out?”

Oh yeah. But they weren’t done. Not if she had anything to say. “You got half your math just fine. Now come here.”

He leaned over her willingly, their torsos brushing lightly as their lips met. She tasted herself on him, and the pleasure that he so willingly gave made her even more determined to not leave him wanting.

Allison grasped his waist, loving the play of the firm muscles under the skin—the way when he twisted slightly the bands wrapping around his torso rose, and she could follow the lines down to his hips. That sexy line she loved to touch.

When she caught his cock in her hands, he groaned into her mouth. “No condoms.”

“Don’t worry. I think I can figure out the angles as well.”

She pressed him away and slipped off the stump.

"What're you up to?" Gabe asked.

"Wrong direction." She tugged, and he followed her lead as she pivoted him and brought him against the stump. He tilted his head, smiling but confused as she leaned in briefly to kiss him. Then she snuck back before he could pin her in place.

She kissed his chest. Bent a little lower to trace around his nipple with her tongue. Licked his ribs, and nibbled her way down his body until there was no way he could misinterpret her intentions.

"Oh fuck, Allison."

His cock was right there, rock solid, a bead of moisture shining along the slit. Allison encircled the base with her hand to hold him steady. Then she licked, taking in his flavour, loving the sounds of his near-tortured groan.

She rested on the grass, the soft earth beneath her knees cradling her comfortably. When she looked up, Gabe had braced himself on the stump, one hand on either side as he leaned back and watched intently.

A memory teased her. "You remember me doing shots with your cousins?"

He nodded.

"The first drink I grabbed was called a Cowboy Cocksucker."

"Ha! No wonder you were beet red." He let out a satisfied moan as she stroked his length. "No need to blush now. I'm the only one watching."

"I'm so glad you didn't say something stupid like 'you know, you don't have to do that...'" Allison teased.

"Hell no. I'm not an idiot." Gabe leered at her. "Any time you want to give me a blowjob, you let me know and I'll be willing to sacrifice the time to oblige you."

"I bet you would."

He rocked his hips, slipping his cock through her clenched fist. “You going to start on that any time soon?”

“Patience. You said you had trouble going slow. Maybe I can help you learn.”

Gabe growled. “Fuck slow. Suck me off. Now.”

She was still smiling when she covered the head of his cock, twirling her tongue over the crest and getting him good and wet. His long, low sigh made her happy, and she imagined he’d closed his eyes in satisfaction.

Then she stopped thinking about what he was doing and concentrated on what she could do to him. Licking his length, her hand easing along the shaft.

Allison brought her other hand up to cup his balls, rolling them in her fingers as she took him deep. Rocking over him slowly at first, taking her time to get him to the point her mouth met where her hand held him.

Fingers brushed her hair, tucking the length behind her ear, and she glanced up, her mouth still full of his cock. Gabe wasn’t relaxed back, eyes closed. He was staring intently at her, pupils gone dark with desire. That made her want to give him more. Make it even better for him.

She caught his hand in hers and held it to her head. When she moved over him the next time, she removed her hand and clasped his hips. His entire length exposed meant there was more she had to work on. More to try to handle, and she relaxed her throat to take him as deep as she possibly could.

“Oh, sweet darling. So fine. That feels so fine.”

Gabe took her suggestion and had both hands in her hair. Twisting the strands up so he could see clearer. There was a slight pull as he moved, and desire streaked through her again.

Giving him the blowjob was suddenly more than payback for the pleasure she’d received. She wanted to reward him. Wanted to give more to this man who was constantly giving, not only to her, but to everyone around them.

She squirmed, and he followed, hips pulling away from the stump he'd been leaning on. As he stood she stared up, willing him to take what she offered.

Wanting him to take.

Gabe brushed his knuckle over her cheek, rocking slowly until the head of his cock bumped her throat. He pulled back quickly.

Allison squeezed his ass on his next motion, driving him a little farther than he'd intended to go, and the guttural pleasure that burst from him made her so damn happy.

A shudder rocked him right before he took control. Her head held firmly now in his palms, he tilted her slightly and slid all the way in. All the way until his abdomen pressed her lips, her mouth stretched wide.

She swallowed around his cock to stop her gag reflex from kicking in, and he trembled.

And broke.

No more slow. No more careful. Just him holding her exactly how he wanted. Plunging in deep three or four times in rapid succession followed by short, hard rocks. He pulled nearly free, resting his cock on her lower lip.

"Lick it."

She teased. Once. Just a touch.

"Suck the head. Just the head." His voice had gone lower. Darker.

Allison licked her lips, tracing around his cock to do so, then closed tight and obeyed. Pulse after pulse, all the while licking and playing. Teasing the slit, swallowing his precome.

"God, so close. I want to..." He dug his fingers into her hair and pulled her forward.

She opened wide and took him all the way, and his cock jerked, heat splaying against the back of her throat. The salty flavour filling her mouth as she swallowed, bits of his come escaping forward and coating his length.

He held her trapped, and she loved it. Loved how he made her feel so beautiful and satisfied. When he loosened his grasp, she licked him clean, working him gently as he softened.

Gabe dropped to his knees beside her and squeezed her tight. His heart still pounding—she felt it against her chest as he held her close.

The sun had moved slightly, and they were now in the shadows.

"It's getting cold."

He chuckled. "The hot sweaty part is done."

He helped her up, brushing the dirt off her knees, this wicked grin stretching his lips.

"You look damn satisfied," Allison teased.

Gabe smiled at her, leaning to kiss her briefly. When he pulled back, his expression had changed. "Fuck it all."

"What? What's wrong?"

Gabe scratched his head and pointed in disgust at their clothes. "This is why you're supposed to strip before you go skinny dipping."

"Oh shit."

All their clothes. Wet. Not just wet, but wet and muddy and a total mess. Somehow they had to pull that on, or at least enough to wear to get home.

Still, she had to smile. Gabe had begun to gather their things, and the first thing he'd nabbed was his hat.

"I don't know. You look like a cowboy to me."

He swung around, buck-naked with his hat on. His burst of laughter as he realized what she was talking about set off her own.

Even with the soaking, sticky garments she had to pull on, there was something magical about the entire morning.

Frankly, she couldn't remember laughing this much in a long time. Not since she'd heard about her mom.

The whole way back to his cabin she held on tight to the sensation.

And wondered if she was crazy to wish for more.

Chapter Sixteen

Her clothes dried during the ride home, so when she spotted Travis's truck still parked outside, keeping a little more space between her and Gabe's impromptu visitors seemed like a good idea.

Gabe didn't like it, but he didn't argue when she asked him to grab her keys. Cleaning up at her mom's was win-win. Privacy for the guys—plus she'd have the afternoon to kick back and enjoy her mom's company.

First, a shower. Something sticky clung between her shoulder blades. She didn't really want to know what, she just wanted it gone.

The Parker family home on the outskirts of town had the best of both parts of Rocky Mountain House. Close enough to access the conveniences and the Timberline Grill, still able to keep horses and have more land than a city dwelling. Allison drove the back lane to the place. Safer to avoid any of the neighbours on the front street than have to explain why she looked like a wet rat.

She ditched her boots before jerking on the sticky porch screen door to wrench it open. The resulting loud creak was familiar. A kind of a homecoming.

She'd barely made it into the kitchen when her mom called from the living room. "Who's there?"

Allison hurried forward to reassure her.

"It's me, Mom. I'm here to hang out for a bit." She rounded the corner, her wet socks leaving footprint marks on the kitchen floor. "I need to hop in the shower first—"

Her mom wasn't alone in the living room. Elle and Paul were there as well. All of them perched on the edge of their seats, tension in their bodies. Elle's and Maisey's cheeks were wet with tears, and Paul was doing his stony-faced thing. The one he did when he didn't want to cry.

Allison's first thought was to ask who had died. Stupid, yes, but with the morning she'd just had, and the secrets Maisey was keeping, it took a moment for the truth to hit home.

"Oh God." Her mom had told them.

Maisey tilted her head to the side, sniffing back more tears. She sighed, then nodded. "They know."

Elle buried her face in her hands, shoulders shaking. Allison crossed the room to her side and hugged her. Words just didn't seem to be coming the way she wanted them to.

What words could possibly make this better?

It had been nearly fifteen years since their father had died. Seventeen years since his first heart attack, and Allison could still remember the turmoil they'd felt as the deterioration set in. Powerless to help him as one attack after the other followed, and his body slowly stopped following his orders.

All the emotions came back so clearly. So brutally overwhelming.

Their house, and their teenage lives, became all about trying to make Dad comfortable. Dealing with hormonal swings and issues of teenage angst were shoved aside as he demanded attention. They'd tried their best to be there for him. It had been such a long, painful journey.

Here they were on the same path, all over again.

Paul stood and paced over to the window, staring out at the fields. He coughed, but it was obvious he spoke around a throat gone tight with emotion. "Mom said there's nothing that can be done. Do you agree?"

"I'm not mentally incompetent, Paul. Why are you asking your sister?" Maisey shook her head. "You think I'm a two-year-old and I made a mistake? I'm not stupid. I know what the doctor said. The statistics on pancreatic cancer are clear."

"There are options. There are always options."

"Oh, Paul. I know you want to make this better, but I already told you. I refuse to do some experimental protocol that might give me two or three more months of pain."

He turned. "But what if—"

"No." Maisey stood up. "No what-ifs. I'm sorry. It's not fair, and I don't want to die—" Her voice broke. Allison went to stand, to support her, but her mom held out a hand. "No, it's okay. I need to make him understand. I need you *all* to understand. I looked at the information. I asked the questions. And I'm going to die."

In Allison's arms, Elle shook.

Maisey snatched up a tissue and wiped her eyes. She took a deep breath before lifting her chin and continuing. "So I choose to die with as much dignity as I can. And to me that means in a way that least impacts your lives."

"Oh God, Mom," Paul blurt out. "You're dying and you think it won't impact our lives?"

"I will not be your father." Maisey spoke each word individually. Forcefully. "I will not take and break you apart like that. I know you're in shock, and I know this is horrifying, but please, *please* understand why I want this."

Allison squeezed Elle's shoulder for a second before releasing her and approaching Maisey. She didn't say anything, just opened her arms and hugged the woman.

Her mom sucked in a quivering breath before accepting the embrace. Then they were all there, Elle and Paul as well, wrapped tight like a cocoon. Crying and struggling to find the way to go forward.

Go forward into the unnumbered days ahead of them.

Paul was the first to pull away. "I need to…I need time."

"You want to do something violent, there's a load of firewood in the backyard that needs chopping," Maisey suggested.

"Firewood? Right now?" Elle sniffed and wiped her hand over her eyes.

"Why not? It needs to be split."

Paul left without another word. Allison watched out the window, and he did head to the back rather than to his car. An hour or so of swinging an axe wasn't a bad idea, really.

"You kids want to come back for a while after you've dealt with the supper crowd at the restaurant?" Maisey asked. "You can get someone else to close."

Elle nodded. "I'll make the calls. I love you, Mom." She coughed through the final word. She straightened her shoulders as she turned to face Allison. "You stink, by the way. What happened to your clothes?"

Shoot. This was not a conversation she wanted to have in front of her mom. "I...fell in the creek."

Her sister raised a brow. "You fell in? Really?"

"Why didn't you change at home?" her mom asked.

Why indeed. Of all the times for her mind to completely blank on excuses. "I was coming over and just figured I'd get cleaned up here."

Elle frowned. "Did you and Gabe have a fight?"

The thought of him going down on her, his blond head buried between her legs as she writhed on the tree stump made Allison smile in spite of the past moment's tears. "No, we didn't have a fight."

Elle lifted a brow. "Did he fall in the creek with you as well?"

Allison bit back a groan, darting a glance at their mom. Little sisters could be a pain in the ass. "I think I need to go get changed, since I smell so bad and all."

Her sister wrinkled her nose, her teasing smile fading as her gaze skimmed over their mom. The taunts and jokes between them might be instinctive, but the reality of Mom's news, fresh and raw, broke into the familiar patterns and tainted everything with sadness.

Maisey patted Allison's shoulder. "You go ahead and have a shower. I'll pop your things in the laundry. You have some old clothes in the bottom dresser in the guest room."

Great. She fled the room as quickly as she could, but not before Elle shook a finger her direction.

It seems there would be a sisterly inquisition in the near future.

Travis was passed out on the couch and Cassidy asleep in the guest room when Gabe snuck in to shower and dress for the afternoon's work. He stopped at the main ranch house to give his ma a quick hug and kiss, determinedly avoided his father, then joined Rafe to go haul feed to the cattle.

His kid brother eyed him with a twisted grin. "You already on your honeymoon or what?"

"Fuck off."

Rafe laughed and tossed the truck keys to him. "Whatever. You seem happy though."

Blowjobs would do that to a guy. Gabe reconsidered. It was a damn sight more than just that, and he knew it. In spite of whatever the hell was going on with Travis, the morning had been really good.

His idea of making what he and Allison had real looked like the right thing to pursue.

"When you guys getting married?" Rafe dragged a couple sticks of beef jerky from his pocket and offered Gabe one.

Before this morning he would have gotten around that question without coming right out and answering it, but now he thought about it. If their engagement were real, when would they get hitched?

"Not until the fall for sure. After harvest, maybe early winter."

"She's going to want a big fancy do, won't she?" Rafe slapped his hand on his knee repetitively.

"Why you say that?"

Rafe shrugged. "Ma was thinking that with the classy restaurant and all, she's probably more used to the fancy stuff. Ben said—"

His kid brother stopped mid-sentence, and Gabe sighed. "Yeah, I can imagine what Ben said. Ignore him."

"It's kind of tough, Gabe. He's not very ignorable when he's at the goddamn table spouting shit all the time."

"Then move out."

Rafe groaned in frustration. "I can't, and you know it. Barely finished high school, I'm not going to make a living with hours at the Home Hardware or something."

"I didn't mean that. I know you want to stay on the ranch. And I'm working on fixing it so we can really make a go of it."

"You said that a couple years back. Things haven't gotten much better."

Gabe knew. To his regret. But that didn't mean he wasn't trying, and the kid needed to know that as well.

"Move over the garage. Make a few meals yourself. Ben is..." Jerk, asshole, bastard—none of the words were the right ones. True, but not the right ones for this time and conversation. "Ben is damn difficult, but he does the job at hand. At some point in the future, who the hell knows, but there might be a miracle and he'll change."

Rafe snorted. "Into the Easter bunny? Or the tooth fairy? Because him changing sounds like a damn fairy tale."

Gabe agreed which made it all the worse. “Move out. I told you that before. Did you talk to Mom?”

“No.”

“Did you haul your shit into the place and settle in?”

“No.”

Gabe pulled to a stop and faced his brother squarely. “Then stop complaining. Either it’s bad enough you want to change it, or you’re just flapping your jaw to flap your jaw. Don’t be like Ben.”

Rafe’s face flushed red. “Fuck you. I’m not like him.”

Gabe understood the response all too well. “No, you’re not. So stop acting like him. Change the things you don’t like. Got it?”

His brother leaned back and eased off the dirty stare. “I get it. You’re still an asshole.”

Gabe laughed.

It was late before he parked the tractor. Rafe took off so he would make it to the dinner table in time, but Gabe carried on to make up for his lazy morning.

He was on the way home before he checked his phone to discover Allison had left him a message. It didn’t sound good, and he put through the return call regretful he’d missed her the first time.

She spoke softly. Tired maybe. “Hey, Gabe.”

“Hey, yourself. What’s this you said about not coming home tonight?”

“Everyone is crashing here. We need a little family time. Mom told them.”

Relief and concern flashed simultaneously. “Ah, hell. How’d that go?”

Allison sighed. “It went.”

“How you doing?”

"Better now than earlier. And nowhere near as good as this morning." Her sadness and frustration came through loud and clear. "I feel guilty for thinking about how much fun this morning was, but damn, at the same time thinking back sure has been a good mental break from the other things we're dealing with."

"You don't need to feel guilty." Gabe pulled into his driveway, noting the empty parking space beside the house. "You want me to bring you anything?"

"You don't need to. I'll be fine."

Of course he didn't need to. But he wanted to. More than that, he wanted to be with her and help support her right now. The revelation was more powerful than the one he'd had that morning. She'd been sneaking under his skin, and it wasn't just the good things he wanted to enjoy.

Allison's voice perked up again. Patently fake. "You go ahead and hit the Coleman gathering at Traders. Say hi to everyone from me, give Puss in Boots a cuddle and I'll see you on Saturday."

They spoke for a few more minutes, but the entire time Gabe was making plans. Bullshit on going out drinking with the guys when she needed him.

Gabe shoved open the door, and stomped into his house, kind of pissed that she would even suggest that he ignore her like that. Fine if the Parkers wanted family time, but wouldn't her family think it strange if he wasn't there? Absentee fiancé—her mom at least would imagine something was up.

He pulled to a stop at the sight of Cassidy sitting smack dab in the middle of the kitchen. The young man looked up slowly from the book he had spread on the table. Puss in Boots, as usual, had managed to find a lap to curl up in.

Cassidy's blond hair was wet from a shower, the bruises on his face colouring up to a variety of rich blues and purples. The split on his lower lip nicely highlighted by the swelling. But he was vertical. Vertical was good.

"You look a hell of a lot better than the last time I saw you." Gabe stepped in closer and held out his hand. "Gabe Coleman."

Cassidy carefully put the kitten on the floor before rising and accepting the handshake. "Thanks for offering sanctuary."

"No problem."

"Travis had to work. He said he'd be back later to drive me to my truck." Cassidy rubbed his jaw carefully. "Sorry about bleeding on your sheets. I'll leave some money for—"

"Don't need to do that." Gabe stared at the other man for a moment, distracted enough to be tempted to go beyond his policy of not asking more information than was offered. Cassidy had to be barely twenty-five and he was built like a bloody tank. It really must have been a fight to get him as messed up as he was.

Cassidy's smile twisted. "I still look like shit, don't I?"

"Worked-over shit," Gabe admitted. "You feel okay?"

"No, but I don't feel like I'm dying anymore. I'll take that as a positive sign."

How do you know Travis? What the hell happened? All the questions he wanted to ask, Gabe shoved down. None of it was his damn business, and over the years he'd had more than enough experience stifling his curiosity. "You need anything you let me know. There're a couple of frozen dinners you can microwave if you'd like."

He ignored his guest and hurried through his shower, packing a bag for the night. Grabbing a nightgown for Allison seemed strange on all kinds of levels. She hadn't been wearing anything for the past week since they usually fell asleep right after wearing themselves out with sex. He'd been waking her up to take her again in the morning. It was heavenly to have nothing but warm woman in his arms before he was even fully awake, the smooth curves of her filling his hands, her softness against his rising cock.

She might have an issue with being naked in her mom's house, though, so he dipped into her drawer.

That was the second weird part. Going through her underwear made him feel like some kind of perverted stalker. He'd have to take the depraved title and stamp it on his head after he grabbed a pair of panties that seemed to have too many straps for a thong. He held the garment up and twisted until he figured it out.

Holy shit.

He tucked his find into the bag before he could change his mind.

His brain was tangled between wanting to see her to make sure she was fine, and needing to bend her over something and thrust in deep. She was driving him insane, and she wasn't even in the room.

Gabe stopped in the doorway of the bedroom. Cassidy had his head resting in his hands, body slumped forward as if totally exhausted.

Damn it anyway. Gabe snapped to an instant decision. If it was the wrong one, he'd take the damages out of Travis's hide for having brought Cassidy to the house in the first place.

"Cassidy."

The blond lifted his head, glassy-eyed stare pulling into focus after only a few seconds. "Yes, sir."

Gabe dropped his bag by the front door before opening the freezer and pulling out one of the dinners. "I'm heating you up a meal. You go on and crash here for the night."

Cassidy went to shake his head, stopping immediately with his fingers pressed to his forehead. "Fuck, that hurt."

Gabe snorted. "Yeah, you might be better to get a solid night's sleep before you try anything else on for size."

"I can't take advantage of you like that."

"Hell, you won't be. You'll be doing me a favour—I've got an emergency and have to be gone all night. Allison's kitten will need some attention. Other than him, you'll have the place to yourself. His food bowl and water are over by the fridge. Pull the door shut when you leave in the morning, and we're square."

Cassidy lifted his gaze to meet Gabe's, brilliant green shining back from his blackened eyes. "Damn decent of you."

"Pay it forward." Gabe grabbed a bottle of Tylenol out of the cupboard and plopped it on the table. "If you need them. Otherwise, stay out of trouble. Maybe we'll see you around sometime."

Cassidy smiled cautiously. "Maybe you will. You're a good man, Gabe Coleman. I won't forget this."

Gabe grabbed his bag and left.

Chapter Seventeen

Elle poked her head around the doorway to mock whisper, "You going to tell me why you smelt like dirt earlier today?"

"You want me to share secrets when you're trying to get out of dishes? Forget it." Allison slipped another plate into the dishwasher.

Paul had gone to the Timberline alone and left them to a girls-only evening, at least until he organized for closing and could return. Maisey lay down on the couch after dinner to rest, and the house had stilled to nothing but the light sounds of the clock ticking and the wind against the eaves.

"I'm working, I'm working." Elle shook the salt and pepper shakers in her hands. "Heavy lifting going on here."

"Heavy? Good grief, don't give yourself a hernia. Besides, you're too young for details on dirt."

Her sister laughed out loud for a moment before cutting off, her smile fading rapidly.

Allison wiped her hands on her skirt and snuck across the room to grab Elle by the arms. "Oh, sweetie, don't do that to yourself. It's okay to laugh."

"It hurts. Like I'm breaking something delicate, or walking into a solemn church service wearing a clown suit. How can I laugh when...?" She dropped her forehead against Allison's shoulder and sighed.

Allison hugged her, petting Elle's head the way she used to when they were younger. The ache inside throbbed like a living creature trying to break free. This was why she'd come back to Rocky. Why she had to be there for the family. She was so grateful to be in the right place to give to them.

"I get it. I really do. Remember, you just heard the news. That makes the pain sharp. I've known for longer and the cut doesn't feel as raw, even though it still hurts. I guess I think Mom would prefer us to laugh than to be all mopey, right?"

Elle nodded as she stepped back. "You going to head out after dishes?"

Changing the topic. Well, it was going to take time for all of them to figure out what they had to do. Elle would deal with the grief in her own way.

"I called Gabe. I'll stay here tonight."

Elle turned on the taps to fill the sink with water, getting the pots ready for hand washing. "Really? You remember you don't have a room here anymore."

"Room thief."

"Hey, I waited years to take over that space. You can sleep in the guest room."

Yeah, she'd figured. "The sun is going to wake me at five in the morning."

Elle pushed her toward the dishwater. "Which is why I switched into your old room so I wouldn't have to get up early all summer long."

Allison dug into the washing, passing the pots and lids over to her sister to dry. It was a bit of a time warp, back to their teen years. Not all the memories of that time were good, not with the long illness they'd faced with their dad. The little chores, though, like cleaning the house or doing the dishes. Those things felt comfortable and familiar. Something to fall back on to help the hurt fade.

Elle hip-checked her lightly. "Dirt. Spill."

It took her a second to figure out what Elle was talking about. Allison grinned. "I'm not telling you the details. You go find your own cowboy."

"If you won't talk, it had to be sex outdoors. Or something sex-like." Elle swung her towel in the air like she was roping a calf. "Yeehaw."

"Oh jeez. Watch yourself, or you'll put out an eye."

"You and Gabe—it working out okay? Like you'd hoped?" Elle leaned on the counter. "When you announced you were engaged, I'll admit it was a shock, but you seem pretty happy lately. You thinking this is really it?"

Allison was torn. Telling the story she'd been sticking to was possible, but there was more between her and Gabe than before. Secrets she wasn't sure she wanted to even share with herself, let alone her sister.

Since it was only pretend on Gabe's part. And wouldn't falling in love with him be about the stupidest thing she could do?

"You're not talking, sis. Stop daydreaming about his ass, and answer the question," Elle said.

"Abs." The word snuck out.

Elle raised a brow. "Abs?"

Allison gave up. It was safer to talk about the physical side of things than the turmoil of emotion in her heart and head. "The man has got the most incredible butt, yes. And arms. And shoulders. But goodness, you should see his stomach."

"Six-pack and all, I bet," Elle teased. "You need to take pictures and post them."

"Hands off." Allison shook her head. "Forget I said you should see him naked. You just daydream about other cowboys and leave mine alone."

"So he's good then?"

Allison twisted to give her sister the evil eye. "You really asking what I think you're asking?"

"Does he know how to burn up the sheets? Yes, I'm really asking. Because I need to live vicariously—"

Elle shut her mouth with a snap.

Uh-oh. “What about that reporter Mom said you’re seeing?”

Her sister snorted. “Was seeing. Once. Maybe twice. It was terrible. He kissed like a wet fish. And I didn’t even try sex with him, not when he pretty much proved he didn’t know where or what my clit was.”

Allison laughed. “I don’t want to know how that happened.”

“I bet your cowboy knows where things are. Tell me you’re at least happily getting all the sex you can.”

A little over a week ago she would have had to lie through her teeth and ignore the sexual frustration she’d been feeling. Now? Now she was free to grin and gloat a little. “Oh. My. God. You have no idea.”

The back door opened, the squeak echoing off the walls.

They both swung their heads to take in *her cowboy* slipping into the house, his broad shoulders just about filling the teeny back entranceway.

Elle was busy admiring Gabe. “Look what the cat dragged in.”

That curious flutter in Allison’s stomach kicked up again. Especially when he looked straight into her eyes, ignoring Elle completely as he marched across the kitchen. He wrapped his hand around the back of her neck and brought their mouths together.

Possessive. Sweet. How was it possible for both those sensations to whip through her? Like he was cherishing her and never going to let her go at the same time.

It might be a show for Elle’s sake, but Allison didn’t care. She slipped her wash-water-wet hands over his shoulders and held on tight. Returning the kiss and savouring his touch.

When he finally let her up for air, she was grinning so wide her cheeks felt stretched. “I wasn’t expecting to see you, but that was very nice.”

Elle snorted. "Nice. *Sheesh*, I need a cold shower after witnessing that. I'll leave you two lovebirds alone. Mom wanted to watch a show and it's on in a bit."

"See you in the living room in a few minutes." Allison meant the words for her sister, but she couldn't take her eyes off Gabe. He held her, his fingers tickling the hairs at the base of her neck gently.

The door to the living room closed with a soft sigh, and still he held her.

The position was comfortable, and she wasn't sure why. "What are you doing here?"

Gabe lowered his voice. "If your family just found out about your mom, and you need to be here, then I need to be here as well."

A thread of sadness wove through her tangled emotions. Oh. That made sense. And yet it wasn't what she'd been hoping to hear, not if she was honest with herself. "You're right. Thank you for coming."

She went to walk around him, to put some physical space between them to help put some emotional space between him and that weird aching sensation in her heart.

He wouldn't let her go. Instead he slipped one arm around her waist and tugged her to his side. Lips hovering over her ear. Secretive. Private.

"I came here for you. Because I wanted to be with you."

Allison looked into his green eyes. The blond waves of his hair stuck out in a mess from under his hat, his concern clear in his expression. His hands on her body were controlling, but careful.

"You wanted to be here? What about the Coleman gathering?" Maybe he hadn't meant his message how it came out. The caring sound of the words—that could be her wild imagination speaking.

He rubbed his hand up and down her back slowly. "Drinking with the guys can wait."

Gabe didn't say anything more, just tugged her against him and held her head to his chest. The steady beat under her ear reassuring and stirring at the same time. He wanted to be with her.

Like a tiny seed of hope in the middle of the coldest winter.

"Gabe?"

"Yeah?"

She didn't look up, just clung a little tighter. "I'm glad you came."

Elle had gone to bed. Maisey had gone to bed. Paul had left and headed back to his place. The living room was down to him and Allison, and if he wanted to be any use in the morning, he damn well better be going to bed soon as well.

He couldn't stand to move. Not with the way she'd draped herself over him while they'd watched TV with her mom. The shows weren't much on his agenda, but the heat of Allison's body snuggled up tight—that he could get used to having around all the time.

When her sister had plopped down on the far side of the couch, Allison had shifted closer to him to make room. Gabe had to adjust position a couple of times to ease off the pressure on his cock. Damn thing didn't care they were in a public place. The longer they sat in the cozy room, the more Allison's scent filled his head. Her perfume, or soap, or whatever it was, tickled his nose and made him long to start at her toes and nibble the entire way up. Stopping a few places along the way for good long breaks.

Worse still was thinking about what she wore underneath the skirt. And that bit of torture was his own damn fault.

Allison sighed. "We could have gone back to your cabin."

"I don't mind staying. Puss in Boots is cared for. Your mom enjoyed having us here, and it's no trouble to drive the short distance in the morning."

"She's going to want to feed you pancakes. It's traditional Saturday morning fare."

Gabe would have answered, but Allison picked that moment to roll and stretch, her breasts pressed to the front of her tight T-shirt.

He couldn't look away.

She flicked a finger under his chin. "You never seen a pair of tits before, Angel Boy?"

Gabe rotated her slightly to let her back rest on the couch, her hips still in his lap. "You and the Angel Boy business. No one calls me that anymore."

"Your family is still known as the Angel Colemans around town. I've heard it."

"Whatever. I'll answer your question if you answer mine." He smoothed his hand over her legs. "And this isn't the question, but what are you wearing? Not that I mind that shirt—shows off your tits nicely. And yes, I've seen that particular pair a few times."

"Hoping for more?" she teased.

"Always," he whispered back. "Fooling around in your mama's living room. I feel like I'm fourteen and hoping for a grope or two."

They smiled at each other, and the ease and comfort between them was wonderful and frightening at the same time.

They'd been having sex, but always on the wild side. Raw and needy, physical release and physical comfort. This felt like there was something new in the room. An edgy, needy part, just not as frantic.

Her breathing picked up as he caressed her leg. "I had old clothes in a drawer. Most things were too small, like this T-shirt. The jeans were all a write-off. The skirt still fits—*oh!*"

Gabe had gathered the fabric in his fingers, a little more bunching up on each stroke. Now he touched smooth, warm skin, letting his hand sneak under the cotton material.

"So my real question is...did you put on those panties like I asked you to?"

Allison bit her lip, then nodded.

He had to suck in a breath of air to keep from shouting out *hell, yeah* or something. He snuck his hand higher, teasing the inside of her thigh.

The house was silent but for the moans of the wind and the floorboards settling. And the increased pants from Allison's lips.

Gabe touched a scrap of lacy fabric a second before making contact with the warmth of her mound. The curls covering her were damp. He forced himself to continue past until the second section of elastic brushed his fingertips.

He'd been right.

It only took a second to lean in closer. He kept his hand cupping her heat, not wanting to let go. "What a nice surprise."

She glanced toward the stairs. "Gabe, not here."

He pressed his index finger between her folds and hit moisture. Heat. That urge to up and drive into her struck again. To lift her legs in the air and rest them over his shoulders so he could line up and thrust deep...

"You're addictive."

"Gabe." She sucked in a gasp as he pressed into her core fully, burying his finger while running his thumb over her clit.

Just as suddenly he withdrew. Lifted his hand to his mouth and licked his finger clean. Her scent wrapped around them, filled his mouth, filled his head.

Her eyes were wide. Her hips had followed him as he'd pulled back, as if she was as reluctant to let him go as he was to leave off touching her.

Please, *please* let her want him as bad as he wanted her right then.

“Where can we go?” he whispered.

Not upstairs where the guest room sat next to the master bedroom. Not on this floor where he knew Elle slept. He didn’t give a damn who heard them, but Allison probably would.

She used his shoulders as a lever to rise, slipping off the couch and pulling him after her. When she opened the front door, he thought maybe they were going to leave, but instead she tugged him around to the side of the porch.

He peered through the darkness eagerly searching for deck chairs. Or a porch swing.

No such luck. One good thing, though, there were no windows on this side of the house. This section of the porch faced the fields and the small horse stable. It was as private as he could hope for.

Impatiently he scooped her up and manoeuvred her until he could claim her lips. Kissing her, wanting to experience her taste and the wild thrill of teeth and tongue, lips and needy gasps. Allison wrapped her legs around him, the layers of her skirt riding up and exposing her long smooth limbs.

He grabbed her by the ass and held on tight. Brought her warmth over his hard cock, rubbing her slickness over him. She was wet enough he felt it through his jeans. Gabe pressed her against the wall and pinned her there as he struggled to gain back control before he simply ripped open his pants and fucked her hard.

Allison caught him by the ears and pulled until their lips met again, just as hungry as he was.

He backed away. She clung to him as he walked the dozen steps to the corner of the porch. Inspiration struck as he lowered her to the top rail.

“Grab on to the upright post,” he ordered, “and spread your legs.”

She threw her arm around the column and squeezed. Gabe lifted her leg closest to the pillar and rested her foot on the railing that headed off at a ninety-degree angle to them.

He snuck his hand under her skirt again and found her pussy.

"Damn, you are wet. So fucking sexy." He slid his fingers through her folds, loving the little noises that burst from her lips.

"Oh God, Gabe. Oh yeah, right there..."

He focused on her clit. The hard little point demanded his attention. Even as he played with her, circling and teasing, he kissed her, their breaths mingling as she got closer to exploding.

Gabe took his time to learn more. When he changed pace, he listened to her response. Concentrated on making her squirm until she cried out and he swallowed the sound. Sucking the call into himself as she writhed on the railing and he held her firmly.

She relaxed a bit, sighing happily, and he straightened up.

"You got a condom?" she whispered.

"Hell, yeah." He pulled it from his back pocket.

"Cocky. That sure you were going to get lucky?" Allison reached down and one-handed managed to pop open the button on his jeans.

He was never going to be around her without one handy ever again. Their time at the creek had taught him that. "That cocky, period. You're in charge. Put this on." He pressed the condom into her hand and took hold of her shoulders.

Watching her fingers move toward his dick was incredible. The actual heat of her taking him in hand was even better. Gabe gritted his teeth together for a second to make sure he didn't lose it while she rolled the latex over his length.

Then he put her hand back on the support pillar, hooked his arm under her thigh. Stabbed forward, little aim, no finesse.

Just damn good luck as he found her heat and buried himself in one persistent rush.

"Oh, yes. So good." She had one arm around the pillar, elbow crooked like she was holding on for dear life. Her other hand fisted his shirtfront. He withdrew and thrust forward slowly. Evenly. At least at first.

Then she started whispering.

"You know how good that feels? With you touching all those places inside? I feel you all over. My lips, my pussy."

Gabe's balls were tight, the shiver of icy cold down his back rising in anticipation as he got closer to the final point. He wanted to be the one blowing her mind and making her crazy but he couldn't speak, just fixated on the sensation of how good it felt to be surrounded by her. Warm moisture, flashes of heat.

He stared down at where they connected and watched his cock slip in again, and he shuddered.

All the while Allison spoke to him. Soft words, but dirty ones. Swear words occasionally, especially after a deep thrust where his groin meshed tight with hers.

He loved it. Loved having this woman be herself. Unique and perfect. The words became confirmation that fucking her outside her mom's house was exactly what she wanted right here and right now. Because, yeah, it was twisted in a way, but sweet mercy, it was good.

Her final *fuck me hard* was too much to take, and he rocked against her again and again, grinding with his pelvis over her clit until she joined him in release. Sheath squeezing his cock, jerking his climax free. Lips fluttering breathlessly against his until they both caught their breaths.

"You've fucked me boneless," Allison complained. Or boasted.

Gabe reluctantly withdrew and supported her as she found her balance on the porch. He dealt with the condom, not sure where to toss it, when Allison giggled faintly.

"Drop it over the railing and we'll grab it in the morning."

He did it, feeling a little stupid. "Make sure you remind me. I would hate for your mama to find that in the garden box."

They laughed together, straightening and organizing their clothing. Gabe turned to allow her to walk ahead of him into the house. Instead she snuck her hand back in his. Painfully sharp hope smacked him, but he tried to ignore it.

It was too soon to say anything. But in terms of starting to let her know he wanted more than casual from her? It had been a positive day.

Chapter Eighteen

Day slipped into night. The next day followed, and the next. Allison was busier than she'd ever been. In spite of the sadness of watching her mom grow weaker, she daily found enjoyable moments.

More than enjoyable, they rocked.

She worked full out at the restaurant, filling the rest of her time at her mom's or putting through calls to help arrange matters for Gabe and the ranch.

No matter what she was doing, though, the longing to be with Gabe remained. She didn't want to avoid the other things, but spending time with the man?

Addictive. She'd stupidly fallen for her own deception.

Or had something changed?

He held her hand while they watched TV, Puss in Boots purring happily in Gabe's lap. He sat with an arm around her shoulders as they talked with family or visited with Maisey. He hugged her at the drop of a hat, and it seemed he couldn't get enough of kissing her, no matter what time of day it was.

The sex? Oh my God, the sex. Even thinking about how they carried on made her flush and tingle.

Her mom noticed her happy glow, and complimented them both on being so terribly in love. "His rough edges are getting worn smooth by caring for you," she shared while Allison helped her one afternoon.

Allison hid her grin by turning to fill the kettle. Something was happening, but she didn't have the nerve to come right out and ask him if the rules had changed on their charade. "He's never been one of the wild ones, Mom. He's hard working and decent."

Maisey patted her arm and slowly moved into the next task she felt had to be done. Allison clung to the happy moments, like spotting bright jewels sparkling in the rough.

Gabe *was* hard working. Which meant he was out in the fields and with the animals in all the different weathers, at all hours. Summer had finally decided to stick around, heat-sweltering days followed by lovely cooler nights as the sun dipped behind the foothills. The little cabin they shared with Puss in Boots seemed to have a steady stream of visitors. Rafe stopped in often. Travis. The twins from the Six Pack Coleman side.

Every time someone visited, Gabe dropped what he was doing to help.

The third time he abandoned his dinner to up and give a helping hand Allison wanted to fuss at him. That she wanted to rant didn't piss her off as much as the fact she had no right to tell him to make his family wait. Gabe helping others—it was just a part of who he was.

Like he'd helped her. How could she be upset with him about that? And the memory of her basically stomping in and begging him to cooperate made her feel guilty all over again.

Guilt mixed with a healthy dollop of longing.

Was it crazy she wanted more?

She'd thought hard about it all week, trying to decide when things had changed. If they really had changed, or if it was her imagination working overtime after the exhaustion of long days and short nights.

Deciding to be brave and straight out ask him was difficult, especially knowing her mom could be gone soon. Having things change between her and Gabe before that happened?

She couldn't take the risk. After would be soon enough to discover if that look in his eyes was something more than wishful thinking on her part.

So she put her plans on hold and took each day in stride. Promising to enjoy every moment as much as possible with Gabe, as well as with her mom. Because she didn't know when either would be snatched from her.

The bonfire before them shot sparks into the indigo-coloured sky. Allison rested against Gabe's side and looked around. "It's a beautiful night."

"Too early yet for the Perseids, but come August we can go lie out on the hill side and watch them all night long."

"Shooting stars?"

"Meteor shower. Hundreds of them."

Oh, what she wouldn't give for a hundred stars to wish on. To miraculously make her mother better. To know her siblings would recover from the coming heartbreak.

For Gabe to feel even a little bit about her the way she'd begun to feel about him.

He leaned back on the low cushion he'd brought along and sighed.

"What's that for?" She spoke softly to avoid interrupting the rest of their company, although she didn't really need to worry. The Friday-eve activity had broken into two this weekend. Some still met at the bar in town while the more hardy of the Colemans made the trip to the bluff overlooking the Baptiste River.

"Just relaxing. It's been a long week."

She agreed. They'd moved Mom to the main floor of the house, shifting Elle upstairs. Her sister didn't want to take over the master bedroom, so ironically, she was back in her original space, sunshine flooding in at a horrible hour.

Allison had teased Elle about it, but the taunts had been bittersweet. Maisey couldn't do the stairs comfortably anymore, although homecare visits meant remaining in the house was still possible for a little longer. The clock kept ticking.

She added her own sigh to Gabe's, and when he dropped his arm around her, she rolled to cuddle against his chest and soak in the warmth and comfort of his body.

Guitar music began, Steve Coleman rocking lightly as he picked out a tune. His girlfriend sang along, her voice a little too high to complement his, but it wasn't center stage Nashville, or even the Stampede fairgrounds. It was the middle of the summer in the foothills of Alberta, and the out-of-tune mashup fit.

You did what you could, you enjoyed yourself.

Jesse threw back his head and howled. A series of yips answered back from the not-so-distant trees, and the crowd laughed.

Another joy of the country. You didn't take yourself too seriously.

"Was that a commentary on me?" Steve taunted. "Because you notice the coyotes didn't start in until you piped up."

Jesse waved a hand, not letting go of the young lady he had under his arm. "I'm not the singer of the group, just thought we needed to speed things up a little. You were going to put me to sleep with your lullabies."

"You don't mind a reason to hit the sack, now do you?" Travis poked his brother.

Jesse shook his head, lifting the woman at his side and depositing her in his lap. "You know I don't."

His date giggled. She didn't seem to mind that he had his hands on her right out in public.

Allison leaned harder into Gabe as the talk got raunchier. Some of it was funny, but maybe she was too old for this kind of fun. It was one thing to talk dirty while they were fooling around, but the public shit talk had lost its appeal.

She would have been happy to just stay home with Gabe. Get hot and sweaty with him and not—

Drat. Stay *home* with Gabe?

She was so gone.

Another truck pulled into the parking area, brakes screeching, door slamming loudly. Gabe leaned forward and Allison went with him, turning to see who was joining the group this late.

Jesse hopped to his feet, dropping his cuddle bunny on the ground in his haste.

"Hey, watch it," she complained.

He grinned and tweaked her nose. "Sorry, darling. I'll be back in a minute with a surprise."

Jesse jogged off.

Allison was ready to suggest they leave as well when loud voices sounded behind them—familiar voices. Angry and sharp, but far enough away to be undecipherable.

"Great. Come on, let's see what's happening now." Gabe hoisted her up and took her hand.

Gabe to the rescue again. Allison went willingly, if only because she figured they could head home after dealing with the situation. She'd had enough, and spending time with the clan wasn't what she needed tonight.

They were still a ways out when she recognized the newcomer as Joel. The twins seemed to have finished shouting at each other and moved to the scuffling part of the program. Joel grabbed his brother by the front of the shirt and laid into him.

"Crap. Stay here."

Gabe pushed her behind him and shot forward. He couldn't move fast enough, though, not before Joel had time to land a snapping hard crack to his brother's chin. Jesse jerked backward and fell to the ground. Joel had him by the collar and was leaning in for more when Gabe stepped between them, catching hold of Joel's fist before it could descend again.

"Fuck off. This is none of your business," Joel ground out.

"Beating the crap out of someone in public is my business." Allison cringed as Gabe shoved himself even farther between the twins.

"It's not someone, it's an asshole who needs a pounding. Now move."

Joel attempted to drag Jesse closer. His brother scrambled to back out of the way. A loud rip sounded as Jesse's shirt tore. He escaped, rushing to his feet, hands at the ready to defend himself.

"*Jesus*, Joel. What the hell's got your panties in such a twist?" Jesse wiped a hand over his bloody mouth, spitting to the side without taking his gaze off his twin.

Joel stood, feet planted wide. The only thing that moved was his chest as he sucked in huge breaths, obviously fighting the urge to take another swing or two. Allison moved in closer to Gabe's side, the sound of the guitar in the distance eerie. Its light-hearted tune didn't make any sense while looking at Joel's expression.

"You really want me to tell you what I'm so pissed about? Maybe if you look over there you'll get a clue."

Joel pointed toward the fire. Jesse didn't bother to look, just twisted his face into a sheepish smile.

"You're taking this the wrong way," Jesse complained.

"How am I supposed to take it, asshole? I went to pick up my date for the night and she was already gone."

Ouch. Allison glanced at Gabe, who shook his head slightly. He squeezed her fingers and tugged her to the side, farther away from where Jesse and Joel faced off.

Jesse held out his hands like a negotiator. "Come on. So I've met Sue. Sorry I didn't tell you, but isn't this really what you've been wanting? For both of us to be around?"

When Joel would have stepped in, fists rising, Gabe grabbed him and held him back. “Punching his lights out won’t get this solved. Talk to him.”

Joel snarled, “Talk? He doesn’t listen. I’ve told him what I wanted, and the jackass ignores me.”

“Because you’re being stupid,” Jesse said.

“Says you.”

Jesse snorted.

“Enough.” Gabe stepped between them and glared at them both. “You guys twenty-two or twelve? Grow up.”

“I’m trying.” Joel dragged a hand through his hair, pacing away before turning back and growling in frustration. “Jesse. I know we’ve got this reputation. But when I tell you I want to date a girl by myself that isn’t some fucked-up code for you to go and try to convince her otherwise.”

“Shit.” Gabe turned his glare on Jesse, and suddenly all three of them were staring his direction.

Jesse shrugged. “Fine. I thought you were goofing off. She’s a nice-enough girl, but nothing special. I thought—”

“God*dammit*, Jesse, it doesn’t matter what you think. It matters what I said. Listen to me next time, you bloody idiot, or I’ll fucking bury you, got it?”

Allison covered her mouth. Even as he shouted at his twin, Joel had evidently decided to let the matter drop. He stepped back, body relaxing. Hands falling to his sides.

“And you.” Joel turned his disapproval on Gabe. “Stop getting in the middle of everyone’s business.”

Gabe laughed. “What? It’s not okay I stopped you from breaking your knuckles on Jesse’s head?”

Joel cursed. “Okay, that part is fine, but it’s not okay you helped him get involved with Sue in the first place.”

What? Allison froze in horror.

So did Gabe. “What the hell are you talking about?”

Joel pointed at Jesse again. “Jackass used your truck to go see her when I was out of town in Calgary. At least he didn’t pull some stupid fuck-upped business of pretending to be me, but still.”

“I had nothing to do with this,” Gabe insisted.

“He didn’t. Totally my fault.” Jesse grabbed his twin by the shoulder. Joel shook him off. “Come on, he was oblivious. You know Gabe always does what he can and never asks questions. I took advantage of his saintly good nature. Just—I’m sorry, okay?”

Gabe’s grip on her had gone tight. Allison glanced into his face to see him pulling back. Closing off. She couldn’t read anything anymore. He’d turned cold.

His expression was similar to what she was used to seeing on his father Ben’s face, and it scared her a little.

Joel shook his head. “Whatever. I’m going home. Tell Sue I said goodbye.”

He turned without another word, feet hitting the ground hard as he stomped away.

Silence. Loud silence.

Jesse cleared his throat. “Thanks for saving my butt.”

“No problem. It’s what we saintly, good-natured type do.” Gabe stepped toward the parking lot as well. Allison let her fingers slip from his, and surprisingly, he let her go. He just walked away, shoulders slumped. She wanted to hang on. To reassure him.

But first she wanted to pick up where Joel had left off and wipe the smirk from Jesse’s face.

She moved in close, forcing him to tilt his head. He looked her over, gaze lingering where he had no right, and sheer willpower stopped her from slugging him. That, and the need to get back to Gabe as quickly as possible.

“You got something to say?” Jesse drawled.

Her hands shook, she was so pissed. "Joel was right. You need to grow the hell up. Gabe's got the biggest damn heart out of any of you, and you choose to use him because of it? Jackass isn't strong enough."

"Now wait—"

"No, you shut up and listen." Allison poked him in the chest with a finger. If she used her fist she would be tempted to take a real swing. "You listen a damn sight harder from now on. To me, to your brother. I've heard about the games you boys play, but this isn't about you anymore, this is about messing with someone who didn't deserve your shit. If you want to goof off, find people who appreciate your screwed-up sense of humour. Gabe will probably forgive you, but I'm not going to, not for a damn long time."

Jesse's lips were pressed together, his usual cocky grin faded from his face.

Allison planted her hand on his chest and pushed. He was too solid to shove over, but the move let her propel herself away from him.

"Allison. Allison, wait. Shit, I'm sorry."

She ignored his calls, eager to get back to the truck. She needed to see Gabe.

He was leaning against the driver's door staring off into the darkening sky. Somehow he still spotted her coming, shifting to vertical as she approached. He pulled the door open, and she crawled in without a word, scooting to the middle and buckling up.

After all her bravery shouting at Jesse, she wasn't sure what to say.

He drove slowly, his body tense beside her. She dropped her hand onto his thigh and he immediately covered it with his own.

They rode in silence the entire way back to the house.

Chapter Nineteen

Gabe burned inside and he wasn't sure what would put out the flames. All the frustrations, all the pain piled up, and he was slowly being crushed.

The saving grace was Allison's presence, and even that he had no right to enjoy. Their relationship was a sham, a fake. Maybe comparable to what Jesse had done. She'd unwittingly used his desire to be there for others against him.

Yet he could have sworn something more was growing between them. He had to believe it. Had to cling to that hope.

Had to know, because waiting any longer was wrong. He wasn't strong enough to let this one ride.

If it had been winter he would have lit the fire, just for something mundane to do with his hands. Instead, he found himself wandering the house. Moving things around. Adjusting chairs. Hell, he probably would have gone out and found a hole or two to dig if Allison hadn't come up and wrapped herself around him.

She snuck her hands under his shirt, pressing her palms to his back. Her cheek resting on his chest. God, he felt as if she was drawing strength from him when she did that, and he didn't have anything left to give right now.

Except, it was Allison, and he would always have something for her. He caught her head with a hand, stroked her hair. Pulled the strands over her shoulders and tangled his fingers in the soft mass.

His heart stopped racing, and when she tugged him toward the bedroom, he went.

She crawled on top of the covers and patted the space beside her. "Come here, Angel Boy."

A snort escaped involuntarily. "I'm not great company right now."

"I gave him hell." Her eyes flashed. "Jesse, I mean."

"I figured that's what you were doing. You didn't have to."

She caught him by the chin. "I wanted to. And you stop it with that suffering-in-silence business. You don't have to be quiet around me. Hell, you've heard me moan and groan and complain more than anyone. If you want to call your cousin a few bad names, I can take it."

The sentiment was nice, but wasted. Jesse was right. Gabe rolled onto his back and stared at the ceiling. "No use. It's true. I do try to be a saint, and look at the results. I'm as fucked for trying to do good as not."

Allison leaned over him, touching his face gently. "What's wrong?"

Make or break time. He'd taunted Rafe to be brave enough to fix the things that needed fixing. Gabe stared into her concerned face and knew this had to change. It was time to move forward. Now he'd find out if it was with her or without.

"You remember my brother Michael?"

A flash of surprise lit her eyes. "Of course."

"I think you'd already moved away when he died."

She nodded. "I still heard. Paul was pretty tore up—the entire grade twelve class was."

Gabe took another breath to brace himself. "It was my fault."

Allison jerked. She sat upright and stared at him, confusion crossing her face. "I…hang on. I thought he got hit by a car."

Gabe shuddered, throwing an arm over his eyes. He had to get to the end of this, but he couldn't bear to watch her as he spoke. "He did. But it was my fault. I was supposed to go out celebrating with him that night. His eighteenth birthday had been only a few days earlier, and he wanted to hit the bars. The Angel Boy Colemans, painting the town red. He was so excited, in that way only he could get. He was like this light in the family, always joking around, making everyone happy."

She grabbed hold of his free hand and gently stroked his fingers.

He was surprised she wasn't running from the room in terror.

Gabe pushed forward. "He'd always looked up to me, and I had promised to take him out once he was legal. Big-brother shit, the older more mature twenty-one-year-old initiating the newbie. Rites of passage and all that. Only I called it off at the last minute."

The pain flared again. If only he could turn back time and change his actions.

"Something came up?"

Oh God. "Had a girl I was seeing, and she'd promised me the moon that night. I ditched him to go out fooling around. It was nothing important, nothing I had to do so desperately. It was selfish and thinking of what I wanted, not what he needed. When he had too much to drink, I wasn't there to stop him from wandering out into the road and getting hit."

Allison crawled over top of him. Surprise made him move his arm as she leaned over and stared down into his face.

She had tears in her eyes.

"It wasn't your fault."

Easy to say, impossible to believe. "I could have stopped him. He would have whooped it up a little, but I would have prevented him from getting shitfaced. Could have driven him home, and he'd still be here. One minute he was alive, the next he was gone."

In that moment their entire family changed.

She tugged on his shoulders. Gabe pulled himself to a sitting position. With her straddling his thighs, their faces were right in line with each other so she could peer straight into his eyes as she spoke. "Gabe Coleman. You don't honestly believe you are responsible for your brother's death."

When he would have looked away, she tilted her head in warning.

He sighed. "We dealt with psychologists. The entire school had grief counsellors in, and one came to talk to the family. She told us how sometimes bad things happened to good people, and that life went on. I heard it, I get it. Doesn't matter what I think, though, because everything changed. Ma lost her joy, Ben got mean and ugly. Rafe was only eight, and you know how hard losing family is when you're a kid."

She knew. Allison knew all too well what kind of pain it was to lose someone you loved.

She leaned forward and covered his mouth with hers. Briefly. Just a caress. Touched her forehead to his and spoke against his lips. "It wasn't your fault."

He breathed in her scent. The taste of her on the air. "I left after that, to hide from the pain and the blame. I was gone for a bunch of years before I realized I was running and there was nothing chasing me."

"So you came back."

"I came back because I loved the ranch, and I loved my ma. And..." He had to do it. Had to finish this. "I came back because Rafe asked me to."

Allison lifted her head, the question clear on her face.

"He got drunk one night. Ben. Losing Michael tore him apart, and he started drinking. When I ran away I managed to avoid most of his mess, but one night he got liquored up enough he kind of lost his mind. He didn't lay a finger on Ma or Rafe, but he smashed a bottle. A piece of glass flew out and hit my kid brother."

She pressed her fingers to her lips, shock in her eyes. "The scar on his cheek?"

Gabe nodded. "I came home. Figured I could at least be a buffer between him and the others."

"Oh, Gabe."

"It worked. He stopped drinking as much because he gets some weird satisfaction out of telling me just how fucked up I am."

Allison cupped his neck in her hands, eyes filled with moisture. "You came home to rescue them, and you've been doing it ever since."

Nailed it. "Even, it seems, to people who don't need saving."

"Fuck Jesse."

He couldn't stop it. He snorted. "No, thanks."

"You know what I mean." She squeezed harder, fingers stroking the tight muscles at the top of his spine. "You're a decent, kind man, and no matter what your motivations were to start with, if you weren't a giving person deep down, you never would have tried to be there for others. Especially not for as long as you have."

"You're doing the same thing, you know. Trying to rescue your family."

She nodded slowly. "When Dad died, I was torn between so many emotions. We were sad he was gone. That he'd never see us as grownups, never grow old with Mom. But I was relieved in a way, because he'd been in pain for so long, and he'd unknowingly made our lives tough during the years he was ill. And then the guilt hit for feeling relief. How could I be so selfish? Everything was all twisted and confusing for the longest time."

Allison dragged her hand over his shoulders and down his chest, her nose wrinkling as if she was trying to figure out how to say something.

"What?" He was so achingly tired from it all, but worry for her and the need to find out more urged him on.

"When I came and asked you to help me. That was wrong of me. I'm sorry."

Gabe pressed his hand over hers, holding her palm against his chest. As good a time as any to see if he was going to get even more wrecked tonight. "I may have a reputation of being a bloody saint, but agreeing to help you? I'll never regret it."

"Really?" She blinked hard. "It was rude, and bossy, and totally controlling. You should have thrown me out from the start."

"Maybe it was a little brash, but if you hadn't decided to take the first steps, I never would have fallen in love with you."

Her heart stuttered to a stop. "What did you say?"

His eyes looked so haunted, but a hint of his smile tweaked the corner of his mouth. "Allison, I know it's crazy, but having you around these past weeks has been the best thing that's happened to me in a long time."

The trickle of fear that had filled her as he'd shared had become a ball of ice as he told her more of the story. How could she possibly find the right words to explain that Jesse was wrong? That everyone who thought Gabe was a person to take advantage of was wrong.

And she'd felt the guilt hard at what she'd done.

Now, looking into his honest face, the ball of ice melted a little as hope lit a flame beneath her. "Oh, Gabe."

He smiled. "'Oh, Gabe, what the hell have you done?' I know we started this thing as a ruse to fool your mom, and I'm totally on board doing whatever necessary to keep her happy. I want you to know it's become more than an act for me. I like having you in my life."

She swallowed hard. "I like it too. I..."

Was she in love with him? Could she even know right now with everything else ramping up her emotions?

Was he really in love with her or just saving her all over again?

He stroked her cheek with his finger. "Don't rush. I don't need you to say anything yet. Hell, if anything, maybe you shouldn't say anything tonight, because I don't want to push you into something you're not sure about."

"I pushed you into helping me," she pointed out.

"Helping you was a given. I was already hooked by those big eyes and the sexy swing of your hips."

She screwed up her courage and kissed him. Long and hard. Taking what she wanted. Giving what he needed. Trying to affirm without words that things were different, and she was good with the change.

She was breathless by the time he released her, his grin stretching from ear to ear. "Mmm, nice."

Allison slowly undulated against him, rubbing their torsos together. "There's more where that came from."

Gabe lifted a brow. "You needing a bit of sexy cowboy? You want me to take off my shirt so you can touch my abs for a while?"

A gasp escaped. "Gabe Coleman, you were eavesdropping on me and my sister."

"Course I was. Had to know if it was safe to come in. Didn't think I'd be hearing about how you wanted to strip me down and take advantage of me."

Oh, stripping him down was a fine idea. But that second part of what he'd said? "Sex isn't why I want you. Just to be clear. You're a good man—"

"You say that one more time and I'm going to feel as if they should put a halo over my picture when they hang it on the wall."

"Well, it's true."

"I'm not a good man. I choose to do good things. There's a difference."

"Not in my books."

If he could be brave, so could she.

"Gabe?"

He nuzzled her neck. "Umm?"

"I've been wanting this to be more than just something to make my mom happy. I've been hoping you were starting to want me. For me."

The sheer joy in his face lit the room. "I want you. Not just want you, physically, although, oh, woman, you are very fine."

She caught his hand and stared intently at him. The little flecks of gold in the green of his eyes sparkled like stars. He rolled her, covering her with his long hard body, and suddenly his expression had nothing to do with being angelically good.

"Let me make love to you."

Even the way he said it sounded different. More intense, more meaningful.

She grabbed on to his shirt and jerked it loose from his jeans.

He helped her, she helped him. One article of clothing at a time, they stripped. When he dropped his shirt to the ground, she reached out and touched him. Pressing her fingers to his abs and tracing the rigid lines of his muscles. She kissed his collarbone, licked the hollow of his throat.

His hands were busy, pulling her top free, reaching around to unhook her bra. The warm air from the open window brushed her naked skin a second before his mouth covered her right breast, and she sighed with pleasure.

He licked and sucked, his other hand coming up to hold her left breast and tweak her nipple until the spot tingled and she squirmed against his mouth.

One side. The other. She wanted to undo his pants and continue the getting-naked part, but he wouldn't let her, instead spreading her over the mattress and continuing to drive her crazy.

"I've rushed and rushed. Every time we've fooled around it seems my brain shuts down, and I've never stopped to savour you. Tonight? I'm in no hurry, so you just enjoy."

Gabe kissed her then inched his lips along her throat as he returned to her breasts. Every touch, every lick, it was as if strings were attached from the sensitive tips to her core, and he tugged them again and again. She squeezed her legs together to try to get some pressure where she needed it most.

He dropped to her belly and played with the piercing there. She was wearing a tiny diamond chip, and as he tongued it, the heat of his breath fanned over her belly.

Bringing her up, taking her higher.

He kissed the center of the butterfly on the crest of her hipbone. "It's beautiful. They all are."

The tiny butterflies she'd had inked on her body were therapeutic and made her smile every time she spotted them. "I needed something to show how I felt. The butterflies were a natural fit."

He fell silent, fingers tracing the outline. "Incredible."

"Life goes on. Changes. I wanted to celebrate that."

Gabe shifted lower and touched her thigh where another of the brightly coloured creatures decorated her skin. He kissed the spot tenderly. "Inspiring."

Then he covered her mound with his mouth, and she was the one being inspired. Long, slow, thorough licks followed. His tongue teasing through her folds, circling her clit. Plunging deep into her core. He clasped her thighs and pushed them up and out of his way, and dove in deeper.

Allison touched his head, dragging her fingertips over his scalp. His tongue drove her crazy, but touching him satisfied her like she'd never expected.

Sexual tension, physical responses. They were there, they hit just right, but it was in her mind that she felt it most. In her heart.

It was more than physical, stirring her deep inside.

He covered her clit and sucked lightly, tongue flicking against the sensitive spot until her tension rose so high she was ready to tip over. Ready, but needing something more. Just a touch to send her flying.

Gabe caught hold of her nipple. It still tingled from his earlier attentions, and as he increased his assault on her clit, he tweaked the tight point. She took off in a wonderful explosion, pleasure shooting over the barrier and setting free.

As the waves rocked her body, he kissed her intimately, slowing as the pulses slowed. Then he rolled her, rising behind her as he pressed his lips to the butterfly on her lower back. The one on her shoulder blade.

The tiny one at the base of her neck.

He licked her neckline. "I like this going-slower business."

She had to agree. "Can you get naked, though? That would make the slow business even better, at least in my books."

Gabe chuckled softly, moving away for a moment. Allison lay in boneless relaxation, wanting more, but satisfied as well.

It was a neat sensation.

Thinking of his words, his confession of wanting more? It was everything she wanted and dreamed of and feared at the same time.

Gabe returned, the mattress dipping under his weight. His warm body settling over top of hers, hard muscles tight to her back, hard length of his erection against her butt.

"Naked as commanded," he whispered.

She twisted her head to the side and gave him her lips. Slowly they tangled tongues and explored each other. Gabe ran his hands over her shoulders and up to her wrists, circling them with his fingers and tugging her arms over her head.

He was full out lying on top of her. Protective. Like he was shielding her.

Her heart ached and was happy all at the same time. Gabe, her guardian angel.

She tried to move her hands, but he had them locked in position. "You planning on tying me up, cowboy?"

"Not today, but now that you mention it, I think we can arrange that."

She shimmied her hips, attempting to rub against him. His cock was a solid weight pressed into her flesh. "You still planning on doing something with that tonight?"

"Hell, yeah. I was having fun watching you squirm, first."

He rose off her, the heat and pressure of his possession easing, and she sighed. Her exhalation turned to a gasp as he raised her hips and buried his cock in her pussy.

"God, Allison."

He gripped her hips tightly and thrust forward again. She was still chest-down to the mattress, arms extended overhead, and the angle he held her hips made him go deep. Filling her, expanding her with his girth. She grabbed on to the headboard and held on for dear life.

Only the wild ride she expected didn't come. He rocked steadily, filling her completely. Groin meeting ass, his fingers bruising her hips. When he forced his thighs farther under hers, she held her breath, it felt so good. Different angle, different slide against her sheath. Teasing and tangling her pleasure into anticipation, and anticipation into need. He thrust in all the way then paused, bending over her and covering her with his body. Heated chest against her back, his arm slipped under her and wrapped around her waist.

"Let go of the bed," he ordered.

Her fingers slipped from the wooden struts, and he lifted her torso, settling her in his lap. Her butt rested against his abs, and she was so damn full she was ready to burst.

He caught hold of her neck and sucked, both hands covering her breasts. Sensory overload began, and she was going to die if she didn't come soon, but she was determined this time she wasn't going alone.

She squeezed around him, and Gabe responded, hands twitching for a second. "Hell, do that again."

Allison laughed and reached to catch hold of his neck, arching her back and luxuriating in his caresses. He slipped one hand between her thighs and teased her clit, and she moaned happily.

Just a little more. Little more.

Gabe growled in her ear. "Touch yourself."

She lowered her hand and her fingers met his. Moisture covered her fingers. He rubbed her clit, stroked along the seam where his cock disappeared into her body, and she shivered.

Gabe placed his hand over hers, joining her in the touch, making it something far more than when she played with herself, looking for release. Not only her, but him, directing, guiding, following her lead as she changed position slightly.

His other arm banded around her body, higher up, and when he leaned her forward against it, he braced her in position.

She would have asked what he was doing, but she didn't care. She trusted him. Trusted he would hold on, keep her safe. Make her satisfied.

The new position allowed him to move his hips again, and he pulled back, his cock brushing the walls of her sheath, sensitivity rising as he slid forward, forcing his way into her core. Deeper. Intimately close, the heat of the evening and the heat of their bodies making them slick. All the while his fingers worked with hers.

Her climax came between one breath and the next, flashing through and shaking her, squeezing her around his cock as she cried out.

Gabe stilled, their bodies sealed, tight and intimate. His cock impossibly hard inside her.

He groaned, the low aching hum brushing past her ear and caressing her entire body. She did that to him. Made him sound like that. Made him needy and hard and hers. At least for now.

His cock jerked, and she felt him release. Felt his hands tremble as he lost control and spent.

They stayed there, locked together for a couple more seconds. Gabe lowered them to the mattress, still spooning her, his cock lodged in her core.

She clutched his hand where his palm pressed over her belly. "Don't let go."

He rocked lightly, the additional stroke of pleasure making her moan. "You got it."

Allison closed her eyes and luxuriated in his possession. In his caring. "Can we do that again?"

"What, have sex?" His laugher rumbled against her body. "I'm pretty sure we can arrange that."

She reached up and caressed his cheek. "That too, but I meant the talking. Telling each other what's really happening. I need that, Gabe."

Because in spite of living under his roof for the past couple of months, she felt she'd barely scratched the surface. This feeling between them? It was big and powerful, but it was just the beginning.

He turned her then, leaving for a moment before coming back to lay her flat out on the mattress, their legs twined together. He stroked the hair off her face and gazed down with those star-filled eyes, and she fell a little further without even trying.

"We can do that. We've got all the time in the world." His deep voice so sure and confident.

Then he touched their lips together, and she pulled him over her, and they started all over again.

In spite of the hurtful words by the fire, and dealing with painful memories, it had turned out to be a magical night.

Chapter Twenty

Time was the one thing it turned out they didn't have. The phone call came at four in the morning not even three days later. Elle's weeping could be heard over the line, and seeing the colour drain from Allison's face made his heart break.

They'd known this was coming, known it was probably soon. But you still hoped for longer than you got.

"Is Maisey…gone?" he asked softly.

Allison shook her head. "Elle called the ambulance. They're taking her to the hospital in Red Deer."

"I'll drive you out. We can pick up Elle if she waits for us."

"Paul's driving her."

Gabe caught Allison against him and squeezed her tight. "Shower quick. I'll make the calls."

He pushed her toward the bathroom, and she walked willingly but in a daze. Gabe realized this was only the start of the day's pain.

The hour and a half drive to the hospital was quiet. Allison laid her head on his shoulder and he held her against him. It wasn't about saving her anymore; it was about being there and being a part of every bit of her life.

He'd been so afraid to tell her how he'd felt. Typical male, but letting her know had been exactly what they needed. The little smiles, the intimate glances they'd shared over the past days. All of it felt different. They were together in a more solid way, which was exactly what she needed right now. Exactly what he'd hoped for, in spite of promising to go slow.

She stopped outside her mom's room and took a big breath. Gabe squeezed her fingers. "Maisey loves you."

Allison turned her face toward him. In spite of the dark lines under her eyes, she was even more beautiful than usual. "That makes it all worthwhile, right?"

"Everything. Every ache, every sorrow."

They walked in together.

Maisey was in bed, the headboard raised so she could lean against the support. Her skin looked paper thin, her body so fragile.

"If you'd wanted to come to Red Deer to go shopping you should have just told me, Mom. I would have let you take a few days off from the restaurant." Allison stepped to the side of the bed and caught her mom's hand. She had to reach around an IV tube and another monitor, but she found a way.

Maisey smiled, and the expression transformed her face to something striking and ageless. Joy had that ability. "You know me. Slacking off any time I can."

Gabe held on to Allison, his arm draped around her waist as the ladies talked. Paul and Elle hurried in about an hour later, and Gabe pretty much just listened. Supported Allison and watched as this family who had so much love and togetherness in them—watched as they prepared to say goodbye.

Sharing with Allison the other night had been like letting go the plug on a barrel. He hadn't realized exactly how tightly wrapped he'd kept parts of himself.

She was right, though. He'd always been like this. Always wanted to save people. Only his tragedies had taken him over and he'd started doing more to save others. He'd forgotten he was allowed to save himself as well. To accept a little saving from her.

When Maisey's eyes closed in fatigue, he tugged Allison to him. Whispered in her ear. "Come on. I'm going to feed you and give you coffee."

"But Mom—"

"Will be okay for a while without you." The nurse who was checking the room nodded at his soft-spoken words. "You need to eat or you're going to collapse, and then Maisey will get out of that bed and kick my butt for not taking care of you."

Even as he said it he knew they both wished Maisey would do exactly that.

The small cafeteria was busy with people grabbing coffees and late breakfast. Gabe moved quickly through the line to return to where Allison sat, her head cradled in her arms. He slipped onto the bench seat beside her and nudged her. "Eat."

She nodded, sucking back the coffee first. They were quiet, the low buzz of voices around them so similar to the familiar noises of the barns. Even in sadness, home called to him.

Something had been running through his brain all morning. He wasn't sure how it would go over, but she'd said to talk to her.

Gabe took her fingers into his. "Allison, this may sound like a crazy idea, but hear me out."

She lifted her head, her tired gaze meeting his. "Crazy idea? What you got planned now, Angel Boy?"

He smiled. "Damn, I left my halo at home."

His quip tugged a smile to her lips. "Tell me your crazy idea."

"We should get married. Right now. In front of your mom."

She bit her bottom lip and her eyes welled with tears.

"Why not? Why not make someone who you love very happy?"

Allison squeezed his fingers. "You still trying to rescue people, Gabe Coleman?"

He shook his head. "Caring isn't rescuing. We started this entire thing for your mom's sake. I'm thinking we may as well finish it while we still can."

Gabe stuttered to a stop at the expression on her face. Damn. He was an idiot for even having brought it up. Besides, the truth was far more layered than he was admitting. He wanted to beg her to not do this just for her mother's sake, but to do it so they could really be together.

He'd never admit that to her, not here and now. Never add that kind of pressure to her already tormented world. Instead he'd offer what made the most sense.

If she wanted to break his heart down the road, he'd let her.

He cleared his throat. "I told you I loved you, and I'm not taking that back. But this doesn't mean that I think you're in love with me. Same rules apply. If you want to call it quits, after—" He didn't say it, but she had to hear it. *After Maisey was gone.* "We'll call it off quietly, no harm, no foul."

She covered their joined hands, holding on for dear life.

"Gabe, you are the best man I've ever known."

"Does that mean yes?"

She nodded.

Allison stared at the flowers in her hand. Three hours later and she was standing beside her mom's bed, waiting for Gabe to return so they could get married.

It *was* crazy.

Maisey reached out and touched her arm, and that delicate balance between joy and sorrow rose again.

It might be crazy, but it was crazily perfect.

"You two sure you want to rush this?" Maisey asked for the dozenth time.

Allison grabbed her mom's hand and held on. "If you ask that again, I'm going to start thinking you don't like Gabe."

"It's not that, and you know it. He's perfect for you, and you're so much in love. I knew from the first minute you told me about him that you'd work out fine. But you're missing all the fun parts of a wedding."

Good grief. "What parts? Making invitations, scrambling to book a church or a hall. Setting up a dinner menu? Mom. I don't care about those things. The guest list is the most important, and I've got that figured out."

Elle burst into the room, breathlessly handing over a small box. "God, I hope I did that right."

Allison hoped so too. She worried for a moment Gabe would think her surprise was stupid, then certainty rushed in and washed away those doubts. The ring might only be a prop for this make-believe wedding, but he'd get the message. He'd understand what she was trying to say.

They'd gone back that morning to give Maisey a head's up of their plans. Mom had been speechless for a moment before smiling so hard Allison knew without a doubt the ceremony was the right thing to do. Gabe whipped her out of the hospital to grab the marriage license. Dropped her off at the main doors with a promise he'd be back as soon as possible.

She'd wandered up to her mom's room in a bit of daze. It was happening so quickly and yet...

He was right. Giving her mom this one last thing to cherish made sense.

That he would go through the trouble to arrange it made something inside her care a little harder for him, and yet she clung to her promise to herself.

Sleep-deprived and emotionally devastated was not the time to make decisions about forever. She cared about Gabe, wanted to be with him. But their entire relationship had been built around a deception.

No matter how drawn to him, she was not going to imagine herself in love. Not until she could claim her mind was clear and it was more than an emotional decision.

The door opened, and Gabe's mom and brother stepped in. Dana went straight up to the bed and no-nonsense offered Maisey a hug.

Rafe stood back a little more awkwardly, looking around at the medical equipment in the room. "I called Gabe to let him know we're here. He said he'd be back within the next twenty minutes."

Allison let the ladies talk quietly, Dana standing next to her mom and holding her hand. They seemed to be doing just fine, so instead she concentrated on Rafe who looked as if he'd preferred to be anywhere other than where he was.

She caught him by the arm. "Thanks for bringing your mom out."

Rafe's bright smile surprised her. "You kidding? Gabe's getting hitched. I wouldn't miss this for anything. It's a bit sooner than he mentioned, but you probably want to tie him down good before the snow flies."

The kid was trying. "True. I didn't want him to get away."

Then she got Rafe to do some rearranging of the room to keep him busy. She had no idea what exactly was going to happen in terms of the ceremony, but even if they changed their minds about sitting or standing, hauling chairs around kept the boy occupied and out of trouble for the moment.

Elle had slipped out of the room shortly after handing over the ring box. Now she returned, Paul entering with her.

Her sister held out a bright blue knit jacket. "Here. Your wedding attire."

Allison shook her head but pulled it on. "You're a goof."

"Hey, you always said you were going to do that 'something old, something new' thing when you got married. Here's your blue, and I suppose your borrowed, since it belongs to one of the nurses in paediatrics. I have to return it after we're done."

Maisey and Dana were paying attention now as well, and the older ladies' laughter brightened the place until it seemed a thousand rainbows had settled in the room.

Allison soaked in the memory.

Paul caught her in a hug. Then he went and helped Rafe, which Allison figured meant he'd had enough of the emotional stuff and all. She let him go and instead looked around with a growing sense of peace.

Yes, her mom was weak. Frail. Leaving them. But the joy in the room was undeniable because Maisey made it like that. Made the love of the family more than enough to help them through this day, no matter what came next.

When the door opened again and Gabe walked in, Allison's heart could barely stand how full it felt. He walked straight over to her and kissed her. Held her close and cradled her against him.

She wasn't sure which one of the guys wolf-whistled, and she didn't care. She gave as good as she got.

"I thought you had to say the vows before you got to the kissing," Maisey teased.

"I ordered the special ceremony." Gabe released Allison, but only enough to slide his arm around her waist and tug her to his side. He offered a smile to Maisey. "We get the good stuff beginning, middle and end."

The man in the suit who had accompanied Gabe came forward. "Levon Tate. I'll be your commissioner for the vows."

Allison shook his hand, then introduced the family. The guilt at pulling another deception over on Gabe's mom and brother passed faster than she'd expected. If anyone would understand, Dana would. The woman stood beside Maisey, offering silent support as Allison's mom shifted into a more comfortable position.

No one said a word about Ben not being there.

Small talk, organizing. Before she knew it she was standing at the foot of the bed, the rest of the family gathered around.

Gabe stood before her. Big, tenderhearted, generous Gabe, who had given and given so much in the months behind them.

Like he always gave.

He took off his hat and laid it on the bed. Allison snatched it up and put it back where it belonged.

Gabe's slow grin broke out. "You want to make sure you're marrying your cowboy, is that it?"

Elle giggled, and the rest of them responded with subdued laughter.

"You know it." She squeezed his fingers and took a deep breath.

They repeated the form vows. Simple. Plain. The generic words were surprisingly intimate. He swore he'd care for her. In the good and bad, in the happy and sad times. Richer or poorer. From then on forward.

She stared up at him, his familiar flannel shirt stretched over his broad shoulders. The cowboy hat she'd pressed back in place tilted so she could see every nuance of emotion that showed. And he let her see it all. The caring, the longing. The passion he felt.

Her throat was tight as she repeated the words.

The commissioner held out his hands. "Well, other than a little signing we're just about done. Who will be the witnesses?"

Gabe nodded at her.

She turned. "Mom, will you, please?"

Maisey hadn't let go of the flowers Allison had placed in her hands at the start of the event. Now she handed them carefully to Dana. Brushed down the front of her gown slowly. "I would be proud."

The book was passed over. Allison blinked hard. So much dignity and love shone in Maisey's every gesture. Paul snapped off another shot, moving around the room to capture everything for them.

Gabe cleared his throat. "So, little bro. You grown up enough to help us make it official?"

Rafe jerked upright from where he'd been leaning on the wall. "Me? I thought Ma was going to—"

"I asked you. Or did you forget how to sign your name already now that you're out of school?" Gabe squeezed Allison's hand, and she stifled her laughter.

"Fu—" Rafe's mouth snapped shut as he glanced at Dana. She just shook her head as he sheepishly stepped forward. "Guess I can."

Allison added her name next, watched Gabe carefully pen his after hers. Strong letters, firm control. Everything done with a purpose, deliberately. Like everything else she'd learned about him, even the little thing with his brother—there had to be a reason.

The commissioner tucked the book under his arm and grinned after he finished the last of the form phrases, the ones saying she and Gabe were husband and wife. "May you enjoy a long lifetime together."

Gabe lifted her chin with his finger, his touch delicate and tender. He stared into her eyes. "Two lifetimes won't be enough."

It might be too soon, the timing was all wrong, but if she was honest, that's the moment she fell headlong in love with her Angel Boy.

Chapter Twenty-One

August passed with a tortuous slowness. The good part was her mom had taken a slight turn for the better. Maisey wasn't well enough to come home—everyone knew that was never again a possibility. The main hospital transferred her back to the small extended-care health unit in Rocky, which meant life returned to a simpler routine. Instead of dropping in at the house to visit, Allison stopped at the center. Her and Gabe sometimes, or her and Elle. Taking in every last moment between continuing on with the restaurant and the rest of their work.

Distracting themselves. Moving forward.

The one thing she'd never, ever expected was for a husband to be a part of the waiting. Having Gabe as a part of her world, as something greater than a friend still seemed impossible. Unreal.

Allison looked across the room at him. His hair had gotten longer in the past while, he'd been so busy running between the work of the day and the time with her.

Time spent fooling around, or resting, or curled up together as she chatted with Maisey. Passionate moments, relaxing ones. Sad and yet needed ones.

Tonight when she'd gotten home from visiting Mom, she'd found him with paperwork strewn over the table. Puss in Boots was curled up in his lap, and Gabe absently petted him as he pored over the papers.

He refused her help.

"You've worked all day. Put your feet up. I'll get this done." Gabe kissed her briefly then turned back to his mess.

That was two hours ago and he hadn't said a word since. Even the kitten abandoned him to stalk imaginary enemies under the bed.

She finished her cup of tea and wandered over to stand behind him. Hands smoothing his tense shoulders as she pressed her thumbs into the firm muscles. "Tough job tonight?"

He leaned his head to the side as she found a knot, twisting as if to keep her focused on the spot. "Least favourite part of ranching, to be honest."

"I hear you." She leaned down and kissed his neck, the warm earthy scent of his skin filling her head and making her ache. "You need to finish this now? Or can I distract you?"

"Can you distract me? Woman, you distract me by breathing."

Allison smiled and trailed her fingers through his hair. "You've gotten a little wild, cowboy. What do you say I give you a trim?"

She scraped her fingernails against his scalp, and he groaned, leaning his shoulders back and pressing their bodies together as much as possible with the chair between them. "You keep touching me and you can do anything you damn well please."

She kissed his neck again before escaping to grab the scissors. "Take off your shirt and pants."

Gabe chuckled. "What kind of trim you aim to give me?"

She was still smiling when she returned to the room. She had to swallow hard to stop from drooling over the sight that greeted her.

He'd followed her orders, all right. Stripped to nothing but his boxers. The chair was farther from the table than before, resting on solid wood floorboards instead of the area carpet.

He had one leg stretched forward as he reclined comfortably. Arms crossed over his broad chest, the dusting of hair bleached from his hours outside. A rancher's tan line ran across his biceps—the deeper golden brown of sun-kissed skin on his forearms contrasting with the paler area usually covered by his T-shirt sleeves. She'd seen him bared to the waist occasionally, wearing nothing up top but a slick of sweat as he worked in the hot sunshine. More often, though, the men laboured on without bothering to strip. No fashion-show outfits, no trying to produce model-perfect tans.

The result was breathtaking. Rock-solid muscles formed from backbreaking labour.

She took her time admiring the view. His chest, his shoulders. When she finally lifted her gaze to look into his face, a lazy grin curved his mouth and heat shone in his eyes.

"You sure you want to cut my hair? Because the way you're looking me over, I'm thinking of all kinds of other things we could do instead."

He adjusted his stance slightly and she spotted another part of him that had grown rock solid and hard.

Allison moved in close, stopping to press her hands on his thighs and lean over him. "Haircut first, maybe other things later."

His fingers slipped around her neck. "Only maybe?"

The kiss he gave her made her toes curl, but this time she wasn't going to give in. She planted her free hand squarely on his chest and pressed herself away.

He was staring at her lips.

Oh yeah, she wanted to take this further as well. "Okay, more than maybe. Now behave."

She walked behind him, first dropping the scissors on the side table where they were easily accessible. Then she gave in to temptation and touched him. Fingers buried in the unruly strands, pulling them into line. His hair was lovely to play with, the light curls at the end sweeping up and under at random. "You've got the most gorgeous hair. Makes me jealous."

"You can have it. Girlie hair—gets to this point and I feel like a sheep."

"Hmmm, so soft." She leaned in, addicted to the taste of his neck. Lick. Nibble. All the while she worked with her fingers.

He reached back and caught her, his hand skimming over her head, holding her to him.

"Cut my damn hair, or I'm calling this off and taking you to the bedroom for some ravishing."

Ravishing would be good. Only...

Allison smiled. Why not? She pulled off her top and slipped her pants down before grabbing the scissors and stepping in front of him.

His mouth stretched in a wide smile.

She held up a hand. "You seem to need distracting. One way or another, I am cutting your hair."

She straddled his legs, moving in close enough her butt rested in the middle of his thighs.

"Nice." Gabe stroked his knuckles along the edge of her bra. "Only, if you're going to be snipping hair, maybe you should take this off. Don't want to get it messy."

She used two hands to guide the scissors, carefully making the first cut. A blond curl tumbled to the floor. "Go slowly and you can do anything you'd like."

What he liked, it seemed, was to drive them both mad. Gabe stayed relatively motionless as she trimmed the front of his hair, careful to toss the snippings to the side. He cupped his big hand around her waist, his thumbs the only things that moved. The gentle brush as he stroked back and forth tickled her skin, sending tiny shock waves like warning signals to the rest of her body to be prepared for the next assault.

When she stood to reach around him, he pulled her closer, making contact between his warm rib cage, her torso. Slowly, as ordered, Gabe slipped his hands to her bra fastener and loosened the clips.

She lifted a section of hair between her fingers, using her knuckles as a guideline for trimming. One shoulder strap fell away. The other. She moved her hand to gather another portion. Gabe carefully caught her wrist, tugging her arm lower until the elastic of the bra slipped free.

"You're very good at working cautiously," she admired.

"It's like harnessing a skittish colt."

Allison laughed. "So now I'm one of your horses, am I?"

"Hmm, I'll cover you any time."

Oh dear. The images his words brought to mind. She let him slip off the other side of her bra before even attempting to return to her task.

She pressed to tiptoe to reach around his neck. Gabe took total advantage and caught hold of her breast, lifting the mound the final bit until he could suck her nipple into his mouth.

She had to concentrate hard to keep control while he played with her breasts.

By the time she'd managed to complete the back, or at least as best she could from that angle, she was tingling and needy. Wet between her thighs, her core aching for a touch. She sat slowly, sliding along his body. Making contact with the solid length of his erection. Both of them groaning out in pleasure and frustration.

"You done?" Gabe growled.

She put the scissors aside and lifted her hands to his hair, fluffing the strands. The cut wasn't perfect, but it was better. "I guess."

The words were still escaping and she was already in the air. She flung her arms around him, clutching his shoulders as he carried her to the bedroom and beyond.

He lowered her to the floor in the shower stall, reached behind her and flipped on the taps. The cold water hit her back the same second his lips covered hers, and her gasp of surprise was lost.

It seemed his hands were everywhere at once. Skimming over her breasts, between her legs. Briefly touching as he stripped away their underwear. She returned the favour, and stroked and played as well, letting her palms roam over the solid lines of his form. He twisted them until water cascaded over their heads, pouring over their faces as they gasped for air.

As suddenly as he'd begun, he jerked the taps off and lifted her again, his cock caught between them as he stared her in the eyes. "That takes care of the hair. Now you're damn well going to get everything you asked for."

The pounding in her blood screamed *bring it on.*

He dropped her to the mattress, water droplets still clinging to their skin. He wasn't gentle, flipping her over onto her belly and dragging her to the edge of the bed. The crinkle of a condom wrapper being ripped open was followed by his hands touching her intimately, a finger slipping into her core.

"You're wet. Ready for me?"

"Always."

His cock nudged her opening, the broad head stretching her. Gabe leaned over her and thrust in.

She screamed. His name? Some other word? She wasn't sure because what followed felt so damn good she got lost in sensation. He fucked her hard, pounding against her ass, fingers clutching tightly. He put his teeth to her shoulder, and for a second she thought he really was going to bite down like a stallion rutting on his partner.

Excitement rose so rapidly she cried out, rocking back to meet him with equal fervour, his frantic gasps and groans adding to her enjoyment.

This is what she did to him. This is what she inspired in the man. Desperate need, urgent desire.

Pleasure bloomed in her core, and she jerked under him, his hard chest pressed to her back even as his hips continued to pulse. He caught her hands in his, linking their fingers, meshing them together as he rested his forehead at the base of her neck and jolted out his release.

Hearts pounding, blood racing. His weight pressing her against the mattress.

Allison let out a long, slow breath as soon as she could do more than gasp. "Holy. Shit."

Gabe chuckled as he peeled himself off her and helped her crawl more fully onto the bed, collapsing beside her. "I can't seem to get enough of you, woman."

"Never knew getting a haircut turned you on so much, Angel Boy."

He stroked his fingers over her naked shoulder as he settled them skin-to-skin. "You cut off my curls—I lost all strength to resist."

"I'm Delilah, now?"

He lifted her chin. "You're mine. That's what you are."

The kiss that followed said the same thing as the words, and wild lovemaking. That she was his seemed so incredible. Impossible.

But the hope of forever hovered, and she was nearly ready to grasp hold of the truth.

Maisey had become frail. Fragile.

Allison kissed her mom's cheek and mouthed "I'll be right back" at him before slipping from the room.

Gabe stared into space. He should be trying to find a solution to his problem, but he was so damn tired. Hopelessness had a way of wearing a man down. No matter how much they'd managed to accomplish over the summer, the numbers just weren't there. In less than a week he had to square up things with the bank, and winning the bet looked impossible.

Ben had taken to showing up every day, not saying anything, still doing the tasks Gabe left written on the board in the barn. Always taking extra time to get in Gabe's face and wordlessly accuse him of being a failure. Gabe was so fucking close to losing the battle, and he had run out of ideas at this point of what could make the final difference.

"Gabe?"

He shot to his feet and stood beside Maisey. "You need something?"

She smiled wearily. "You're always ready to do things, aren't you? I like that about you."

Gabe took her hand, holding it carefully. Parchment-like skin stretched over her thin bones. "Be pretty boring to sit all the time, I'm thinking. You want me to take you drag racing down the halls in your wheelchair?"

Her laughter came, thinner, more brittle, but still full of joy. "I think I'll stay here. But I do want to talk to you before my daughter comes back."

"What's up?" Gabe pulled his chair over with a foot and settled where Maisey could see him.

"She's stubborn."

"I wonder who she gets that from?"

Maisey lifted her hand and shook her finger in his face. "Stop sweet-talking me and listen."

"Yes, ma'am."

"I know she's worked hard over the years to become independent. And I'm proud of her. But I want to give her a gift, like I gave Elle and Paul, and she's been refusing me."

Gabe leaned forward. "That sounds strange. When did Allison ever turn you down?"

"Now." Maisey sighed heavily. "It's not as if I can take things with me, Gabe. You know that."

Her sense of humour had grown on him. "Well, not unless you've got special arrangements made the rest of us don't know about."

She smiled then gestured beside the bed. "In the file. That stubborn girl of mine has argued with me twice, but I'm smart enough to get what I want."

Gabe followed her pointing finger and pulled out an envelope addressed to Allison. He slipped the thin parchment open to discover an astonishingly large cheque.

"Maisey, what the hell is this?" Manners totally forgotten.

She raised a hand, palm toward him. "Hear me out. It's for Allison. I know the children will get money when I'm gone, but that's not the same. This is from *me*. I want to give each of my children something for them to use as they please, and I want to do it while I'm still the one in charge of the giving. The other two accepted it, why can't Allison?"

He opened his mouth to protest, then stopped.

What she said made perfect sense. A cheque now, or a lump sum from the estate down the road—it didn't seem to make much difference to him, but if it was important to her, why not? He'd gone out of his way to fast track a wedding partly to make this woman happy.

Why on earth would he argue with her now over something so basic as money, as shocking as the amount might be?

"You're right. It's your money and you can do what you want with it."

Maisey's eyes gleamed. For a second he spotted the mischievous streak he'd always loved about Allison. Seems she came by it honestly.

"You are a fine young man." Maisey leaned back on her pillows and smiled contentedly.

"You're only saying that because I'm wrapped around your little finger right where you've got all the men in your life." Gabe cradled her hand again, scared to squeeze for fear of hurting her.

"And don't tell her about it until after I'm gone," she commanded.

Only Maisey would go there so boldly. It wasn't his first choice, but would keeping this secret really hurt anything? "I promise to keep the money safe in trust until Allison is ready to receive it."

Maisey nodded absently. "Now, let me rest. It's so hard keeping up with you children."

Gabe remained where he was as she closed her eyes and fell silent. He didn't want to pull away because she had him trapped, fingers now literally wrapped around his.

Generous, loving...he was so glad he'd gotten to have this woman as a part of his life, even for a brief while. Another kind of family—extended family by choice, not blood.

The ache inside was going to kill him. So much history was tied up in his own extended family—the Six Pack, the Whiskey Creek, and the Moonshine clans all brought something unique to the mix.

He didn't want to lose his bet. It would be like letting down the entire family, not just his ma and Rafe.

He didn't want to lose what he had growing with Allison. One minute he was certain she was ready to confess how she felt about him, the next moment the occasion slipped away.

He was stuck in the middle of a rocky place and an impossible decision, and it seemed there was no choice he could make that would be the right one.

One way or another, he had to do something he was going to hate like hell.

Chapter Twenty-Two

Allison leaned her head against the windowpane. Not even the warmth of Puss in Boots in her arms could force her gloom away. The rain streaking down the other side of the glass echoed her mood perfectly.

Mom was fading, but not so quickly it made any sense to spend every moment in the hospital waiting for the final curtain to fall. Every night since the Labour Day weekend, Gabe had dragged her home when Maisey fell asleep. And every night Allison said her final goodbyes in case it was the last time.

Morning didn't dawn bright and clear in her heart, so the rain they'd woken to on this Wednesday seemed appropriate. Gabe grumbled about the weather, then left to start his day, promising to take a break and meet her for lunch.

The front door slammed against the wall, frightening Puss into jumping free and hiding under the couch. Allison jerked from her musings, wondering what had Gabe so riled. Shock turned to dismay when Ben Coleman stumbled around the corner from the porch.

"Where's that goddamn son of a bitch?" he snarled, water dripping from his slicker, his wet hair plastered over his forehead and halfway covering his eyes.

He looked mad. Insane-type mad, and Allison backed away, edging into the living area. "He headed to the ranch early. Said something about the harvester. Look in the barns maybe?"

She wanted him out of her house. At the best of times Ben was frightening. This version of the man terrified the living daylights out of her.

Ben stopped in the kitchen area, looking her over with disgust. "You're so satisfied, aren't you? All smug that you two pulled one over on me."

If she'd ever wanted Gabe to walk in unexpectedly, this would be the moment. "I don't know what you're talking about. Ben, let's go to your house and we can find him. You can talk to—"

"He used you, you know. Nothing changes about that one. Just like he's always been. Untrustworthy, unreliable."

Gabe unreliable? Good grief, if she weren't shaking from having Ben glowering at her she would have laughed at the idea.

"He's not here," she repeated. Allison pointed to the door, praying Ben would take the hint.

He stepped a little closer and her heart skipped a beat. "You give him the money, girl?"

Allison hesitated. "What money?"

Ben's face lit with a twisted kind of delight. "What money, she says. Oh, so did the boy fuck you over without your knowledge? Doesn't surprise me one bit. Bet that's why he started up with you in the first place, planning to take advantage of your bank account."

Her mind whirled as she tried to figure out what he was talking about. If anyone had taken advantage of anyone at the start, it was her using Gabe. "Ben. If you want to discuss the ranch and money, you need to find your son. I'm not involved in that part. I gave him suggestions for changes, and I helped with applications—"

"And he helped himself to your money and paid off the goddamn bet."

She froze. "A bet?"

"That he could turn this shit-hole of a ranch around with your help. Your help, indeed. It's not information he married you for."

Something inside went icy cold. The rain outside could have turned to snow for how frigid it was in the room. "He is turning the ranch around. The changes that have been approved, and all the plans he's got in place, are incredible. Within five years the Angel Coleman section will be a fully organic operation."

"Five years? He didn't have that long. He had until this week. Tuesday, he waltzed into the fucking bank and cleared everything off, and I know that's fucking impossible. Where the hell did he get the money?" Ben kicked the nearest chair, sending the heavy wooden object flying into the table.

Allison looked around for an escape route. "I don't know. Ask the person who can help you, because I don't know."

Ben stomped a couple paces forward, grabbing the back of another chair. His knuckles turned white. His voice one step up from a growl. "I don't want to talk to him, or see him. Just the sight of him makes me sick. Told him that years ago when he killed his brother, and every fucking day since he was stupid enough to come back and I—"

"What?" Absolute fury flared inside at his words; the fear and the cold vanished in a blaze of anger. She might be confused over the bet, and the money, and whatever the hell else Ben was going on about, but this? She understood completely and wouldn't accept. "Shut up. You shut up, right now, Ben Coleman. My God, you really said that to your son? Gabe did not kill Michael."

Ben snapped his mouth closed, features twisted in anger, and threw the chair he held to the side. It crashed to the floor, and Allison cursed herself for being all kinds of a fool. Trapped in a house with a man she didn't trust. Great time to go off like a crazy woman.

Still, rage gave her balls. She snapped up her arm to point at the door. "Get out. Get out of my house."

"If you had any sense you'd dump the bastard. He's used you."

"And I used him. It's called a relationship. Something you don't know anything about."

She wanted to go on. To rant at him. To scream. That he'd actually accused Gabe of killing Michael, and continued to torment him for this long was incredibly perverse and hugely wrong. This is what Gabe had come back to? What he'd put up with to save his family from the man's poison?

Puss in Boots raced across the floor. Ben swung a foot that just missed the little thing as he scurried for safety.

Allison nearly lost it. Everything in her wanted to rush forward and hurt Ben. To punch and kick and cut him like he'd been cutting into Gabe's soul over the years. Logic made her stand her ground and simply scream the word again. "Out."

If he didn't go voluntarily, she wasn't sure what she'd do. Trying to dodge past him would be her only chance. Snatch up the kitten, and make a break for it. The rain against the window spattered in gusts, a syncopated sound. Not reassuring and calming like rain could be, but violent and hurtful. Destructive. Cold.

Eerily like the man in front of her.

Ben stared at her for a minute before glancing around the cabin, his face gone expressionless again. He turned to go.

A soaking wet Gabe burst in wearing no coat, only his drenched T-shirt, water dripping from the brim of his hat.

Ben jostled past his son in an attempt to leave.

Quick as a whip, Gabe snatched hold, the muscles in his biceps bulging as he fixed Ben in place. "Not so fast. What are you doing here?"

Ben jerked his arm, but Gabe held him. "Telling her the truth. That you're a cheat and a thief and no better than a goddamn murderer."

Allison stepped back as Gabe rushed forward, slamming Ben against the wall and pinning him in place. As glad as she was to see Gabe, this isn't what she wanted. "Gabe, let him go. It's not worth it."

"He's not worth it," Gabe spat out, shoving his father toward the door as he released him.

She folded her arms around herself, holding in the shaking that wanted to take control. Gabe stepped to Allison's side, keeping an eye on Ben the entire time.

He darted a glance over her, then placed himself protectively between them as he snapped at his father. "Rafe said you had a problem with me. If that's so, then you talk to me. Not Ma, not Allison, not Rafe. You be a goddamn man and deal with me, you understand?"

"Because you're calling all the shots now?" Ben taunted. "As soon as I tell my brothers how you won the bet, they'll back me up on kicking your ass out of here."

Gabe laughed. "You're wrong. It's all dealt with, square and proper. The bank is happy for the next year, and that's what you dared me to do. Hell, it's what you couldn't bloody well do yourself."

"That's not true."

"You hoped I'd fail so you could blame me, like you've blamed me for everything else that's gone wrong over the years. Even Michael."

Ben sputtered in anger. "Don't you talk about him. Don't you ever talk about him to me."

"You talk about him all the time, don't you? Reminding me I was supposed to be there to save him." Gabe stepped forward, his cheeks flushed, hands fisted at his sides. "Well, I wasn't and every day I regret it, but I wasn't the one who told him to go out and have a good time. I wasn't the one who slipped enough money into Michael's pocket he could drink himself into a bloody stupor."

Ben's face went white, his hands trembling. "How did you know that?" he whispered.

"Michael called me." Gabe snapped. "Already into the liquor. He teased me to come join him. Said he was flush with cash and he'd forgive me for being a stick in the mud. We could both have a blast on the money you'd given him."

Oh God.

Gabe took a deep breath, dragging his hand through his hair. "That's the end of it, Ben. I won't meekly accept your taunts anymore. Michael's death is not your fault, but it's not mine either."

Ben's eyes reflected guilt even as anger twisted his features. The pain of what he must have felt would have made Allison more sympathetic if she hadn't discovered the man had deliberately tormented Gabe for years.

As it was, Allison wanted to grab hold of Gabe and offer her support. Let him know he wasn't alone. Wanted to hold him until all the pain had vanished.

Ben straightened, his gaze turning on Allison.

Gabe spoke softer. Slower, the calm man who she'd come to know so well pulling himself to the foreground. "It didn't work, Ben. Your plan to get rid of me. I won. Admit it."

Ben's anger still roiled. He should have retreated after that revelation, but it seemed as if all his focus remained on hurting Gabe. Allison wondered what the man thought he could possibly say to defend himself or recast Gabe as the villain.

But when he spoke, it wasn't about Michael at all.

"Did Mrs. Parker give you money?" Ben demanded.

What a ridiculous question. Now Allison understood what Ben had been accusing Gabe of earlier. She waited for Gabe to deny it.

Nothing came.

Nothing but confusion.

"How do you know about that?" Gabe stammered.

Ben sneered. Allison was already turning away to focus on Gabe. "My mom gave you money?"

He hesitated then nodded. Her stomach turned over.

"Ask him if it was before or after you two got hitched," Ben gloated, his words thrashing out like a whip being cracked.

The implication was clear. That Gabe had only married her for money.

After all her dealings with Gabe over the past months, and the knowledge of how twisted and hurtful Ben was and always had been, knowing whose word to trust was simple.

Ben was on the losing side.

Yet a part inside her felt ill at the thought of being used. If it was only about money, there was no need for Gabe to extend the deception beyond their initial relationship—she'd already committed to help him if he helped her.

She looked into his eyes and saw the fear there. The hurt. The resigned acceptance that someone else was about to falsely accuse him. To take from him without giving.

In this case, without giving him a chance.

All their time together gave her the courage to lay her hand gently on his arm and trust him.

Trust him to not tear her fragile heart in two.

"Gabe. You had a bet with your father. How did you manage to work things out?"

He answered instantly. "I sold some land."

"What?" Ben roared as Allison blinked in surprise. "You had no right to do that. You had—"

"I goddamn did have the right. We still have the same amount of land as we had before. The section I traded with the Whiskey Creek clan is worth more on paper, so they paid the difference. That's where I got the money. That's why we can make a go of it for another year until the changes Allison and I implemented turn into profit-making ventures."

"You've got no signatures. You've got nothing from me to make that land exchange legal," Ben protested vehemently.

"They're family. *Real* family who give a shit that we all survive. Uncle George saw the merit in the swap, even without your approval upfront. It's not as if they weren't getting something of value, and the land is still all in the Coleman name. Uncle Mike and Uncle George helped me last Friday. We did up a rough draft and signed it with a gentleman's agreement. The Whiskey Creek Ranch transferred the money into my account and I went from there.

"If you want to be petty enough to throw the entire Coleman spread into chaos out of some perverse need to hurt me, you're a sorrier son of a bitch than I thought." Gabe grabbed Allison's hand. She held on for dear life.

Ben turned without another word and walked away.

The cabin was strangely quiet for a minute. The rain pounded, water dripped outside the open front door, but something peaceful came in to replace the violent storm that had been roaring through the room moments earlier.

Allison stood in silence, not sure what to ask. What she needed to know. In the midst of the entire chaos, and the fear, one thing had registered the hardest.

The only thing she really needed was Gabe.

Chapter Twenty-Three

He was still sopping wet, but damn if he could wait a minute longer. Gabe hauled Allison against him. Pressed her head to his chest and dug his fingers into her hair.

Clinging to her and trying to convince himself she was safe.

"I was so damn scared." Her voice shook.

Something inside exploded. Ruthless anger at his father. "If he comes near you again I swear I'll—"

"I don't care if I am scared, I'll kick him hard and run. Mean, cruel, ignorant bastard." Allison reached up and caught his face in her hands. "You are not any of those things he accused you of. You're good and you're kind, and should be proud of everything you've accomplished. And you're a saint for not sharing what you knew about him sooner."

She kissed him and he took it all in. The stroke of her mouth against his, the way her breasts pressed tight to his chest, the moisture soaking her as well. The way her words poured in and stroked his aching soul.

Then she released him, pulled back her fist and punched him in the gut. Or tried to—he caught her before the blow could land.

"Hey, what's that about?"

Allison jerked her hand free and crossed her arms in front of her chest as she glared at him. "Why was that the first time I heard about the bet? And what the hell is going on with my mother giving you money? I just about got whiplash from being jerked around during that conversation."

"I can explain."

"Make it snappy. I'm pissed at you."

He chuckled. "I noticed."

Her glare got hotter, and he rushed to clarify at least parts of the question. Gabe slipped past her to close the front door and pull off his boots as he spoke.

"The bet started the night—good Lord, it seems like years ago now—Canada Day. After the picnic. The same day everything first came out with your mom."

The memory burst over her. "The first day we made love."

"That too. There wasn't any reason to tell you, not in the middle of what else was going on. Plus the bet didn't really matter."

She frowned. "What? How can you say that?"

"It didn't," he insisted. "We were already doing everything we could to make changes, and you knowing I had a deadline wouldn't have effected what you suggested, would it?"

She wrinkled her nose. "No. I guess not."

"You know not. All along you've talked about being realistic. Even though accepting the bet wasn't sensible, it was my only choice. I still feel kind of sick at the final solution. I guess it's worth losing some prime land if it means surviving the extra years we need for transition."

Allison shook her head. "Stubborn fool."

She grabbed him by the hand and pulled him into the bedroom.

"Not stubborn. Just..."

"Trying to save me the worry?"

She'd got him on that one. "Yeah."

Allison pushed him toward the bed. She nabbed a towel from the bathroom and threw it at his head. "Now you're a dumb fool."

Gabe stripped off his shirt and rubbed the material over his torso and head, waiting for the final shoe to fall.

She removed her sweater, the one he'd gotten soaked by hugging her while dripping wet. Stepped in front of him and stilled his hands. How someone so much smaller could seem to loom over him was rather impressive.

"What about my mom?"

He groaned. "She swore me to secrecy. Do I really have to tell you the details?"

Her eyes rolled upward and she grimaced. "Dammit, did she sweet-talk you into accepting money for me?"

"What was I supposed to do?" he complained. "She turned those big eyes on me, and it was like watching a puppy beg. I couldn't say no."

"And you didn't think you should tell me?"

He caught her and stopped her fidgeting, trapping her hands in his and pulling her between his legs. "I couldn't tell you because she asked me not to. Keeping the gift a secret wasn't hurting anything. The money is in a separate account, and I can sign it over anytime you want. Only I think you should pretend it's not there, that you don't know about it. That would make your mom the happiest."

"Happier pulling one over on me than me saying thank you?"

He nodded.

She snorted. "You're probably right." Allison buried her face against him and snuggled in tight. "Oh God, Gabe, I'm so exhausted."

He held her. Little by little their breaths synchronized, the tension in her body fading. She had one palm pressed to his naked chest, slowly tracing designs with her fingertips.

He felt every stroke as if she were permanently branding him.

"Why were you soaking wet and not wearing a jacket?" she asked.

That one was easy. "When Rafe came bursting into the barn to tell me Ben had tore off, madder than a hornet, I jumped. I'd parked across the way and had to run through the field to get to my truck to make sure you were okay. I didn't trust him."

He'd driven like a damn madman. Having something happen to her because he wasn't there in time—even the thought of it tore him up inside.

Not being a part of her life would be nearly as bad. No way he could let this go for any longer, but hell if he could decide the best way to convince her this was real.

He could blurt it out, or arrange to take her out for dinner. Maybe wait until they'd finished fooling around, but none of those options were right. He'd already said he'd loved her, but it seemed to need repeating.

Bigger. Louder.

The heavy rain dancing on the ceiling had changed to a steady fall, the wind calmer, and inspiration hit.

"Come on." He scooped her up. Ignored her squeal of protest as he carried her through the house and out the front door.

They were both instantly soaked, his hair completely wet this time with his hat abandoned.

Allison clung to his neck and laughed. "What are you doing, you crazy cowboy?"

He walked in his stocking feet all the way across to where the trail led up the small rise at the back of the cabin. "I need to show you something."

Gabe placed her down carefully, her bare toes resting on the thick grass. He knelt on one knee and pulled her to sit on his thigh, her eyes level with his.

Allison shook her head as she laughed, one arm looped over his shoulders. "Rain dance? Harvest ritual I'm not aware of?"

He would totally make sacrifices to the gods of nature if he had to. "I want you to know what I'm offering."

The little crease between her brows that appeared at his words was cute, but he refused to be distracted. He pointed back where they'd come from. "One nearly finished rustic cabin."

Her frown broke into a smile. "Gabe?"

He kept going, pointing over the rise, passing his hand from east to west. "One section of not yet, but on its way to being self-sufficient, organic grazing and seed land."

She fell silent as he caught her right hand and pressed their linked hands against his chest. "And one slightly beat-up heart. All of them are yours. For real. Forever."

Her bright gaze darted over his face. "What are you saying?"

"I'm saying I love you. And I think you love me. Isn't it about damn time you admit it?"

She bit her lip and sniffled once. Then again. Then the sniffle turned into a smile and she laughed. Softly at first, then louder. Laughter that carried over the land and the little cabin, and filled his heart with exactly what he needed.

It was infectious and addictive. Her smile, the sound of her joy—

There it was again. What she'd brought to him. Joy. In the midst of the tears, in the midst of the rain.

She stroked his cheek, wiping the moisture away, and he savoured her touch. Loved how in the middle of trying to save her, she'd saved him.

Gabe played with the ring that adorned her finger. "Does the fact I made you laugh mean yes?"

She leaned closer and whispered in his ear. "It means I love you too."

The words hit like a branding iron. Scorching deep, permanently marking him, and he couldn't have been happier.

He caught her by the cheeks, cradling her face, and kissed her. Full out, no holds barred, marking her as much as she'd done to him. The rain streaking down to baptize them with a fresh, clean start.

When they separated, she shook her head in wonder. "Never expected this to happen when I raced over to your place at the start of the summer."

"One season of changes." He brushed her lips with his thumb and spoke softly as he leaned in for another kiss. "I can hardly wait to see what we can accomplish in five."

Chapter Twenty-Four

The scent of autumn in the air warned winter approached, but for one more week Indian summer had burst out bringing glorious hot days and sultry starlit nights. A light breeze danced over the tall grasses to set them swaying, the river beyond them gurgling and rushing forward like usual.

Allison tipped the container and let the ashes trickle out.

Elle clutched the fingers of her other hand hard, Paul's hand rested on her shoulder. Sorrow lay like a blanket over them all, only the pain wasn't unbearable.

Sending her mom off on a day that screamed happiness seemed appropriate.

A few steps behind them the horses shuffled their feet. Gabe stood patiently holding the reins as he waited for the family to finish saying goodbye.

They'd been saying it all summer long.

"I miss her, but I'm..." Elle shook her head sadly as she turned. "I'm glad she's not suffering. That she's happy and at peace, and there's nothing that can hurt her anymore."

"I love that we were all there when she went." Allison snuck her fingers free so she could wipe the tears from her eyes. "Smiling—just like always."

Paul didn't speak at first. Cleared his throat and stared over the land. "I understand better now why Mom did it. She wanted to be strong for us, didn't she?"

"She *was* strong. To the end." Elle caught them both in a tight hug before stepping back and blowing her nose into a hankie. "I've got to go. I love you guys."

"Mind if I walk with you?" Paul asked.

Elle shook her head.

"I'll come by the house in the morning," Allison said, "Right after breakfast."

Paul leaned over and kissed her cheek, "See you at the restaurant in the afternoon." He tipped his head toward Gabe. "Take care of her."

"I will," Gabe promised.

Her brother and sister walked slowly back toward the trail that led to where they'd parked. Allison watched them until they disappeared into the trees.

It hurt terribly to have Maisey gone, but her family—they were still there for each other. Their family hadn't disappeared when their mom died.

She tucked the small box back into Patches's saddlebag and turned to find Gabe at her side, his love-filled eyes staring down.

"You were the best daughter she could have ever hoped for."

Allison rested her cheek against his chest and gazed over the land. He rubbed her back, his strength and power right there for her to cling to if she needed. But what she appreciated even more was how he let her go when she straightened. How he accepted her tight hug.

He didn't just try to save her, he let her save him as well.

"Ready to ride for a while?" Gabe passed her the reins.

Allison swung into the saddle and nodded. "You never did point out the section of land you switched with the Whiskey Creek Colemans. Can we get there from here?"

He laughed. "Gabe's Folly? Sure, I can show you that."

"Oh no, did the crew name it already?"

"Hell, yeah." He pointed toward a shallow ford in the river, and she tugged the reins to direct Patches that way. "You knew it would happen. Not sure if it was one of the Whiskey Creek girls, but probably not. Karen wouldn't care, since it doesn't affect her precious horses. Tamara's still too busy getting into everyone's business in other ways. I figure it was someone on the Moonshine side."

Allison was quiet for a minute as a whisper of guilt rose. "I never did tell you something."

Gabe took her offered fingers and squeezed them before the horses stepped too far apart, breaking their handhold. "A secret? Hmm, those aren't allowed, right?"

"Right." Ever since they'd turned this fake marriage into a real one. "Way back when I first contacted you, it was Tamara who'd snitched about Mom being sick."

He chuckled. "Tell me something I don't know."

"What?" That was good, yet surprising. "All this time you knew? How?"

"You told me."

The splash of the water sounded rhythmically as the horses paced forward. Allison searched her memory for a time or place that she'd shared that bit of info. "I...was sure I hadn't."

"Oh, darling, first day out you were spouting all kinds of things. Sleep-deprived, you don't do so good. You'll never get a job as a secret agent." He grinned at her. "Don't worry, I know how to keep my mouth shut."

"A little too well." She took it in. His love, his acceptance. Gave it back. "I think you need to open your mouth more often."

"Hmm, now that's an invitation I'm happy to take you up on."

He reached for her and she laughingly pulled Patches out of reach. "No. No sex on a horse."

"We've had sex everywhere else," he pointed out.

True. "You've very inventive, I'll give you that. Now hush and show me this land you foolishly traded for."

He sighed. "Four more years until things are completely switched over. We'll just keep our heads above water until then, if no more disasters go south."

Which partly meant Ben. He'd stopped fighting the changes, and he'd stopped taunting Gabe, but he'd grown even colder in some ways.

Allison avoided him as much as possible.

They rode in silence, both deep in their own thoughts as the land passed under the horses' steady stride.

She knew finances were going to be tight. She also knew if it really came down to it, the money her mom had given her would be the first thing they'd use. The funds were hers to spend as she pleased. Not even Gabe, *especially* not Gabe, would deny her the right to use them however she chose.

Allison stared across at her husband—Lord, the word still made a chill zip along her spine—and admired him all over again. From his boots on up to his firmly positioned hat, he was hundred-percent Canadian free-range cowboy.

And hers. Heart of gold and all.

Gabe shook his head. "I like your smile."

He slipped off Hurricane, tethering him to a nearby bush. Allison dismounted as well, securing Patches before stepping forward to accept Gabe's outreached hand.

"Look and weep. She's right there. We actually own both sides of the waterway now."

Allison gazed over the section Gabe pointed out. Checked to the south. The north. The river wove its way along the western border, about the farthest thing from a straight line possible. "This piece?"

"Uncle George said he felt a little guilty for switching the north section with me. In exchange he got a parcel you could use a straight edge on—you could fall asleep in the tractor and the lay of the land would nearly steer you home."

A little bit of hope brightened inside her. “So this piece that he gave you? He hasn’t planted it for a while?”

“No. Pain in the ass to do anything here, he said. He’s had the horses out for a few years at least. Karen would know more, she keeps all the records.”

Hope budded and grew, ready to bloom full out if given a chance. “Gabe, don’t go laying wagers or anything yet, but you might have struck gold, not foolishness, in your switch.”

He looked her over intently. “Explain.”

“What were you going to do with this bit of land?” she asked.

“Turn the cattle out. Let it lie fallow. I wasn’t sure yet.”

She smiled. “How about checking with Karen, and if it has been sitting for at least three years, you can get a jump on your plans. At least in terms of starting a few animals or maybe plant some alfalfa out here. You don’t mind a little extra work to cultivate, do you?”

Gabe’s jaw dropped, and a light came on in his eyes. She could see him calculating and reasoning through her suggestion. A shortcut, not everything they needed, but it would certainly help.

He snatched her up and swung her in a circle. His laughter rang out, carried down the hill and over the land. They twirled until they tangled and fell. Gabe caught her on top of him, breaking her fall.

She twisted until she straddled him. His firm body stretched out under her, the fading green grasses a cushion under them both.

He caught her hands and twirled her ring lazily. “I love you.”

Her heart leapt. The words were becoming more familiar, but she never got tired of hearing them. She lifted his fingers to her lips and kissed them briefly in response before teasing him with a pout. "You know, there is one more secret I have. Well, it's not a secret. Only you've never noticed."

He raised a brow, dropping his hands to her thighs in a caress that promised she'd soon have something to think about other than organic regulations and pieces of land.

But not before she was ready. She pointed at his ring. "Take it off."

Gabe sat up and pulled off his shirt. Allison slapped a hand over her mouth to stop her burst of laughter from escaping. "I didn't mean your clothes."

"If you're not clear, woman, I'm going to take the interpretation I like best."

Smiling, she traced the outline of the tattoo begun on his skin. He'd had the phoenix designed to burst from flames on his lower back, one wing stretching over his left shoulder, and the other wrapping around his ribs on the right.

Said he'd been inspired by her tattoos.

"Still think you should have had the wings burst over both your shoulders," she teased.

"Don't need to give you more reasons to call me angel, now do I?"

"I love how I can see a piece of this no matter which way you turn." Her fingers moved slowly along the intricate design of the feathers, colour still needing to be added.

"Everything feels new. I feel reborn. You gave me that."

"We gave to each other." Allison kissed his chest and tugged on his ring. "Now take it off before I hurt you."

He humoured her, pulling the ring free, the one she'd had prepared so quickly back before she even knew this marriage was going to be real. Gabe handed it to her.

She held the plain gold band carefully at an angle. "Look. What do you see? Inside."

Gabe leaned closer, squinting slightly as he focused in. "Butterflies? You put butterflies on the inside of my wedding ring."

She dipped her head. "I did. Because you deserved to break free as well."

Her cheeks were flushed. Butterflies. What had she been thinking? The glorious phoenix marking his skin was far more appropriate than the delicate little creatures she'd picked out.

Gabe slipped his ring back on. "I think that's pretty amazing. Thank you. Thank you for wanting that for me."

She shrugged. "It's only butterflies."

He caught her chin in his hands and stared into her eyes. The tenderness she saw there, the love—it made her speechless.

He brushed their lips together for a second. Spoke against her mouth. "And they only live in places that are healthy, right? So I want to see whole flocks of butterflies over this land. Over our house. If I have to tattoo butterflies on me to prove it, then I will."

He shushed her protests and stood them both, his shirt abandoned on the ground. Allison couldn't figure out what he was doing until he twisted his back toward her and pointed. "Look. Look closely at the fire."

She pressed her palm to his skin, framing the section. This was the only area fully coloured. Deep crimson and brilliant gold mingled together as they rose to form the feathers covering the bird's chest. She'd admired the tattoo a hundred times since he came home to show her.

Now for the first time she spotted it. The tiny outlines of dozens of butterflies, their wings meshing into each other's like some drawing by Escher. A thin line of them escaping from the fire and flying upward, hidden in the plumage of the phoenix's breast.

When he turned, she trailed her fingers over his body, not wanting to let him go.

Gabe tilted his hat back slightly. Grinned.

“Rabble,” she said.

His grin twisted. “What?”

“A rabble. A group of butterflies is called a rabble. Or a swarm, or the really pretty name is a kaleidoscop—”

He covered her mouth with his hand. “I love you, Allison.”

When he slipped his fingers off she leapt, wrapping herself around him and clinging tight. “I love you too, Angel Boy. I’m so glad you’ve found your wings.”

“We can fly together.”

About the Author

Vivian Arend in one word: *Adventurous*. In a sentence: *Willing to try just about anything once.* That wide-eyed attitude has taken her around North America, through parts of Europe, and into Central and South America, often with no running water.

Her optimistic outlook also meant that when challenged to write a book, she gave it a shot, and discovered creating worlds to play in was nearly as addictive as traveling the real one. Now a *New York Times* and *USA TODAY* bestselling author of both contemporary and paranormal stories, Vivian continues to explore, write and otherwise keep herself well entertained.

Website: www.vivianarend.com

Blog: www.vivianarend.com/blog

Twitter: www.twitter.com/VivianArend

Facebook: www.facebook.com/VivianArend

Nothing comes easy. You've gotta work for it.

Rocky Mountain Desire

© 2012 Vivian Arend

Six Pack Ranch, Book 3

Matt Coleman always figured at this point in his life, he'd be settled down with a family. Since his ex split for the big city, though, no way will he give anyone else the chance to drop-kick his heart. Physical pleasure? Hell, yeah, he'll take—and give—with gusto, but nothing more.

Hope Meridan is working long hours to hold on to her new quilt shop, going it alone since her sister/business partner ran off. Sex? Right, like she's got the time. Not that she doesn't have the occasional dirty fantasy about Matt. Fat chance he'd dream of knocking boots with her—the younger sister of the woman who dumped him. Nope, she'll just have to settle for the F-word.

Friends would be far easier if there wasn't something combustible going on between them. And when casual interest starts to grow into something more, their tenuous bond strengthens in the heat of desire. But it may not survive the hurricane-force arrival of the last person either of them ever wanted to see again…

Warning: Small-town rivals, men in pursuit and family meddling—in good and bad ways. Look for a cowboy who knows how to rope, ride and rein in a hell of a lot more than eight seconds of sheer bliss.

Available now in ebook and print from Samhain Publishing.

CPSIA information can be obtained at www.ICGtesting.com
Printed in the USA
LVOW06s1520120913

352189LV00002B/3/P